THE QUOTIENT OF
MURDΣR

Ada Madison

BERKLEY PRIME CRIME, NEW YORK

THE BERKLEY PUBLISHING GROUP
Published by the Penguin Group
Penguin Group (USA) LLC
375 Hudson Street, New York, New York 10014

USA • Canada • UK • Ireland • Australia • New Zealand • India • South Africa • China

penguin.com

A Penguin Random House Company

THE QUOTIENT OF MURDER

A Berkley Prime Crime Book / published by arrangement with the author

For information, address: The Berkley Publishing Group,
a division of Penguin Group (USA) LLC,
375 Hudson Street, New York, New York 10014.

ISBN: 978-0-425-26270-2

PUBLISHING HISTORY
Berkley Prime Crime mass-market edition / November 2013

PRINTED IN THE UNITED STATES OF AMERICA

10 9 8 7 6 5 4 3 2 1

Interior map by Dick Rufer.
Cover art by Lisa French.
Cover design by Lesley Worrell.
Interior text design by Kristin del Rosario.

Berkley Prime Crime titles by Ada Madison

THE SQUARE ROOT OF MURDER
THE PROBABILITY OF MURDER
A FUNCTION OF MURDER
THE QUOTIENT OF MURDER

ACKNOWLEDGMENTS

Thanks as always to my critique partners: Nannette Rundle Carroll, Jonnie Jacobs, Rita Lakin, Margaret Lucke, and Sue Stephenson. They are ideally knowledgeable, thorough, and supportive.

Thanks also to the extraordinary Inspector Chris Lux for continued advice on police procedure. Chris is always available to answer my questions—often the same one for every book—or to share a laugh. I'm so lucky to have met him.

Thanks to the many other writers and friends who offered critique, information, brainstorming, and inspiration; in particular: Gail and David Abbate, Sara Bly, Mary Donovan, Margaret Hamilton, Diana Orgain, Ann Parker, Suzanne Bilge Rasmussen, Jean Stokowski, Karen Streich, and Ellyn Wheeler.

My deepest gratitude goes to my husband, Dick Rufer. I can't imagine working without his support. He's my dedicated Webmaster (minichino.com), layout specialist, and on-call IT department.

Thanks to my very helpful editor, Robin Barletta, and the staff at Berkley Prime Crime.

Finally, my gratitude to my Primary Care Editor, Michelle Vega. Michelle is a bright light in my life, personally supportive as well as superb at seeing the whole picture without missing the tiniest detail. Thanks, Michelle!

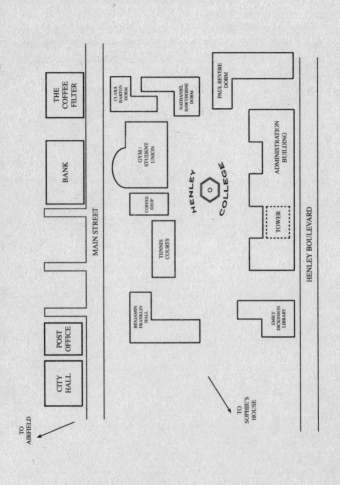

Don't spoil my circles!

—ARCHIMEDES

CHAPTER $\sqrt{1}$

Four seasons aren't enough to please some New Englanders. The administrators of Henley College, in Henley, Massachusetts, gleefully wedged in a fifth this year—our first ever January Intersession. Four weeks of classes, three credits each, and thirty-one days of braving the winds on an icy-cold campus.

Brilliant.

"You know you love teaching, anytime, anywhere, Sophie," more than one of my friends said every time I whined about the extra load.

"Yeah, yeah," I admitted, acknowledging that I couldn't get enough of class prep and student interaction.

But now, two weeks into the so-called term, a pipe somewhere in the nether regions burst, and the heating system went out in Benjamin Franklin Hall, home to the mathematics and science departments. After shivering through my nine o'clock calculus class, I carried my mug of coffee and laptop into the faculty lounge, hoping someone had started water boiling on the hot plate. During my free hour, I could give myself a steam facial and warm up at the same time.

I wasn't the only one with that idea. I set my computer down and joined two other department chairpersons—the tall, heavily mustachioed Ted Morrell, from physics, and the much smaller, strawberry blond Judy Donohue, head of biology—standing at the side table, where the hot plate occupied a prime position. I squeezed between them.

"I can't teach maxima and minima in a freezing classroom," I complained to Ted, the most senior faculty member in Franklin Hall. "What good is having a physicist in the building if you can't fix the plumbing?"

"I'm on it, Sophie." Ted saluted and smiled. He spared me his standard speech about the difference between science and technology. According to Ted, physicists were busy trying to understand the universe; it was the engineers who were responsible for fixing its leaks.

It sounded like a cop-out to me.

No one wanted to argue with Ted, however, since he was our go-to guy for any computer problems in the building. In deference (or not) to his age, we called him our One-Hundred-Year-Old Geek, the techie who could unfreeze your bits and bytes or recover the file you thought you deleted.

Our laptops lined up on the conference table, the three of us engaged in a time-honored New England winter tradition, hovering over the steam from two pots of boiling water, talking and drinking our coffee in a half-bent position while the bubbles gurgled away. I hoped someone who needed boiling water for tea would join us so I'd feel less wasteful and environmentally unsound.

This morning we also eyed a pink pastry box next to the hot plate. It was the Chemistry Department's turn to supply goodies today, and a chem major had delivered the box earlier. Ted patted his flat stomach, making a calculation before indulging, then went for a cruller. I followed his lead, promising myself an exercise routine soon, and broke off a small piece of cinnamon twist.

Judy sucked in her stomach, then let out a breath and admitted, "I pass, because I just walked by a hunky, very buff guy in the basement fixing our heater, and I might want to go back and introduce myself."

Ted and I pretended not to get the connection.

To add to the January woes, parking on campus had become a nightmare. Large vehicles and heavy equipment for the renovating and reopening of our carillon facility had taken over the lots on the east and north sides of the Administration Building. Besides the bell tower, the landscaping at the back of Admin was also getting a makeover.

Franklin Hall had its own lot next to the tennis courts at the other end of campus, but the displaced cars had moved in on us. This was as good a time as any to gripe about it.

"Someone was in my spot today," Judy said. "A dirty old blue Citroen." She brushed the front of her spotless wool jacket, as if she'd inadvertently leaned on the scruffy vehicle.

"Probably someone from the French Department," Ted joked, halfway through his cruller. "But where else are they going to park?"

"Anywhere but my spot," Judy said, stomping her feet. For circulation or for emphasis? Probably both. "They could at least remove some of that equipment that they're through with. I'll bet they're never going to use that backhoe again."

"It's all for a good cause," I offered, and hummed a few notes of the Westminster Chimes. Thanks to a generous donation from a group of alumnae, Henley College's Music Department would once again have a full program of carillon studies and regular concerts.

"Listen to Ms. Arrives-at-Dawn Knowles," Ted said, flicking a crumb of powdered sugar from his mustache. "You still have your spot."

"That would be *Dr.* Arrives-At-Dawn Knowles," I teased. "But you have a point."

Usual construction delays and a late December snow had slowed the carillon project, but the remaining work was fairly weatherproof, and we were promised a concert in the spring.

In spite of the inconvenience of the parking situation, most faculty and students were thrilled about the restoration and upgrading of our carillon. Comprising fifty-three (formerly forty-eight) bells, the instrument was housed in a tower attached to the sprawling English Gothic Administration Building. A system of wires and ropes linked the oversize keyboard, much bigger than those of a regular organ, to the bells' clappers. It was hard to believe that the present construction zone, with ugly equipment, scaffolding, and black and yellow caution tape, would soon give way to beautiful music from the tower.

Judy shook the box of pastry for a better view of the bottom layer, then succumbed to a piece of Danish that had broken loose. "I know, tsk, tsk," she said, as if someone had reprimanded her. "You're being so good, Sophie."

"Uh-huh." I didn't share my reasons for holding back—there were more goodies in my immediate future, and I wanted to save my appetite. I planned to share cake with my class after my eleven o'clock seminar, then enjoy lunch with my boyfriend, search-and-rescue hero Bruce Granville. Medevac pilots didn't often get a regular lunch hour, so I'd jumped at the chance to meet Bruce downtown.

"We don't have our parking lot back, but at least the excruciatingly dull special faculty meetings are over," Judy said.

I nodded, recalling endless hours of meetings to decide details that should have taken five minutes each. Should we charge admission to climb the tower for a tour? (No.) For attendance at a carillon concert? (No.) Should the players be called carillonists or carillonneurs? (The former.)

Whose names should be inscribed on the new bells to be installed? (Big donors, of course.) Which shade of gray should we use for the walls, "sea salt" or "samovar silver"? (Who even remembers the final decision?)

"Notice, no one in administration ever mentioned the real reason the carillon program was cancelled to begin with," Judy said.

"Knock, knock, Doctors?"

Our longtime, diffident janitor, Woody, stood at the door, his smile broader than usual. He knew we'd be pleased to see the load he was ready to pull into the room—a gray metal cart with two shelves full of small space heaters.

Three variations of enthusiastic thanks, plus a round of applause, caused a light flush to appear over Woody's face. We invited him to share the wealth of sugar in the pink box.

Woody scooped up a jelly donut and placed it to the side on a napkin. "For after I set these up," he said, pointing to his cart. "Thank you, Doctors," he added.

"Thank you, Mr. Conroy," Judy said, but I was unsure whether he'd recognized her tease. We'd long ago stopped trying to coax him into using our first names.

Five minutes later, life-giving warmth radiated from the coils of a heater at the back of the room.

We moved from the hot plate and arranged chairs around the heater, while Woody cleared the way for a second unit at the front of the room.

Judy's earlier comment came back to me. "What do you mean 'the real reason' for closing the tower?" I asked her. "I thought it was sealed off because of some building code violation and we didn't have the money for retrofitting."

Judy pointed to our colleague from physics. "Ted would know better, but what I heard was that twenty-five years ago, toward the end of the spring semester, a young woman jumped from the tower. A sophomore French major, right, Ted?"

Ted nodded, frowning, closing his eyes.

I drew in my breath. "A student jumped from our tower? That's why the tower was sealed off?"

I looked at Ted for more information. He'd been at Henley forever, an icon in horn-rimmed spectacles. I'd lost track of how long ago we'd celebrated his thirtieth anniversary. But Ted wasn't in a sharing mood today. He opened his laptop, finished with the tower conversation.

Even with the new source of heat in the room, I felt a chill. Maybe because of the horrible image now in my head. A girl falling from the tower, hitting concrete, breaking bones, bleeding . . .

I thought back. I'd been born and raised in Henley, but twenty-five years ago, I was a college student on the West Coast. Had I been so self-centered that I wouldn't have paid attention to such dramatic news in my hometown? Granted, I was three thousand miles away and it occurred more than half my lifetime ago, and it made sense that my mother wouldn't have wanted me to focus on it. Still . . .

I finally caught my breath. "How come you knew this and I didn't?" I asked Judy.

Though Judy was five years my junior, we'd joined the faculty the same semester, fifteen years ago. She'd arrived straight out of grad school, skipping the phase I'd been through, where you try gainful employment in industry before giving in to your first love, teaching.

"I heard bits and pieces my first year here. I haven't thought about it in a long time," Judy said.

"They quit having all those live music concerts and we put in that electric system. Nobody was supposed to talk about it," Woody said, packing up his toolbox.

"A very good idea," Ted offered, without lifting his eyes from his keyboard.

"Yes, sir, Doctor," Woody said, taking Ted's message to heart, and, I guessed, wishing he'd never contributed to the conversation.

"The real answer to your question, Sophie, is that everyone

knows you're no fun when it comes to keeping gossip alive," Judy said. "That's why no one brought it up with you."

I didn't know whether to say "Sorry" or "Thanks."

Ted gave Judy a disapproving look, and she quickly explained. "I didn't mean that this was gossip. It must have been an unimaginable tragedy for her family, of course. For everyone at Henley."

Judy had a way of being flip that annoyed Ted—the straightest arrow in the building—at least once a day in my experience, but we both knew she never meant disrespect.

The natural questions were swimming around in my head. Who was the girl? Why did she jump? How did her family handle it?

I didn't have to ask. Judy tuned in to my vibes. "The girl was from an influential family in Boston." She snapped her fingers, remembering. "Her father was a high-profile lawyer, if I recall correctly, and headed to Washington. The first rumors were that she was depressed over a boyfriend who'd just dumped her. But they never did verify that she was depressed or that there even was a boyfriend."

"Maybe she was flunking her classes?" I offered, knowing how high the stakes were for some students.

Ted cleared his throat. "No one really knows why anyone does anything," he said, in a sweeping pronouncement. "What does it matter, anyway?"

"I just found it strange that so many rumors persisted, even after the suicide ruling," Judy said.

"You think the boyfriend was a cover story?" I asked. "There was another reason she jumped from the tower?"

Judy shrugged. "Anything is possible. There could have been more to it. Something embarrassing to the family. I'm pretty sure the girl's father was running for office. Sometimes that alone is enough to doubt what you see in the press. The girl—"

"Kirsten Packard," Ted interrupted. "The girl was Kirsten Packard, and her father was in the state's attorney general's office, running for election as US attorney, which he won. He served his country in that capacity, and died a few years ago."

There was a finality to Ted's tone. He might as well have said, "Zip it," or, more suited to him, "Now can we please drop this topic?" But Judy, who never met a rumor she didn't like, wasn't finished.

"I even heard that someone might have been up there with Kirsten," Judy said. "In the tower. And that's why the Packard family wasn't eager to have an investigation."

As much as I sympathized with Ted, I couldn't resist. Trying to establish a reputation to match Judy's? I hoped not. "So she might have been pushed by this other person?" I asked.

Judy raised her eyebrows and gave me a slight smile, as if to commend me for guessing what she had in mind.

We both turned to look more closely at Ted, Woody having slipped out by now.

"You were on the faculty back then, Ted. What do you think?" Judy asked.

"No comment," he said, and continued to work at his keyboard. He acted as uncomfortable as if he himself had been in the tower with Kirsten that day. But the look was more that of a sad father than of a witness to murder.

"I don't get it," I said. "Why would a parent not want an investigation if they suspected their daughter was murdered?"

"Politicians, you know," Judy suggested, shrugging. "It's all about image. A murder investigation digs up all kinds of things besides a murderer. Family secrets and skeletons. Maybe the girl . . . Kirsten . . . was into something that got her killed. Suicide is neater. Well, not neat, but you know what I mean."

"Right," I said, as if either of us were an expert in the matter. "One more question, Ted. Did you know Kirsten personally?" I asked.

He took a deep breath and gave a slight, slow nod. "I didn't have her as a student. She majored in romance languages, I think. But her roommate was a physics major so I'd met Kirsten once or twice."

Ted stood and walked to where the coffee urn and the hot plate kettles were both going strong. He refilled his mug with our less-than-gourmet coffee, carried it back to his seat, and bent over his keyboard again.

I was curious to know why Ted didn't leave the lounge and the conversation that seemed so distasteful to him. Maybe he wanted to keep tabs on the wild imaginings of his colleagues. Was he protecting the victim for some reason? Though he claimed not to know her, he certainly would care about the image of the college where he'd spent the better part of his adult life. Or maybe he simply couldn't face the even colder office wing of the building.

"Let's lighten this up a bit, shall we?" Judy said, surprising me. "Give us a puzzle or a math riddle, Sophie."

I snapped to it. "Of course," I said, and scanned my mental list for a puzzle I hadn't already told them. The first riddle that came to me was a cute entry that I'd seen in the kids' section of one of the magazines I submitted puzzles and brainteasers to.

"How many eggs can you put in an empty basket with a six-inch square bottom, three inches high?" I asked.

Judy made a *pshaw* sound. "You're off your game, Sophie. The answer is, only one. After that the basket's not empty. And those dimensions are to throw me off. Like a red herring in a mystery."

Judy was right all around. Not just about the number of eggs and the clever distraction, but about the fact that I was off my game. My heart wasn't in it. It was heavy with the thought of a student in distress.

Unless the corollary legend was true and someone had pushed Kirsten out the tower window. Another horrible scenario.

Ted clicked away, neglecting to offer his usual challenge to me with his own joke. *An electron walks into a bar. . . .* Judy's laptop bonged awake. The coffee klatch had come to an end.

In my office, I sent a quick text to Bruce, confirming our lunch date, and gathered my class materials. At the last minute, I picked up my down jacket, in case Woody hadn't yet set up a heater in the classroom.

I heard a noise behind me and turned to find Judy in my doorway.

I invited her in, but she declined. "I know you're on your way to class, but I had a thought."

I cupped my ear. "I'm listening."

"Fran would have been here at that time. Twenty-five years ago."

Not a thought. More of a fact. Fran Emerson, my colleague in the Mathematics Department, had been at Henley at least as long as Ted. She was off this semester, teaching in Rwanda on a Fulbright.

It took a minute, but I got it. "You want me to call Fran in Africa and ask about a twenty-five-year-old event?"

"Would you?"

"That's a crazy idea."

"Just a thought," Judy said, as she turned and walked away.

"Crazy," I called after her.

"Curious," she said, her voice echoing after her. "Scientists are curious."

"Yes, but biologists are crazy."

I walked down the hall to my classroom, Kirsten Packard's death still weighing on me, almost as if she'd been my own student.

Most faculty members who'd been around awhile and were even the least bit approachable had at one time or another counseled a student who was on the edge. I certainly had. It was a sobering, frightening experience. Though Kirsten's death had occurred a long time ago, it pained me to acknowledge that one of us had failed to save a young life.

I hoped my current students were all in a happy state, glad to be alive.

And that no one was out to get them.

I stood in the doorway before entering the room and pulled out my smartphone. I clicked on the world *clock*.

Almost eleven o'clock in the Commonwealth of Massachusetts. Nearing five o'clock in the evening in Rwanda. Not that I needed to know.

Curious, crazy mathematicians.

CHAPTER $\sqrt{2}$

My second class of the day was a history of mathematics seminar, one that I'd led for the last few regular semesters. The sessions provided an opportunity for me to call attention to often little-known pioneers in obscure fields. And to throw frequent parties.

If I had any notoriety on the Henley College campus, it was as the driving force behind the combined lecture-cum-birthday parties for the Franklin Hall departments. Every week, we honored a worthy contributor in mathematics, physics, biology, or chemistry—which, by the way, was the order of the floors in the building, bottom to top.

Though they hated to acknowledge it, the Chemistry Department was closest to the roof for safety considerations, as the department most likely to explode. That was also the reason we monitored the kinds of demonstrations chemists were allowed to bring to the parties. No nitroglycerin for the presentation on October twenty-first, Alfred Nobel's birthday, for example.

In my mind, the ideal party, like today's, honored a female mathematician and featured an undergraduate presenting a paper on her work. The ideal party also came with cake.

Jenn Marshall, a sophomore math major, was the seminar leader for today. She was already in the classroom, setting up her props. I stepped over to help her with an easel and a large poster. As the two of us petite women juggled with the ancient, low-tech instructional aids, I compiled a mental wish list for that big donation that might come someday from a satisfied, highly successful Math Department alum.

"Sorry we had to abandon the seminar room," I said. "It's always nicer when we can sit around the table, but I thought a smaller room with direct sunlight might be warmer." I saw that Woody had been here with his magic appliances, and added, "And the space heater will do more good."

Jenn nodded and mumbled something like, "It's okay."

Moving a couple of chairs around, I spied her backpack in the corner of the room.

"It looks like you finally replaced that threadbare old backpack I've been teasing you about. I didn't really mean it when I asked if you'd had it since first grade."

I laughed at my own humor, but Jenn said simply, "I know."

"You must be excited about your first talk," I said, trying another tack. "Good work on your bullets. The poster looks great."

"Yeah, I guess," Jenn said, again without the enthusiasm I'd hoped for.

"Poor departments have to make do," I said. "One of these days we'll have the equipment to do this electronically. But at least we got rid of our abacus."

Jenn barely acknowledged my final attempt at humor. I'd worried about her lately. Usually an animated young woman, ready for the challenge of a good math problem or a fun puzzle, Jenn had been dragging her thin body around the building the last couple of weeks. I chalked it up to the extra work of the Intersession.

Jenn was a scholarship student, and like most who were on financial aid, she worked several hours a week on campus. She also loved music and had taken up the carillon as soon as she'd heard about the restoration of Henley's program. She spent many evenings in a practice room in the tower, but she often had to travel to a church in Boston when construction precluded her entrance to our tower.

Now Jenn looked less than thrilled about the task before her, and I wondered if she had too many commitments this year, and too little sleep. Maybe I'd take her aside later and see if I could help in any way. I could certainly extend the deadlines on her assignments and maybe talk to the other Franklin Hall faculty about easing up on her student aid duties.

Eleven AM and the bell signaling the start of class rang down the corridors of Franklin Hall. The antique mechanical clock in its wooden frame had been in the vestibule of the first floor, the math floor, since the building was opened in the nineteen forties. Some of us thought it should be featured in the college orientation brochure along with the vintage furniture in the parlors of our Administration Building.

My seminar students, whose number seemed to go from one to twelve in seconds, filed in and settled down for the last hour before lunch.

After my preliminaries, including my apologies that we had to wear scarves and hats in the classroom, I took a seat. Jenn Marshall stepped up to enlighten us about Gertrude Mary Cox, born in 1900, a pioneer in the development of applied statistics.

"Her birthday isn't today exactly, but I thought it would be okay to have cake anyway," Jenn began, even before mentioning Cox's work.

She seemed surprised that a round of *Woot, woot* erupted for her, accompanied by clapping, muffled as it was by the presence of gloves on most of the hands.

Jenn plunged in and talked about Cox's pivotal book, published in 1950, which brought order and insight to the design of statistical experiments. Especially for a sophomore, she did a respectable job clarifying the then-new methods of increasing the accuracy of experiments and analyzing the results. My heart went out to her when she paused in her presentation to pull a pink and white ski cap over her long, straight brown hair. I wished I'd thought to bring a cap of my own. Jenn did well tackling various aspects of induction ("going from a small sample of something, like people, to the whole population," she explained) and randomization ("like, close your eyes and don't look when you choose, like a piece of candy or something," she offered).

During the discussion, Andrew Davies, another sophomore math major, raised his hand. "I read that the title of Gertrude Cox's master's dissertation was 'A Statistical Investigation of a Teacher's Ability as Indicated by the Success of His Students in Subsequent Courses.'"

Another round of *woots* and applause, this one aimed at me, as a dozen heads turned to their professor in the back row.

"Sorry, Dr. Knowles, I had to mention it," Andrew said. "Of course, we all know you're the best, and soon the whole world will know because we're all going on to do great things."

Someone, namely a short, dark-haired male sophomore, was looking for brownie points.

"Yada, yada," I responded, then cleared my throat and gave the dude a look that I hoped said, "Thanks. Now let's move on."

On the other hand, I was grateful for this cheery little respite in a competent but otherwise lackluster seminar by

Jenn. Rescuing her from a tough semester moved to the top
of my to-do list.

At one point Jenn held up a photograph of Cox. She
reminded me of my mother, Margaret, who wore her hair
the same way back in the day, in neat, tight rows of waves
across her head, starting at the edge of her forehead. After
Margaret died, I found boxes of the thin metal clips that
formed those waves, more serious looking and functional
than the decorative plastic versions I saw today.

I paid as much attention as I could to the rest of Jenn's
presentation, but with thoughts of my late mother alternat-
ing with made-up images of the deceased Kirsten Packard,
it was difficult. I kept trying to picture Kirsten, who would
be about forty-four by now, had she lived. *Gulp.* My age.
With relief, I tuned in again to Jenn's unemotional recita-
tion of Cox's awards and a string of "first female to . . ."
accolades.

I checked the clock at the back of the seminar room.
Only fifteen minutes until cake, then lunch with Bruce.
Statistician Gertrude Cox would not have been proud of me
today, distracted and inattentive. Neither would my mother
have approved. I heard both women shout, "You're the
teacher. Focus!"

Jenn left the room as soon as the seminar was over,
passing up the cake. Thanks to me and the rest of the students, by twelve thirty, the cake was gone. The party was
over, and the students drifted out. I gave as many as I could
a smiling "take care" and a "good job" pat on the shoulder
and headed out the door myself. If they were wondering
about my extra dose of nurturing today, they didn't say.

The small city of Henley—population less than fifty
thousand—was situated almost halfway between Boston,
Massachusetts, and Providence, Rhode Island; about an
hour to beaches on Cape Cod (my choice of vacation spot),

and a straight two-hour shot to the beginning of frigid ice-climbing terrain in New Hampshire (Bruce's idea of fun).

Bruce and I had been together more than five years. Our relationship survived probably because first, Bruce loved the Cape as much as I did; second, I never felt compelled to join him in any activity that required more gear than a SWAT team showed up with; and third, we both enjoyed regular trips to Boston.

Today, however, thanks to my commitment to the January Intersession, the farthest we'd go would be to a Thai restaurant on the edge of town.

Bruce had the day off but had agreed to on-call status since we were grounded anyway. If the Bat Phone put out an all-hands emergency call, he'd be a no-show for lunch and I'd be on my own. I'd been present in the double-wide trailer of Massachusetts Shock, Trauma, and Air Rescue, widely known as MAstar, a couple of times when the compelling, ear-piercing sound rang through the so-called building. I'd watched in amazement as Bruce and his buddies stopped mid-sentence, geared up, and headed for the chopper in well-choreographed movements. It couldn't be easy trying to sleep—or eat or talk or relax—knowing that at any moment the souped-up phone would blare out a summons to the team. Maybe to a crash scene, maybe to a simple transfer job, transporting a patient from one facility to another.

Though I had no problem dealing with the vagaries of Bruce's schedule, I was glad I always knew my own schedule at least a semester in advance. That was one reason I'd left a lucrative job at a frantically run software company to take up residence in the ivory tower.

I carried my laptop into Pan's, our Thai restaurant of choice, and took a seat against an interior brick wall that had been painted a shimmering gold. I divested myself of gloves, hat, coat, scarf, and extra sweater and fluffed my short hair. Without the benefit of a mirror, I smoothed my one highlight, a jagged stripe of gray hair about an inch wide that ran off center at the top of my head. The artifact had been placed there by Mother Nature herself, though many thought it was by my own hand.

I drew a welcome warm breath. The smell of curry and a mash-up of special Asian spices told me we'd chosen the right spot for a cold day.

"Hot lemon tea for Miss Sophie," my favorite waitress, Toi, said. She smiled, placed the cup in front of me, and padded away in tiny red slippers.

She was out of sight before I finished my "Thank you."

Toi knew to let me work while I waited for Bruce. She also knew that Bruce would order a dish he'd never tried before and I, after much ruminating, would stick with the crab Rangoon. If I had to wait too long, the lovely, dark-haired Toi would treat me to a small sampler plate of appetizers—crispy tofu, spicy shrimp, and a pot sticker.

No one could call me adventuresome. That's what Bruce was for. I'd attached myself to a guy who, after a tour in Saudi Arabia with the US Air Force, took a job that involved dodging telephone poles, satellite dishes, power lines, and trees as he soared to heights of several thousand feet piloting a rescue helicopter.

I opened my laptop and booted it up. What to do first? Class assignments could wait. Brainteasers for a new magazine contract could wait. Even email from my best friend, Ariana Volens, who was wisely spending the two coldest weeks of the season with an aunt in Florida, could wait. The big question was, could I wait before calling Fran in Rwanda to ask her about Kirsten Packard's fall from the tower?

I decided to collect as much information as I could before resurrecting Fran's memory of a terrible time. I searched on Google for the long-ago student's name and year of death. Immediately, all irrational hope vanished that my friends Ted, Judy, and Woody were somehow mistaken, or that I was, having missed the fact that they were talking about a new movie or a thriller they'd all just read.

Pages of hits rolled down the screen. I'd ceased to be amazed at what was so easily accessible on the Internet and wished I'd had such a resource through my own school years. I clicked on the first few links and read articles from the local newspaper archives. Not much information besides what I'd learned in the Franklin Hall faculty lounge. After a "thorough investigation," Kirsten's fall was ruled a suicide. Her body had been discovered on the front steps of the Administration Building, at the base of the tower, in the early morning by students practicing for a race.

I shut my eyes against the nasty image, but curiosity propelled me forward.

I pulled together a scenario from several reports: Two freshman roommates had been running on campus. As they approached Admin from the east, they claimed, they heard a single, brief chime from the carillon. This was verified by others in their dorm rooms. At the same time, the runners "thought they saw something drop from the tower," then noticed "a pile of clothes or something" on the top step of the building, spilling over to the second step. They ran up the stairs to check and saw the deceased, sprawled out. Since the front door of Admin was not open, they'd immediately run back to their dorm and called nine-one-one.

The next day, I read, Kirsten's father, a state's attorney, made a brief statement, expressing gratitude for the outpouring of sympathy to him and his family, and requesting that their privacy be respected. The funeral services were for family and close friends only. No special memorial was held in the campus chapel, a departure from the usual practice in a faculty or student death.

I found no mention of a boyfriend, good or bad, and suspected his existence was born of word of mouth and in less formal areas of the media, like profiles or column pieces. Or the tabloids, I thought, and looked around the densely populated restaurant to see if anyone had read my trashy mind.

Only one photograph of Kirsten kept showing up: what appeared to be her high school yearbook picture. I was surprised at the poor reproduction. I'd gotten used to the crisp images of current online newspapers. But Kirsten's image had the look of a fourth-generation photocopy, devoid of detail, a grainy version of a long-haired young woman wearing an obligatory drape across her shoulders, like every other girl in her class. The photo gave me no clue as to what Kirsten might have been like. I wondered what she would have looked like now, what career she might have had as a language major. A linguist for the United Nations? A teacher? A literary translator? What had the world missed?

I made a note to check later, to search the *Boston Globe* and other media for wider, national coverage. I could also pull up Henley College alumnae newsletters, though I doubted any mention would have been made of the tragedy. It wasn't exactly material for recruiting brochures.

I complained a lot about nomophobes who couldn't disconnect themselves from the net, their phones, texting, IMing, Facebooking, but now I had to admit a video gone viral at the time of Kirsten's fall would have served my purposes well.

Not that I was clear on what my purposes were.

"One thirty, Miss Sophie. A little something while you wait for Mr. Bruce," Toi said, leaving a plate of familiar samples.

"Mmm, shrimp. Thank you," I murmured, but she was gone as quickly as she'd come.

A small glitch in my screen caused my eyes to blink, and when they refocused on the article I'd been reading, it was on the word *investigation*. A *duh* moment. Bruce's best friend since college, and therefore a constant presence in my life, was a detective with the Henley Police Department. Before calling Africa, I could call downtown Henley, USA.

Detective Virgil Mitchell had left the Boston PD and come to Henley only a few years ago, but I was sure he'd have heard about Kirsten Packard. I paused, envisioning an orientation meeting where detectives new to town were briefed on every crime and tragedy in the history of the department. Unlikely. But wouldn't an event like a campus suicide forty miles away reach Boston? If not, surely he could find out about Kirsten Packard and answer some questions for me. And if he knew already, Virge should have told me, I thought, with a mental pout. It had happened on my campus, after all.

Which brought me back to why. Why did I care so much? Was it simply that I didn't like being out of the loop on such a dramatic occurrence at Henley College? Was it the natural curiosity of a mathematician and puzzle-maker?

All of the above, I guessed, but there was another factor, the "unfinished" factor. I was convinced that if Ted and Judy had simply related a story with a definitive ending, no loose ends, I would have filed it away. Sad, but nothing to capture my attention. The Kirsten Packard story, however, was anything but finished in my mind. I couldn't understand why a family wouldn't want a full investigation into the death of a young woman. I certainly did.

The fact that Jenn Marshall and Andrew Davies, both sophomore math majors, were part of the new carillon program also nagged at me. I couldn't shake an unfounded but growing feeling that I should be worried about both of them. I'd meant to ask Ted if the late Kirsten Packard had been a carillonist. I couldn't imagine why else she would have been in the tower the night she died.

If Kirsten hadn't committed suicide, maybe something about being a carillonist caused her death. Not that I had any idea *what*. I couldn't stop myself from wanting to solve the mystery. If in fact it was a mystery. I had only Judy's store of gossip to rely on. And everyone knew the flights of fancy Judy Donohue was prone to.

Another looming question, based on reality: Didn't I have enough to occupy my time without chasing a past event that had nothing to do with me? With Fran off teaching in Africa, and an adjunct faculty member on medical leave, I was back as chair of the department this year. The chairmanship meant an exponential increase in meetings and endless hours spent accounting for each ream of graph paper and every half hour of student aide work. Plus, the compressed January sessions gave me two extra classes; a third puzzle magazine had asked for submissions from me; and my latest research paper sat in a file waiting for me to prepare the final version for publication. Weren't millions upon millions of people waiting to read my paper on an approximation method for solving differential equations? In between all these projects, I had a life. Didn't I?

Whirr, whirr, whirr. Whirr, whirr, whirr.

Speaking of my life. Bruce had programmed my phone to sound like helicopter blades. He claimed he'd recorded the sound of the newest Eurocopter at MAstar, and I hadn't had time to prove that he'd simply chosen "whirring blades" from the ringtone menu of his phone.

"I'm on my way," he said. "You okay?"

"Ten-four," I said, feeling jargony. "Did your number come up this morning?"

"Yeah, but it was one of those Mickey Mouse trips where a VIP needs an emergency taping up for a handball match. The rest of the crew was on a real mission, so I took the old copter and drove the guy."

I loved that Bruce "drove" at two thousand feet in the air. If he had his way, we'd have picnics in a hovering helicopter instead of formal lunches with tablecloths and napkins.

"Want me to order for you?" I asked.

"I've been dreaming of the rice-wrapped squid and an

exotic dipping sauce. Ask them to surprise me with the sauce and a side."

Scary. "Done," I said.

"You sure you're okay?" he asked.

"Why wouldn't I be?"

"Uh, I thought, you know, with the . . ." He paused and clicked his tongue. ". . . event. On campus."

How did Bruce know what had come up in the Franklin Hall lounge this morning? It wasn't out of the question that Ted had called Bruce—they were gym buddies—and told him I seemed upset. But that would be out of character for Ted. And I didn't think I'd exhibited that much upset behavior once I got over the initial shock of Judy's revelation.

"How did you know—?"

Silence. The line, or the tower, or whatever was between cell phones, was dead on his end or mine. Unless Bruce had cut me off.

No problem. I'd see him soon for a face-to-face explanation. But I couldn't rid myself of an uneasy feeling that I shouldn't be okay, in Bruce's mind. Was something wrong with Bruce himself? I thought I'd heard "campus event," but between the high-volume chimes-and-string music in the restaurant on my end, and the lunchtime traffic on his, I could have misheard. Maybe he wasn't referring to Kirsten Packard. But I'd just left campus an hour ago. What could have gone wrong?

I tried to remember Bruce's schedule for today. Did he have a doctor's appointment this morning? Did he come away with bad news? Of course not. He'd texted me all through the morning, his usual practice when he didn't want to interrupt my class with the *whirr, whirr, whirr* of a regular call. He'd gone to the gym, taken his car to the shop, flown a customer to a med center, come back, and headed for Pan's. Hardly time for an X-ray or a scan or a long medical consultation.

I punched his number a few more times before settling back and waiting patiently. Or not so patiently.

I was too jittery, wondering what was up with Bruce, to continue my research into an event that must have rocked the campus twenty-five years ago. Too mentally fractured to read and comprehend information. I pulled up the contacts list on my phone and touched the international number under Fran's name. I heard the click over to voice mail and hung up without leaving a message. I had too complicated a question for the limits of a phone service, smart or not.

I leaned against the gold wall and resorted to plan B, my relax-while-playing-a-game mode. I treated myself to a selection from a bookmarked site that promised an improvement in my core cognitive functions. Who couldn't use a little of that? I clicked around the colorful display, dragging and dropping, rearranging parts of a picture. Completing the scene in less than three minutes was a win. Plan B was better than plan A, I told myself. Not only was I having fun, I was improving my brain's health, and also working—gathering game recommendations for my students who were preparing to teach math in grade school.

Twenty minutes and seven wins, two losses later, both Bruce and Toi arrived at my table, the latter with our steaming, fragrant meals. I wondered if Toi had been watching the door, waiting for Bruce. Her smile said she was pleased at how the timing had worked out.

Why wasn't I smiling, too? Maybe because Bruce's greeting was neither as cheery nor as casual as befitted a midweek lunch. He gave me a longer hug, with a value-added back rub. No jokes. No, "Hey, what are you doing the rest of your life?" once he was seated.

"What's wrong?" I asked.

His eyes widened, as they did when light dawned. His

forehead became deeply furrowed, all the way up to his dark widow's peak.

"You haven't heard," he said.

I had the sinking feeling that this wasn't about twenty-five-year-old news. But Bruce was sitting across from me, healthy and fit, ready to dig into his squid. How bad could it be? "Please tell me, Bruce. What haven't I heard?"

He took a long, slow breath. "One of your students, Jennifer Marshall, was found on campus about an hour ago, badly beaten. She's in a coma at Henley General."

My heart jumped; my hand jerked. My fork flew across my plate of crab Rangoon and smashed into my teacup. My heart raced to catch up.

CHAPTER $\sqrt{3}$

When my heart slowed to normal again, Toi and Bruce were mopping up lemon tea and fried batter from the table in front of me. They brushed away my attempt to help.

I began to dress for the outdoors, focused on leaving Pan's, getting to the hospital to see Jenn. I buttoned my sweater, added my coat, tucked my scarf into my lapels, all in somewhat of a fog.

When I was fully outfitted, hat and gloves in place, I dug my keys from my purse and started toward the exit.

"Hold on, Sophie," Bruce said, putting the last soggy napkin on the tray Toi held out. "I'm driving you home."

I shook my head. "I'm going to the hospital."

While we argued, Toi had been working; she reappeared with our meals wrapped in plastic, ready to go.

After a few rounds of what might be termed a debate, during which I insisted on driving myself to Henley General in my Honda, and Bruce insisted on taking me to my home in his Mustang, we compromised.

"Tell me again how this is a win-win?" Bruce asked from behind the wheel of his Mustang. We were headed in the direction of Henley General. He'd cranked up the heat as far as it would go. I knew the gesture was solely for me. This was a guy who played with ice, deliberately heading for the most frigid parts of the world with a Windbreaker and maybe an extra pair of socks.

"I gave in on the part about driving myself," I explained.

Bruce grinned. "Right. I still don't see why we're going to the hospital. Everyone who needs to be there already is."

"Except me."

His grin broadened into a resigned smile.

"And you've told me all you know?" I asked. "You don't know exactly where on campus she was found, or who found her, or who attacked her, or any other details?"

Bruce shook his head at all my questions. "Sorry. I know whoever attacked her took her backpack, which is not surprising. But Virge is there. And we're only ten minutes out. ETA two forty-nine."

Usually I loved Bruce's emergency language; today it was too real. "Virgil. Of course. That's how you knew about this"—I waved my arm, unable to bring myself to finish the phrase—"this, in the first place."

He nodded. "My man on the force. Intel faster and better than the police scanner."

Virgil always gave MAstar a heads-up if there might be a chance they'd be needed at a trauma site. Not necessarily a homicide, I reminded myself. And when Henley College was involved, Virgil was likely to also call Bruce directly. I wished I could get my own name on the short list.

"Jenn made the presentation at our seminar this morning," I told Bruce. "She did a really great job." I had no trouble raising my evaluation of her Gertrude Cox performance from "adequate," which was what I'd thought of it at the time, to "stellar." It seemed important to lift Jenn up and keep her at the front of my thoughts. As if she could hear me. As if that would matter in her survival.

"She's a math major, right?" Bruce asked.

"Yes, and she's very talented in music, also. In fact, the Music Department chair worked it out so she doesn't have to pay the usual fee to practice at other venues with operating carillons."

"She practices at other schools?" Bruce was kindly feeding my need to talk about Jenn.

"Schools and churches. She and Andrew Davies often travel together to Boston."

"He's her boyfriend?"

I shook my head. "I don't think so. Just a friend. Another sophomore math major, from the West Coast."

"Where's Jenn's family?"

"They live in Fitchburg."

"A local girl. If fifty miles is local."

"Her poor parents," I said, suddenly broadening my scope of concern. "They struggle as it is. Her dad's a house painter. He depends on new construction for steady work and there's not much of that these days. They don't need this. Their daughter—"

"We're almost there," Bruce said, pointing to the blue hospital sign at the side of the road. He looked over at me. "You doing okay?"

I nodded. "I'll be better when I know Jenn will be okay."

I thought of how I'd given the seminar students a special bon voyage pat after class. *Oh no, Jenn had rushed out early. She hadn't gotten the pat. No wonder . . .*

It wasn't often that superstition took over my brain, but when it did, it was uncontrollable, a serious detour in my wiring. I ended up making connections no logical person, let alone a professional mathematician, should make. Freely associating current carillon students with one who fell from the tower twenty-five years ago, relying on good omens and reassuring phrases to ward off bad luck. What was next? Rabbits' feet and horseshoes?

I sat back as we passed the Henley Public Library, surrounded by a patchy green and brown lawn and bare trees. Mounds of dirty ice from the December snowfall lined the pathways that wound through the lawn and dotted the curbs of the sidewalk. I had the urge to have Bruce pull over so I could take down the remaining Christmas decorations around the front entrance. The wreath on the door looked as haggard as I felt and was less appropriate than ever with Jenn in the hospital.

I needed a timeline for the day, a dose of reality. I shook my head, determined to return to the rule of reason, though it bothered me to realize I might have been enjoying special service at Pan's restaurant while my student was being attacked on our own campus.

Jenn had left Franklin Hall just before noon, right after her seminar presentation, probably to avoid any attention or an overdose of congratulations. She might have walked over to the Mortarboard Café, the campus coffee shop, for lunch. Or to the library. Or to any place, as a matter of fact. I started to choke up again as I remembered her silly knit ski hat, with pom-poms on the ends of the ties. It fit the image I had of her as an innocent grade school child. Never mind that she'd written a stellar paper on tensor analysis last term.

I returned to my timeline, recalling that I'd headed for Pan's soon after the party ended and reached the restaurant by one. Bruce had called me about one forty, while I was eating my appetizer. I'd foolishly thought he was referring to Kirsten Packard as the campus "event," but he'd already heard about Jenn by then. That left only about an hour window during which Jenn could have been attacked. In broad daylight. It made no sense at all.

Bruce's muscle car seemed to shrink, until even my five-foot-three frame felt cramped in the seat, the dashboard and windshield moving in on me. While I'd been sipping hot tea and searching the web for information on a long-ago death, Jenn was under attack.

"I hope she makes it," I said, half to myself.

Bruce put his hand on my knee as if to steady me, or brace me for a collision.

Henley General Hospital was undergoing renovation, making it harder than ever to navigate the various wards, wings, and their offshoots. Whoever thought of putting colored stripes on the floor for navigation was onto something, except they'd forgotten to provide a key to the code. Would following the yellow line take you to the cardiac unit? Or to the ICU? Did the red line lead to obstetrics? To the laboratory? There was no clue. The result was a grid without documentation. It looked like a maze in a puzzle book. During my time of frequent visits in the last months of my mother's life, I'd often thought of copying and submitting the floor pattern to fulfill my puzzle-of-the-month contract.

The hospital receptionist had sent us up two flights, on the blue path, which came to a dead end at Gastroenterology. Fortunately, Detective Virgil Mitchell was on a path to coffee at that point and we met in front of a vending machine.

He gave me a hug, which always left me feeling like I'd plopped onto a comfy couch. Virgil used his great height and considerable bulk to advantage in many ways. Better not to be on the receiving end of it in physical combat, but for sheer comfort, he was the best.

"How is she?" I asked, as soon as I was standing on my own again. With Bruce's arm around me, that is.

Virgil cleared his throat. I recognized the strategy he used when he realized he'd better shed his clinical vocabulary, born of years in law enforcement and many unpleasant visits to this facility and others like it. If challenged, I'd have bet that Virgil knew where all the colored lines on the hospital floor ended up.

"We don't know yet. They've induced a coma. And we're just waiting."

"Where was she when—"

"Along the side of the dorm," Virgil said. "The one at the northeast corner of the campus."

"Clara Barton Hall? That's not Jenn's residence hall. She lives in Paul Revere, at the front of the campus, on Henley Boulevard."

"A busy street," Virgil said, as if Jenn should have been walking there instead of on a non-busy campus pathway.

"Did someone actually beat her? I mean, badly?" I had no idea where those questions came from. Apparently in the recesses of my mind, something like a seizure or heart attack for a nineteen-year-old student sounded better to me than an attack by another human being.

Another serious throat-clearing on Virgil's part. A young man in green hospital garb pushed a large cart of food covered with stainless steel lids in front of Virgil, giving him a minute to form his answer. "'Scuse me, please," we heard from the worker, in the wake of a most unappetizing odor. I wondered what meal, or excuse for a meal, was served in the middle of the afternoon.

Virgil took a breath and answered. "Yes, there was an attack."

Cops were like PR people, I realized—those who declared "Mistakes were made." Passive voice was their friend. Virgil wouldn't say, "Someone beat your student," but rather, "There was an attack." As if a change in grammatical structure could soften the brutality of what had happened. I fought back tears as I tried to face the facts.

"Do you know who did it?" I asked.

I knew I shouldn't put Virgil on the spot so soon. Bruce

had been thoughtful enough to buy a coffee for Virgil and now handed it to him. But I seemed to have lost control of my breathing and of my thoughts.

"Three kids were leaving the dorm after some meeting and they saw the end of it. The attack. They ran over and the guy took off. Two of them chased him, but didn't catch him. The other stayed with Jenn and called nine-one-one. She was lucky." Virgil looked at me and changed his judgment. "Well, not lucky."

"The kids saw who did it?"

"Not exactly."

"How about we go to the cafeteria," Bruce said, taking my arm. "You can't see her now anyway, Sophie, and the staff will know where to find us as soon as she's able to talk."

"The coffee's better there, too," Virgil said, after taking a sip of Bruce's offering.

Better coffee for Virgil. It was the least I could do. Not that I was finished interrogating him.

With a table full of Jenn's student friends along the back wall, the hospital cafeteria looked like an ordinary day at Henley's campus coffee shop. I recognized Jenn's roommate, Patty Reynolds, and other residents of Paul Revere Hall, including fellow math major and carillonist Andrew Davies. Clear plastic drink cups dominated the long orange table. The mood was decidedly solemn.

Not surprising, there wasn't much levity at any of the tables in the room. Except for the maternity ward, I guessed, there was little joy in any hospital. I noted a family that included a small child with a solemn face, picking at a couple of burgers; a set of older adults talking softly; and two men, who seemed to be at odds about something, sitting at a table in a dark corner. They looked like hard workers, with worn jeans and muddy boots, not unlike the construction workers on the Henley campus.

I sent a small wave to the students' table as Bruce, Virgil, and I approached a neighboring table where Jenn's parents were in deep conversation with Randall Stephens, chair of Henley's Music Department and our most accomplished carillonist.

"You've never heard her play the carillon?" I heard Randy ask Mr. and Mrs. Marshall. His loud, deep voice echoed off the ugly walls. "You must. Jenn has a great gift. She's one of my best students. You know those bells in the tower weigh tons. Literally. Our largest bell weighs nearly five tons. Nine thousand, seven hundred and forty pounds."

Mrs. Marshall's eyes widened, and she gave Randy an interested look. Good for him, I thought, keeping Jenn's parents busy and also singing their daughter's praises. Mr. Marshall leaned in closer, cupping his ear. The Marshalls—both on the short side, like Jenn—were wearing what I was sure were their best coats, the ones they'd worn to the last Parents' Day event. Their narrow shoulders seemed even less able to support the heavy garments today. My guess was that they'd just arrived after a long drive from Fitchburg, made even worse during rush hour.

Randy appeared pleased to have captured their attention, and though the grieving parents said nothing, he continued in his sure basso tones.

"You see, the keyboard and bells are in different parts of the tower. The keys—they're called 'batons' and they're much bigger than piano keys—they're linked to the bells' clappers by an elaborate network of wires and ropes. Yes, that's right. And your petite daughter makes the keyboard sing." He made firm balls with his hands. "Carillonists have to use closed fists as well as their feet." Randy made pounding motions with his arms and fists, which, to me, looked too much like he was beating someone. He might have realized it himself, since he stopped abruptly and said, "I'll arrange for you to hear Jenn's practice concert as soon as we're all back to normal."

He sat back and took a deep breath, as if exhausted by a performance, and the Marshalls followed suit.

I admired Randy's attempts to keep the Marshalls distracted, and, even more, his confidence in Jenn's future. I wanted eventually to talk to her parents, but I didn't want to break Randy's rhythm. If he had them thinking of something other than their daughter's comatose state, even for a few moments, I could wait my turn. I had a feeling there would be plenty of time later.

I nodded to Randy and gave him a sort of thumbs-up as Bruce, Virgil, and I took seats at the far end of the table, where the pale yellow wall faded into a light blue. The effect was not aesthetically pleasing, but rather looked like the painters had run out of yellow. The cafeteria color scheme was probably thought up by the same guy who painted the stripes on the hallway tiles.

Andrew Davies left his table and squatted beside me. His eyes were ringed in red, his jet black hair disheveled in a way that suggested he'd been running his hands through it.

"What can we do, Dr. Knowles?" he asked.

As strange as it sounded in the circumstances, the question fit Andrew's personality. A problem solver. I'd always known that he'd make a good engineer, his professional goal.

After a minute, I thought of something we could do. We could gather information and pool our intel to help the police find Jenn's attacker.

"Andrew, do you know the guys who interrupted the attack and called nine-one-one?"

"Yeah, I know who they are. Three guys from the Commuter Council. They'd had a meeting in Clara Barton this morning and were on their way to lunch at the Coffee Filter."

It made sense. The Coffee Filter was a shop across Main Street from the Clara Barton dorm. Had Jenn been on her way there? Unlikely. First, that would not have been the shortest route for her from Franklin Hall. Second, for Henley College resident students like Jenn, the Coffee Filter was much more expensive than the Mortarboard, the café on campus, which gave residents a package deal with a discount. I couldn't imagine Jenn spending half her hourly wage on coffee and a scone at the upscale Coffee Filter.

I looked around the cafeteria. "Are they here? The commuters?"

Andrew shook his head. "The cops talked to all the guys right there on the spot. Now they're down at the police station."

"Probably to sign statements."

"Yeah, I think so. Hey, Dr. Knowles, do you think you could come over and talk to us?" Andrew gestured toward a table two down from where Randy was still talking to the Marshalls. At my table, Bruce and Virgil were head-to-head about something I couldn't hear. "We're all a little freaked out," Andrew continued. "It would be nice to, you know, just talk or something."

I could hardly wait. Without attracting anyone's attention, I stood and followed Andrew to the students' table. I was eager to learn what they had heard. Perhaps one or two of them had been close to the scene, albeit too late to protect Jenn. I envisioned myself in a conference with Virgil later, where we'd each have something to contribute to the investigation into who attacked my major and why.

Maybe I could help give Jenn's story a happier ending than Kirsten Packard's, which still weighed on me, and about which I could do nothing.

As I took a seat between Andrew Davies and Patty Reynolds I felt my cell phone vibrate. I realized I hadn't checked it for a couple of hours and saw that I had ten voice mail messages. I didn't bother to click over to my email. I'd get to them all later.

For now, I checked the current caller ID. And LOL'd.

Of all the news I could have received, the offer of food was among the best.

Bruce had dialed me, cell to cell, from two tables over. I looked up and smiled at him.

"How about a turkey sandwich? Chips? Chocolate chip cookie?" he asked, cell phone to cell phone.

"It's not necessary to—"

"Or, I can go to my car and get your crab Rangoon."

"Funny. I'll take the sandwich, thanks."

My thoughtful boyfriend had figured out that all I'd eaten today was a piece of supermarket cake and two Thai shrimp. I nurtured a slim hope that the turkey sandwich wouldn't come from the same kitchen as the food on the cart that had passed us in the hallway.

CHAPTER $\sqrt{4}$

Nothing made me feel at home like sitting with a group of students, no matter what their majors. Even in a hospital cafeteria. Even with a less-than-gourmet sandwich and a stale cookie. It might as well be written on a poster that travels with every teacher: "When young people look to you for guidance, for comfort, for hope, you have no choice but to forget your own problems and tend to theirs."

Bruce had delivered enough food for the whole table, six servings of everything. Then he'd whispered in my ear, "Do your thing, teach," and returned to Virgil.

"They won't tell us what's going on," Patty said.

I almost said, "Welcome to the club." Instead, I tried to be a good facilitator. "Everyone has a job to do, and their first priority is getting Jenn back to health," I said.

"I heard someone say they induced a coma. What does that even mean?" a striking young blond woman asked. She'd been introduced by Andrew as Willa Lansdale, a music major whose family had contributed to the new carillon program.

Willa's question I could handle, thanks to pseudo medical training from Bruce's pals. I'd often been entertained and educated by his flight nurses while visiting him at MAstar.

"They've given her an anesthetic to protect her brain. She must have had a lot of swelling and they need to reduce it by controlling the blood flow." I stopped, realizing I'd come to the end of my knowledge, all anecdotal, of how the brain worked.

I saw a familiar look on the students' faces. The look that said they could tell this wasn't my area of expertise. Maybe I could work the conversation around to numerical simulation of a partial differential equation.

My turn to ask a question. I scanned their faces. "Did any of you have a chance to talk to the guys who came to Jenn's rescue? Do you know if she said anything to them?"

"Like who her attacker was? You wish," said freshman Brent Riggs, who'd been at Jenn's seminar this morning.

"There's all kinds of rumors going around campus," Willa said.

"Yeah, like, I heard someone say the guy was wearing one of those bright yellow Henley College sweatshirts," said a student I didn't know, possibly attracted to the table by the wealth of food.

"No way," said Brent, the loyal freshman. "Couldn't have been one of ours. I'm tweeting about it. So everyone knows it was an unauthorized person."

"You can't be sure," another said.

"My roommate heard that after the thug got away, one of the Henley commuter students was leaning over Jenn and he heard her say 'money.' Just the word 'money,'" Willa offered. She pulled the sleeves of her sweater down over her hands, to the tips of her fingers, as if she were trying to protect herself from a fate similar to Jenn's.

"Money? That would be the last thing anyone would mug Jenn for," Patty said.

"He took her backpack," Willa said.

"That doesn't mean there was money in it," Patty responded. "She just bought a brand new laptop, but she kept it in our room."

"Whatever," Willa said. Student speak for "I don't really care enough to continue this conversation."

I tended to agree with Jenn's roommate. Jenn was one of the least likely students to be walking around with a wad of cash, but I tucked the information away to relate to Virgil. Maybe it would connect with something he knew.

Another student, with tight brown waves in her chestnut hair, spoke up. "I'm Lauren Hughes, Dr. Knowles. I'm not in your classes, but I know how great you are with my friends who are your majors"—she leaned into Andrew—"and I just want to say you're cool, you know. I wish I had a head for math. I'd so major in it."

Nothing wrong with accepting a compliment, I decided, and resisted the urge to tell her everyone's head was pretty much the same and with effort and the right support, anyone could major in math, or physics, or music.

Except for me. I could never *get* music. Unlike many math and science people who seemed to drift toward music. Albert Einstein, for one, who was proficient with the violin, and Peter Knowles, my father, for another, an accomplished mathematician and pianist. He'd died when I was a toddler, and all through my childhood, I'd made several attempts to learn the piano, in an effort to get close to my absent father, but it never panned out. Maybe there was something to this wiring theory after all and I'd never be a musician. On the other hand, I'd never tried the carillon. I made a fist with my hand and studied it. A possibility.

"Do you think we're all in danger?" Lauren asked. "I've always felt safe on campus, but maybe that's not realistic. I mean, maybe we should all be worried now?"

"Or, maybe Jenn knew the guys from home or something," Willa suggested.

Patty frowned. "You're saying because Jenn doesn't live in Henley she brought this on herself? Like she invited some lowlifes from her hometown to campus?"

"That's not what I meant," Willa said.

"Well, whatever you're thinking, this is not Jenn's fault," Patty said.

"She didn't say it was," Lauren said, her voice soft, her words tentative.

"Not directly, she didn't," Patty countered.

"Not indirectly either," Willa said, defending herself in a forceful tone.

Uh-oh. Not that it was a surprise that today's dramatic event would bring out underlying tensions and prejudices. No matter how much we tried to get past class distinctions at Henley, an undercurrent of strained relationships was always there. Scholarship students versus those fortunate enough to afford full tuition, commuters versus residents, town versus gown. And a mugging on campus was the perfect trigger to bring the hairline fractures to a breaking point.

In front of me was a cross section of Henley's resident student population. Andrew often joked about his "extensive portfolio of loans" that his grandchildren would be paying off. Willa's family was in a position to give generously to the school, including a donation to the carillon program, though Willa herself wasn't interested in studying the instrument. Andrew had introduced her as strictly "a violin person." From my tenure on the admissions committee I knew that Patty and Lauren were somewhere in the middle of that spectrum, with limited financial aid, like Brent.

I allowed one more round of "Yes, you did" and "No, I didn't" before I stepped in.

"Let's think about how to give Jenn the support she needs when she wakes up, and how we can help the police find out who did this to her," I offered. "And Lauren's question about safety is a good one. We should all be a little more cautious until this guy is caught. I'm sure there'll be extra security on campus." Not quite true; more like a hope than a certainty. So far there'd been no official memo on the incident. Unless it was buried in my untouched email collection.

I glanced around the table. Lauren's eyes were cast down, almost hidden by her long, wavy brown hair. Brent and Andrew both had screwed up their mouths, their fingers tapping the table (Brent) or squeezing a drink cup (Andrew); Patty and Willa were in a face-off.

"No one is blaming Jenn for this," I said. I hoped for an apology or at least confirmation from Willa, whose words had started this thread, but I heard nothing other than a few sniffles from Lauren.

"So what can we do?" Andrew asked.

I looked over to where Bruce and Virgil had been sitting, at the same long table as the Marshalls and Randy Stephens. The table was empty.

If a call had come from the doctors, it would have been directed to Jenn's parents, or possibly to Virgil, who'd been hoping to talk to Jenn. I'd been left behind. And here I was the one with the big "money" clue. I blew out an annoyed breath.

I stood and addressed my impromptu class. "Why don't we all go up to the waiting area and find out if Jenn's awake. If we can't see her we can at least say hello to her parents. I'm sure they'd love to know her friends are here and ready to support her."

The students shuffled around, packing up and tossing lunch wrappers. Like typical resident students, they'd scarfed down every crumb; like a typical spoiled professor, I ate only the cookie and a bite of turkey and discarded the rest. We all headed to the elevator together, Patty and Willa, both tall and thin, keeping at arm's length.

As for my two friends, Bruce and Virgil, who had neglected to advise me of a call or notification from above, I'd deal with them later.

Henley General's ICU waiting room had been refurbished since my last visit several years ago, during my mother's final days. I counted myself among the fortunate in that I'd had no reason to return, nor to cause others to return because of me.

Now, except for a small family gathering in one corner, the occupants of the newish mauve chairs with arms of polished dark wood (or shiny plastic) were members of the Henley community.

Randy Stephens was with a new group of student visitors, some of whom I recognized. Music majors who knew Jenn, I assumed. They talked in low voices or paced across the carpet, a lighter shade of mauve than the chairs and featuring a leafy pattern.

I spotted Ted Morrell, whose introductory physics class Jenn was enrolled in during the regular school year. He sat slightly removed from the others, flipping through an issue of a news magazine, several months old, unless the hospital had changed its ways.

"I'm glad you came," I said to Ted.

He nodded and waved his hand in a gesture that said it was nothing. I knew he was here to offer support to a student he had in class, one he knew I was close to. I wondered if Ted was also thinking of another long-ago campus incident. More likely, I was the only one fixated on a cold case that wasn't even a case.

On impulse, I approached Ted with a question.

"Just curious," I said. "What was Kirsten Packard's roommate's name?"

Ted frowned and shook his head, clearly taken by surprise, which had been my plan. "I don't remember."

I laughed and pretended not to notice his perturbed response. "What? Come on, Ted. You know every physics major since the beginning of time."

"It was twenty-five years ago and I don't remember," Ted said.

He turned the page of the magazine, shook it in place, adjusted his horn rims, and lowered his eyes to his reading. I didn't for a minute believe Ted's protestation. Henley's Physics Department had always been small, its faculty and majors very close. Why wouldn't he tell me Kirsten's roommate's name? I left him to his reasons.

Bruce, anticipating my pique about not being alerted to the call from the doctors, came up to me with a sheepish look. I'd considered saying something like "Why didn't you take me with you?" But did I really want to sound like a grade school kid who wasn't picked first for the infield?

He put his arm around me and led me to the chair he'd abandoned. "You looked so comfortable talking to your class, I didn't want to interrupt."

"It's not as if I was napping. But thanks," I said, taking his seat.

"I knew you'd figure it out soon enough." He checked his watch. "And you did. We just got here. The Marshalls and Virge are in with the doctors."

The student contingent from the cafeteria took seats on the chairs that lined the wall. The row of framed photos above them were meant to give comfort, I supposed, with their innocuous renderings of trees and meadows and, for a change of pace, a close-up of a dandelion blossom. I wasn't sure what kind of image it would take to ease my mind. Maybe a Rubik's Cube. Or a wall-size crossword puzzle. If my friend Ariana were here, and not wisely in sunny Florida, she'd have handed me materials for a beading project. I had to settle for one of her deep-breathing exercises.

After a few minutes, during which only a low hum of voices and a rustling of dog-eared magazine pages broke the silence, Mr. and Mrs. Marshall came through double doors off the waiting area, Virgil following close behind. The Marshalls wore a forlorn look that suggested no change in Jenn's status, rather than something better—or worse.

"There's no significant change to report right now," Virgil announced, as softly as he could while still encompassing the whole Henley crowd. "They're recommending that we all go home. She's in good hands and they know how to reach us."

He couldn't have done better if he'd read from a script.

Resigned, we made plans for the next few hours.

Patty had had the presence of mind to make arrangements for the Marshalls to stay overnight, or as long as needed, in an area of the Clara Barton dorm reserved for special guests or visitors in extenuating circumstances.

"I'm sorry it's the dorm near where Jenn was mugged," she whispered to me. "But at least they won't have to make the long drive home to Fitchburg in the dark. And I gave them Jenn's smartphone so they can keep in touch more easily. They only had one old-fashioned flip phone between them."

I commended her for her thoughtfulness, then had an idea of my own to put to the assembly. As much as I longed to bury my head in a puzzle right now, like one of the logic puzzles bookmarked on the phone in my purse, there was something more important that needed my attention.

I made the rounds of the small groups and invited them all to my house. A much more comfortable place to wait for the update on Jenn's condition, with better food.

"That's cool, Dr. Knowles. Willa has a car and we can take some kids," Andrew said, with a strong hint that he and Willa were a "we," though earlier it had seemed that Andrew and Lauren were a couple. And earlier than that, I'd considered it might be Andrew and Jenn who were a twosome. It was hard to tell these days.

"Yes, very cool, Dr. Knowles," Virgil said, with a know-ing grin. "And how handy that we'll all be together when the call comes." His strong hint was that I had an ulterior motive wrapped in my generosity. There might have been a grain of truth in that.

I loved the parties in the Ben Franklin Hall lounge, but I usually kept gatherings in my home to a small number of close friends. Pizza nights with Virgil and Bruce, consist-ing of lots of cheese and tomato, drinks, a movie, and war stories. Beading sessions with Ariana, who labeled my jewelry-making attempts "obsessively symmetric," and a few other women who were customers in her downtown Henley shop, A Hill of Beads. Working dinners with Fran, where we generated plans for the department, sometimes joined by Judy, who helped us solve the world's problems in between laughs over Fran's grandchildren or Judy's failed dates.

I missed my girl buddies. They allowed me to be ratio-nal, yet encouraged the occasional crazy idea. Such as call-ing Fran in Africa, once our time zones were compatible, to ask what she remembered about Kirsten Packard and her fall from the Admin tower. I knew I should let Fran know about Jenn, but I didn't want her to worry when she was a continent away. I hoped if I waited just a short time, Jenn would be fine, the thug would be in jail, and Fran could hear a complete, happy-ending story, or I could skip it entirely until she returned.

This afternoon was a different kind of gathering in my little cottage. Not quite a wake but certainly not a party. The commuters had gone home straight from the hospital; the residents had arrived at my house in two cars. Dorm students seldom passed up a chance for a meal off campus. The same might be said for Ted, whose wife was visiting relatives in Ohio. He'd asked if my invitation included teachers.

"Only full professors," I'd said, happy that he felt free to ask.

"I guess that means me, too," Randy had said, decidedly not a surprise, given his new closeness with the Marshall family.

I shared food and drink at the campus coffee shop with students often enough to know the current fashion in snacks and beverages. Thanks to masterful vehicle logistics by Bruce, we used both cars to pick up enough supplies to cover all tastes. I thought I owed everyone something more nutritious than pizza at dinnertime, so I chose a large roasted chicken and what my mother would have called "the fixings."

I hoped the Marshalls would feel comfortable in my home and with Jenn's friends. I wanted them to feel as welcome as possible, though nothing could make up for the terrible state their daughter was in.

It took very little time for my small space to become warm (my heating system was working) and inviting (Bruce had spread out a buffet on my kitchen island). Soon my coatrack, a relic from my grandparents' home, was bulging with parkas, scarves, and extra sweaters. Backpacks and boots were strewn on the floor in the entryway. As much as I valued my privacy, I liked the look and the sounds of friends making themselves at home, eating and drinking as if they belonged.

The students had located some of my favorite kitchen items. A pie plate with the numbers of the value of pi around the edge. A smaller version that was a tiny condiment bowl in which the numbers of pi, starting with "three" at the bottom center, spiraled out to the rim. A snack plate with a crossword puzzle design, with the solution stamped on the back.

When I heard Lauren laughing in front of the open freezer door, I knew she'd found my ice cube tray, which held cubes in the shape of the letter pi. "I knew you were cool, Dr. Knowles," she said.

"Icy cool," Patty added.

I felt my home had passed some kind of coolness test. All was well.

Virgil mingled more than he would have if I'd had a purely social party with our peers. A widower and single father, Virgil didn't get out much, in his own words, and didn't feel the need to. His son was in college, the threshold for when Virgil said he'd think of dating again, but so far there was no sign of that. When Bruce or I would broach the subject, he'd shut us up with, "All the good ones are taken," or "It's not like Franklin Hall, you know. We don't have a party every week down at the station."

This afternoon I knew Virgil the Cop was in investigative mode, listening to the students' conversations, trying to pick up information about Jenn Marshall as informally as possible, in a way that wouldn't spook the kids. A thought came and went quickly—that Virgil might think one of these students was Jenn's attacker. I wished the thought had never entered my mind.

Once I was sure everyone was taken care of, I mingled also, seeking out the Marshalls. I realized I'd been avoiding them all afternoon, since I couldn't bear to see them so sad and I had no idea what to say or do that might cheer them up or give them hope.

I hadn't expected to see Jenn's parents again until March, for Pinning Day. Henley's custom was to celebrate sophomores who made their selection of a major field with a pinning ceremony that included parents. Sophomores officially declared their majors on that day, and faculty presented students in their department with a traditional Henley College pin. I hoped the Marshall family would all be in good health by the time the Math Department was ordering the refreshments for that day.

I couldn't locate Mrs. Marshall, but I found Mr. Marshall as I wandered to the family room, which was attached to my kitchen. Possibly having heard enough from Randy Stephens about Jenn's musical prowess, he had cornered two of the students.

"What's security like on campus?" I heard him ask.

"The dorms are always locked; you can't get into any of them without a key card," Lauren answered, expertly balancing a plate and a drink. I was reminded how easy it was to entertain students; they didn't require perfect Martha Stewart linens and place settings. They seldom needed a fork.

Willa held up her key card. "Yeah, everyone needs one of these. Technically."

"What do you mean?" Mr. Marshall asked.

"You're not supposed to be able to get in without a card, but we all know how lax it is. Someone holds the door for you, or even a stranger, maybe. Or you go in and you know you're going right back out, so you put in something to keep the door open so you won't have to bother with your key again."

"There's always a person at the desk in the lobby," Lauren said, defensive.

"A police officer?" Mr. Marshall asked.

Willa raised her eyebrows. "LOL," she said. If Jenn's father didn't understand text lingo, he didn't let on.

Lauren shook her head. "No, it would be a student. But they get training." I couldn't swear that Lauren was lying, but I'd never heard of Dorm Lobby Desk Training, unless it was to point out the nine-one-one code for emergencies.

"That's not much protection," Mr. Marshall said. His tone was gentler than his words, though both were heavy. He seemed to be trying to figure out why his innocent young daughter was three miles away in a coma instead of poring over her textbooks in a warm, well-lit dormitory room.

"And what about outside the dorms? On the campus?" Mrs. Marshall seemed to appear from nowhere to ask the question. She held a glass of water with both hands.

The group fell silent. And no wonder. Who could defend safety on our pathways with Jenn Marshall still hovering between life and death?

Willa gave it a try. "Some of us have phone apps," Willa said. "Like, I have Circle of 5. I just hit a button and a message goes out to five contacts that says 'Come and get me' and shows where I am." Andrew shot her a questioning look. "They're all big guys," she added. I guessed Andrew, a rather small guy, wasn't in Willa's Circle of 5.

"We also have an escort service if we need it," Lauren said.

"But they take forever to show up," Patty said. "Meanwhile, you could be waiting alone out there for, like, a half hour, to get from the library to your dorm. So you just figure, never mind, and go for it yourself."

Neither Mr. nor Mrs. Marshall showed signs of satisfaction with the offerings. I didn't blame them.

Brent stepped up. "Nothing like this has ever happened before," he said.

Not quite true, but Brent, as a freshman in only the second coed class in the formerly all-women's college, wouldn't know any better. I chose not to correct him and hoped Mr. Marshall wouldn't go through the archives and find out that there had been one or two other nasty incidents over the years. And if he went back far enough, he'd find that one of the tragedies involved Jenn's favored carillon. Or at least the tower that housed it.

I left the group, not eager to get caught up in a campus security discussion with the parents of an attack victim. I headed for the opposite corner of the kitchen–family room area, where Virgil sat at my breakfast table, facing the patio door while talking on his cell phone. I sauntered by, as if I weren't on a mission, knowing I'd find enough busywork in the vicinity to allow me to eavesdrop on his side of the conversation. I cleared the countertop, trashed used paper plates, and slowly loaded the dishwasher with glasses and mugs.

My mission was a wipeout, however, since all I heard was lots of "okays," four or five "uh-huhs," and a final "That's it?"

He hung up and smiled at me. Not giving a centimeter.

"How's the investigation going?" I asked, wiping a platter with extra attention.

"Fine."

"Any hot leads?" I laughed, attending to my drying chores as if the china were much more important than his answer and I was asking only out of politeness.

Virgil laughed in response, reached over to a bowl of cherries, and helped himself to a handful.

I gave in and took a seat across from him. I pushed the bowl toward him, ever the gracious hostess. "Please, Virgil? I have something to bargain with. A clue."

"You mean"—he made quotation marks with his fingers—"'money'?"

I hated being late to the party.

CHAPTER $\sqrt{5}$

With a party in full swing in my home, there were too many interruptions that kept me from charming Virgil into giving me news of the investigation. I would have been happy simply to learn what his buddies on the force were doing while he was surreptitiously interviewing students and waiting to speak to the victim.

Had the police put out an APB for the attacker? Was there a contingent of Henley's finest on the road, searching for the guy? Where? Did they think he was still in town? Were the techs combing the crime scene for hair and fibers? Looking at security footage? I shivered at my next thought. They might be waiting for the results of tests that would determine whether the brute left his DNA on Jenn.

I realized I had no description of the attacker, except that he was a lone male. I wondered how much detail the commuters had been able to provide in their witness statements. Was he wearing a baseball cap? A Red Sox jacket?

(As if that would narrow it down.) Surely not a Henley sweatshirt, as the rumor had suggested.

I was about to ask Virgil if perhaps the man had gotten into a car on Main, the wide street that ran between the Clara Barton dorm and the Coffee Filter, when Ted came into the kitchen. He showed me the lifeless black screen on his smartphone.

"Dead," Ted announced. "Any chance I can use your computer for a few minutes? I have to get back to people about my paper for the heavy metals conference in Atlanta this summer." He smiled. "Everything you ever wanted to know about tungsten under pressure."

"No problem," I said, pointing down the hallway. "Find Bruce and he'll take you back to my office."

"Okay if I print?"

I nodded. "Of course. It's a standard system; printer's right there."

Ted was replaced quickly by the long-legged Willa, alerting me that "the boys" were messing with the jigsaw puzzle laid out on a card table in my den, as my mother always called it. Poor Willa had a lot to learn.

I'd set the puzzle out for Melanie, Bruce's niece, who was due for a weekend visit, but I was happy to have anyone else work on it. When completed, this one would show a symmetry drawing by M. C. Escher, a pattern of repetition consisting of a man on horseback. Should we pay attention to the figure in light orange, traveling to the left? Or to the figure in dark orange, traveling to the right?

"Tell them to knock themselves out," I said to Willa. "There are a lot more puzzles where that one came from."

She walked away, her mouth twisted in displeasure.

After many futile calls to the hospital during the evening, spirits were low, but a community had formed around Mr. and Mrs. Marshall, who'd thanked me and Patty profusely for not leaving them stranded in a motel.

"Mr. Marshall and I are indebted to you, Dr. Knowles,"

Mrs. Marshall said, pulling me away from the students. "I don't think we'd get this kind of attention at a big school."

"But maybe the security would be better," Mr. Marshall said.

I was taken aback, not sure who else heard him. The situation clearly had a great impact on the gentle, down-home man. Fortunately, I realized immediately that, although I knew the stats for big and small campuses, this wasn't the time to recite them.

"Be sure to call me if there's anything I can do," I offered, as Patty Reynolds arrived to take them away.

Patty had assumed leadership of most of the guests, as well as the management of the Marshalls' stay in Clara Barton. Patty told me she'd make sure they were okay and if there was any news about progress in Jenn's condition or in finding her attacker, she'd let me know. Would that Virgil could be so forthcoming.

"Thanks for this, Dr. Knowles," Patty said, flailing her arms to encompass my little cottage. "This was the best way to spend such an awful day. I'm with Lauren. I'd so major in math if I could do it."

Nice to know that students were lining up to sign on to my department, if only they had the head for math. I wished Fran were here to appreciate my internal sarcasm. I'd waited too long to call her and now it was one in the morning in Rwanda. I couldn't take the chance that even night owl Fran would be up. Though she might not mind being awakened if the motive was strong enough, her husband, who'd traveled there with her, probably wouldn't be too happy.

The students left, promising to stay in touch. I promised the same and said good-bye. Ted waved sheets of paper at me as he made his way through the kitchen, indicating a successful session at my computer. Randy, who'd spent most of the time talking to the Marshalls or Ted, blew me a kiss, shouted a dramatic "Thank you, doll," and followed Ted out the back door.

" 'Doll,' huh?" Bruce said.

"That's Randy," I said. "He conducts a regional orchestra down in Barnstable County."

"That explains it," Bruce said, slicing the air with his arms, attempting to mime an orchestra leader, but looking instead like a helicopter pilot gone mad.

I gave the house a once-over. I checked each room, fluffed pillows, and picked up paper cups and plates and crumpled napkins as I traveled. I'd closed off my bedroom at the end of the hallway, leaving the guest room and den for my visitors. Ted had left my office as neat (or not) as he'd found it, except for an opened bottle of water sitting on an MIT coaster, one of a brass and leather set bestowed on me as a conference speaker.

I found no stray guests lurking in the corners.

We were down to Bruce, Virgil, and me. I felt I should bring out pizza and beer and a deck of cards. As if that might erase the events of the day.

The three of us took our drinks of choice—sparkling water for me and Bruce, coffee for Virgil, looking to a long night—to my den, which held almost no remaining signs of our recent gathering.

"Pretty neat crowd," Virgil said from his spot on my new leather recliner. Bruce and I took the old couch. From the way Virgil inspected the room, I guessed he meant to define the attendees as "not messy," as opposed to "cool dudes."

I sat through about fifteen minutes of small talk. How polite all the students were; how nice of the faculty, Randy and Ted, to come; how Virgil's son was spending his winter break (not in a cleverly devised Intersession, it turned out). We covered how well done the chicken was and how tasty the side salads. When we got to whether it would snow again this month, I'd had all I could take.

Not that Virgil didn't deserve a break. He'd been on the phone more than off since he arrived at my house, squeezing himself into a corner, scribbling on a pad of paper, even stepping out onto the freezing patio for privacy for one call. But I was eager to get to work.

"What's this guy look like?" I asked Virgil. "The one who attacked Jenn."

Smooth move, I thought, slipping in a casual question. A bit out of context, but good timing, since Virgil had pulled the lever to send the recliner to a non-upright and locked position.

Why, then, did Bruce and Virgil burst out laughing?

"Real subtle, Soph," Bruce said, slapping my knee for effect.

Ignoring my boyfriend's gesture, I leaned forward, toward Virgil. "I want in," I said. "How's that for not subtle?"

"I was just about to ask for your help," Virgil said.

I turned my head away, the better to look at him sideways. What kind of joke was this?

"Really," Virgil said, sensing my skepticism. "We have a lot of security footage and I think it would be helpful if you and some of the kids looked at it."

Now we're cooking. I took a deep, exhilarating breath, put my feet up on the coffee table, and fired away.

"We can gather the students and see if anyone recognizes the attacker or spots someone unfamiliar on the video." I grabbed a pad and pen from the holder on an end table and made notes as I talked. "Someone who doesn't fit in for any reason. Someone too old, too young, not dressed right. Carrying something out of the ordinary." I paused, tapped the pad, and drew a line to start a new list. "Where are the cameras? I know we'll have footage from the dorm and from the Student Union building next door. The camera on the guard post at the library entrance is a good spot to check also. And we can see if the Coffee Filter has a camera. If not, the bank right next door to it surely will. We should go back, maybe a few days, and look at earlier footage. Maybe a week."

"So, you'll help?" Virgil asked.

"I'll think about it," I said, shrugging. "I'm kinda busy."

It was the best laugh all day.

We wrapped up the conversation about the Marshall girl, as Virgil named her. He promised to email or call me with a time when we could review the relevant security footage. I nagged him to have it ready tomorrow and he humored me with a solid thumbs-up.

My jobs were to find a room on campus for the viewing and make a list of students likely to be helpful with the project.

"Round up the usual suspects," Bruce said.

"That's all you've got, Bruce? *Casablanca*?" Virgil asked.

Bruce, whose goal was to watch a movie every day, and quote from one as often as possible, put on a sheepish face. "Tough day," he said. "Give me a break, Virge."

We gave Bruce a pass, especially since he was all but out the door for his regular shift at MAstar, which began at nine PM. "Serving and protecting in the air," he always said, but I suspected tonight there was a DVD on the schedule also. He needed to refresh his inventory of suitable movie quotes.

As Virgil was struggling into his heavy coat, I remembered what else I'd wanted to talk to him about, before Jenn Marshall captured all our attention. I was surprised to realize how long it had been—a couple of hours?—since I'd thought about Kirsten Packard.

"Can you hang back a minute?" I asked Virgil.

"Sure." He let his coat fall onto a chair and returned to the recliner. I made a mental note to talk to Bruce about a possible birthday present for his friend.

"Ready for a beer?"

"More coffee, please."

"Still on duty?"

He gave me a questioning look. "You tell me."

"I'll get the coffee."

I hurried to the kitchen, grateful for Virgil, Bruce, and all their ilk, who were never truly off duty.

It was hard to decide on a tactic for presenting my carillon theory to Virgil. I chose a slow lead-in. "I learned something interesting today," I said, setting a tray of coffee and cookies on the small table next to the recliner. I took the couch again, and in about ten minutes, I'd told him all I knew about Kirsten Packard. "Did you ever hear about the case?" I asked.

"Sure. Cops talk about twenty-five-year-old cases all the time, over donuts."

"Virgil!"

He lost the grin. "I'm sorry, Sophie. I know this is an intense time for you. I'm trying to help you take a step back. It's not your job to solve cases, hot or cold. Maybe I was wrong to ask you to look at the footage around today's attack on your student."

"No, no." I rushed to correct Virgil and dismiss the worst possible outcome—that he'd cut me out of Jenn's case. Those of us who never served in the military or law enforcement were at a tactical disadvantage; that is, we were no good at tactics.

"I'm just curious about Kirsten Packard. Ted Morrell and Judy Donohue—she's the biology chair—said there might have been a cover-up back then."

"They were there at the time?"

"Ted was there. He's been at Henley forever."

"And he said he thought there was a cover-up?"

I lowered my eyes. "Maybe it was only Judy."

"Who wasn't there at the time?"

I sighed. "Right."

"What makes you think it's easy to find out about something that happened twenty-five years ago? Problem is, there's too much of this DNA stuff on TV where they come back right after the commercial with the key to everything." Virgil shook his head and let out a syllable or two of disgust. "Or they hit a button on a computer and they get a list of every case back to the beginning of human history where the killer used a hammer."

"I know, that's unrealistic. But I just read that they found new documents about the day President Lincoln was assassinated."

"You don't say," Virgil said, feigning interest.

I continued in spite of his attitude. I was a teacher, after all. These working conditions weren't new to me. "A researcher discovered the records of an army surgeon who was at Ford's Theatre, in the next box, when Lincoln was shot. He was first on the scene, you might say, the first doctor to treat the president, and we're just now reading his report. How about that?"

"How about that?" Virgil echoed.

"Historians are calling it the equivalent of buried treasure. A firsthand account. Untainted."

"Did they find out anything?" Virgil asked. "Some new facts of the case?"

"Well, no, but—"

"Exactly."

I'd lost track of the point I was trying to make, but it was my own fault for taking us back to the Civil War.

"I know it seems nuts," I said. "But maybe there's a connection."

"Between . . . ?"

Virgil wasn't making this easy for me.

"I'm just saying—a girl is killed twenty-five years ago, and the tower is closed off. Then the tower is reopened and another girl is attacked."

Virgil blew out a breath, looking understandably confused, trying to process what I'd suggested. "The connection between the Marshall girl and the nineteen eighties girl is your bell tower?" He lifted his arm and twirled his fingers in the air. If we'd been playing charades, I might have guessed "ringing bells." Or "crazy theory."

The theory sounded lame, even to me, its originator. I didn't need Virgil to point out the holes. The girl's fall from the tower twenty-five years ago was what motivated closing the tower. Today's girl was attacked half a campus away from the tower, on the ground. And, in fact, the tower wasn't open yet. Also, there'd been no mention in the newspaper accounts of whether Kirsten was a carillonist. I'd almost asked Ted while he was in my house, but it seemed neither the time nor the place. I needed to let Ted think I'd dropped the matter before I could surprise him again with a query.

I felt I'd been working on a maze that I now discovered was really two mazes with nothing in common except one bend in the road.

"Sophie?" Virgil said. Thinking he'd lost me? Pretty close.

I stood and cleared my head. "Never mind," I said. "We should probably call it a night. I know you still have work to do."

"You sure?"

"Uh-huh."

I heard great relief as Virgil pushed his bulk off the recliner and grabbed his coat. I was relieved, too. Another two minutes and I was sure he'd have recommended therapy. Or something more serious, involving heavy doses of psychiatric meds and a skeleton key.

Could it be? My day had begun with simple calculus problems. It was now after nine in the evening, cold and windy in Massachusetts; three in the morning in Rwanda. Not a great time to call Fran. Unless she'd be thrilled to hear that a snowstorm was predicted for the weekend in the southern part of the state, namely, Henley, and she'd be missing it. I doubted Fran would have to worry this winter about polishing calf-length boots.

For another possible distraction, I could call Ariana in Florida for a simple chat. But, first, it was prime dating hour in Florida, and second, in spite of what I'd told Virgil, I wasn't ready to call it a night on Kirsten Packard.

Being, for the most part, a dutiful teacher, researcher, and puzzle-creator, I thought I'd better check my email. But not without sustenance. I raided the leftovers on my kitchen counters and in the fridge and made up a plate of the least nutritious morsels I could find. A few potato chips, two cookies, and a sliver of previously frozen strawberry shortcake. Tomorrow I'd balance it all out with a real dinner, I promised myself. I took the food and my laptop back to the couch. Tomorrow I'd also exercise, by the way.

My email inbox was overflowing. A quick glance told me there was nothing from Fran. I'd been hoping for a note saying, "Please call me at any hour of the day or night for any reason at all."

As I read notes from students, mostly about Jenn Marshall and not homework, I kept track of whom I might invite to the screening of security videos. I identified only two others besides the friends who'd been at my home this evening.

I emailed an invitation to all of the students, asking them to be ready to appear, time and place to be announced as soon as I knew.

I picked at the shortcake, which was mediocre at best, the kind of frozen dessert that has the smell and taste of ice, no matter what the ingredients listed on the box.

Skipping to puzzle business, I noticed a note from one of my magazine editors. I opened it, not ready for trouble. But there it was.

I'm writing to introduce myself—I'm your new copyeditor and look forward to working with you. By the
way, on the most recent crossword you submitted,
I took the liberty of changing the wording on some
of your clues. I don't think it's anything your going
to have to check, however, since we're going to
press soon. (signed) Kenny Simmons

What? This was completely out of line with our procedures. And what copyeditor didn't know the difference
between *your* and *you're*? I'd already gone through rounds
of revision on the puzzle. I'd assumed I'd already seen the
final copy, ready for print. And what adult, if he was an
adult, still called himself Kenny?

My reaction was far beyond reasonable for the situation.
And I thought I knew why. Nothing had gone well today,
starting with a trip to the faculty lounge, where all I'd
hoped for was a little warmth and friendly conversation,
and ending with this. This Kenny person.

I'd have to drag out my contract with the publisher of the
magazine and see what kind of recourse I had. The puzzle
was my creation, and while it was not up for a Pulitzer, my
name, or at least my pseudonym, was on the page, and I
should be allowed to see the copy before it went to press.

This was no time to respond to Kenny, but I couldn't
take the chance that I'd be too late. I sent a quick reply
for now.

Thanks for checking in, Kenny. Please do not send
the copy to press until we talk.

I hit send, hard enough to break my fingernail. Now I
really was ready to call it a night.

CHAPTER $\sqrt{6}$

I didn't expect my Friday to begin so early. When my phone rang at four in the morning, I'd just gotten to sleep. At least that's how it felt.

I was barely able to make out Fran's voice from across the Atlantic, due in some part to the winds rattling my windows. "Sophie, I got the news about Jenn Marshall. Poor kid. I hope she makes it."

"Me, too," I managed.

"You must be crazy upset. Why didn't you call me?"

In spite of my sleepy fog, I laughed. "I didn't want to wake you."

I heard a quick intake of breath, followed by a chuckle. "Omigod, Sophie. It's the middle of the night for you. I miscalculated. Don't tell anyone I can't subtract. It's ten o'clock here; don't ask me why I thought you'd be just getting up."

"No problem," I said.

I envisioned Fran slamming her hand against her head. "Last night I called my sister in Chicago and got that wrong, too. I need to make myself a cheat sheet with all the time zones."

"It's great to hear your voice," I said, now fully awake. "I've been dying to talk to you. Never mind the time."

I knew I should ask first about how she and Gene were doing with the challenges of a different culture, whether they missed their grandkids, what it was like to teach on another continent, whether Fran's wardrobe of flowing, colorful pants outfits was suitable overseas. I hadn't talked to her since our Christmas call, nearly three weeks ago. She'd just arrived at KIST, the Kigali Institute of Science and Technology, and was eager to tell the world about today's Rwanda and the impressive economic gains it had made. Since then, with both of us so busy, there had been only quick emails back and forth. But rather than ask how differential equations came across in another language, the first question out of my mouth this morning was, "How did you find out about Jenn?"

"Randy Stephens is friends with Jim Hollister, the new guy in Henley's Budget Office, and Jim knows Gene from the business network in town," Fran answered. "He called Gene this morning. Or last night." She paused and laughed. "Or tomorrow."

"Good one."

I might have known. Henley was a small town-and-gown community. News of Jenn's attack had gone from one academic department to another and then out to the business world that Fran's husband was part of. It was the kind of chain I was seldom included in, however, because as Judy advised me, I can't be trusted to keep the chain alive. Maybe I didn't have enough friends. As I filled Fran in on the meager details I had of Jenn's status and the progress of the investigation, I was surprised she didn't already know more than I did.

When we'd sufficiently expressed our horror and disgust at what had happened to Jenn, and our sympathies for her parents, I turned the conversation to an earlier blemish on Henley College campus life.

"Do you remember an event on campus twenty-five years ago? A sophomore named Kirsten Packard?"

"Of course. The suicide from the tower."

I'd already decided it wouldn't be useful to ask Fran why it had never come up between us. "What do you remember about it?" I asked.

"Well, the whole thing, actually. She jumped from the Admin tower one morning. Very sad."

"I'd never heard about it." Neutral enough.

"There was quite an effort to keep it all quiet. For a while we felt the administration had installed bugs everywhere, ready to fire a faculty member or expel any student caught talking about it. They closed off the stairway in the tower right away. Put a wall up, actually, so there was no access. That's when they installed the electronic chimes to strike the quarter hours. Then, after a generation"—I knew Fran meant not twenty-five years, but four years, a generation in academic terms—"it became less and less newsworthy. The construction for the new carillon program is bringing it all back for some old-timers, I guess. Is that how you heard?"

I gritted my teeth and renewed my decision not to ask Fran why she hadn't thought of mentioning this during our fifteen years together, or even in the last months during the new construction.

"It came up with Ted and Judy yesterday."

"Ah, Ted. He took it pretty hard."

I sprang to attention. "What do you mean? How was Ted affected?"

"He was very close to Kirsten."

"The roommate connection," I offered, remembering that Kirsten's roommate had been one of Ted's physics majors.

"Right," Fran said. "Ted and Kirsten's father, Vincent

Packard, were roommates in college. I think Ted was Kirsten's godfather, in fact."

Whoa. I paused to absorb the little detail Ted had neglected to mention. He'd said he hardly knew Kirsten, and certainly never mentioned a connection with her prominent father. Better not to distract Fran with that omission now, though. I had more to learn.

"Do you remember hearing anything controversial about Kirsten's death?"

"That someone might have been up there with her. Pushed her, you mean?"

That's what I mean. "Or that it was an accident?" I said, to soften my query. "Any talk that there was a cover-up of some kind?"

"There's always talk when something like that happens, especially when a prominent family's involved. The most sensational stories likened Kirsten's plight to Patty Hearst's."

I had to think back. "The nineteen seventies kidnapping?" I asked.

I was in kindergarten or first grade when the newspaper heiress's abduction and eventual conviction for bank robbery made international headlines. I'd seen documentaries since, and I was at a loss to see the connection with Kirsten Packard, except that they both belonged to wealthy families in the public eye.

"It was just a few blips in some tabloids," Fran said. "Not enough to last too long. The story was that the privileged Kirsten had hooked up with some bad guys and, like Patty Hearst, got involved in a couple of bank robberies. Maybe she was forced into it, like Patty was by her captors, maybe not. Remember—well, you wouldn't remember— when Hearst was kidnapped, she was a nineteen-year-old college student."

"Like Kirsten."

"Like Kirsten," Fran echoed.

I hadn't seen any reference to the Hearst case, nor any

suggestions of wrongdoing on Kirsten's part in the links I'd explored. But then, I hadn't gotten around to the tabloids. "Did anything ever come of those rumors?"

"Nothing. They were very short-lived, as they would be with the Commonwealth's attorney general stepping in. Packard was in the AG's office at the time. Not that I think the rumors were true in the first place, but you never know, do you? By the way, why all the interest?"

Blame it on the poor international connection that I didn't answer, but instead asked another question.

"I know it was a while ago, Fran, but do you happen to remember if Kirsten was a carillonist? Is that why she was up in the tower that morning?"

"Hmm. I'm trying to recall. I never paid much attention to the music program back then, and Kirsten wasn't a Franklin Hall major, so I can't say."

"She majored in romance languages, I think," I said, trying to trigger more memories.

"That sounds right." Fran paused. Too long for a simple breath or a sip of water. Uh-oh, she was putting it together. "Wait a minute, Sophie. You're thinking there's a connection between Kirsten Packard's death and what happened to Jenn Marshall?"

"Why would you think that?" My voice came out higher than usual.

"Uh—because I know how your mind works?"

"Never mind." I didn't need Fran to tell me how foolish—out of character, I liked to think—I was being. How the Kirsten Packard case had captivated me in an inexplicable way, with an intensity that was exacerbated by Jenn's attack.

"How are your classes going? How do you like Rwanda?" I asked.

I knew that would do the trick. Before we hung up I'd learned more than I needed to about Rwanda's new system of roads, how KIST was its first public technological institute of higher learning, and the emphasis the East African country placed on entrepreneurship and economic growth. She promised to send photos of her students and colleagues and ended with, "You've got to come here sometime, Sophie."

"Sure," I said.

We both knew I didn't mean it. Starting with facing inoculation needles, all the way to learning another language, I had a list of reasons why I'd probably spend all of my teaching career on American soil. I was glad Fran was so enthusiastic, however. I was interested in her work and her goal to bring more applied math, rather than theory, to the math department there.

We hung up. I'd certainly learned a lot from Fran, more than from people in my own time zone.

But I still didn't know whether Kirsten Packard had played the carillon.

At almost five in the morning I decided it wasn't worth trying to go back to sleep for a couple of hours. Besides, my head was throbbing, my mind reeling from the realization that Ted must have known Kirsten all her life. Why would he have tried to keep that a secret? I wondered if Judy knew. I doubted it, since, unlike me, Judy was one of those who could be trusted to share a rumor.

Before I could get to searching for old bank robberies, there was the matter of Kenny, the new copyeditor on my puzzle magazine, to straighten out. I read his email again. Not a good idea to become agitated at this hour of the morning, but what a nerve! He talked about changing my crossword clues as if he had merely shifted a comma or dotted an *i*.

I brewed coffee and pulled a hard copy of my contract from my file cabinet. Ten legal-size pages of fine print, some of it in bold letters, some of it redacted, a plethora of margin notes. My eyes glazed over appendixes and items in even finer print, identified with tiny Roman numerals. I'd never needed an agent. I simply signed my contracts, relying on good relationships with my editors and with my tax man. Now I understood why no one wrote longer works without an agent to interpret for us laypeople. I plowed through the pages, making notes on what I'd have to come back to later.

No sooner did I have a handle on what I might say to Kenny on the next round, than it was time to get ready for class and drive to campus. If I wanted to protect my parking spot from a construction worker, that is.

True to my "she-who-arrives-at-dawn" epithet, I was early enough to park in the lot by the tennis courts, now hibernating under a black tarp. I sat in my car and checked a text from Bruce, on duty at MAstar.

"News?"

"None," I texted back.

Repeated communications through emails, texts, and phone calls among Virgil, the most involved students, and the hospital had turned up nothing new.

Bruce and I closed our final texts with a long line of *xoxoxoxox*, which made up for the nasty way I'd started my day, steaming over Kenny.

At this hour, seven twenty in the morning, with the sun low in the sky, the campus was peaceful and beautiful. Last night's wind had cleaned the air. I'd never share my theory with Ted, who taught an undergraduate class in meteorology, but it made sense to me that the wind had swept away atmospheric debris, leaving fresher, unpolluted air. The scattered patches of ice reflected the bright rays and seemed whiter than they did during the busy day.

I hadn't been on campus since I left for lunch yesterday, and it was hard to grasp that it had since become the site of a brutal attack.

I exited my car and felt the brunt of an early January morning. The air was windless, but cold, cold, cold. I dabbed my nose and my watery eyes as well as I could, manipulating a tissue with heavily gloved fingers. I pulled my scarf up over my mouth, trying to breathe through the holes in the knit pattern. Ariana had given me the scarf, and I didn't remember in time that it was more of a fashion statement, in bright shades of red, than effective protection against a New England winter.

I was close to Franklin Hall and could have ducked inside after a brisk three-minute walk. And though it wasn't warm and cozy in the building this week, there were at least some protective walls and space heaters. But I walked in the other direction, toward the spot where Jenn had been attacked. I headed that way without a lot of thought, shuffling along the pathway, weighed down by what felt like ten pounds of clothing, plus the awareness that one of my student majors lay in a coma at Henley General.

I passed the Mortarboard Café and the gym and arrived at the narrow path between the Student Union and the Clara Barton dorm. I positioned myself in the middle of the path, where the three commuters might have been when they saw the attack.

I expected to see crime scene tape, but apparently the police were finished scooping up evidence. I looked up to the right at the dorm windows. Had there been a student at one of them yesterday afternoon? Someone whose daydreaming had been interrupted by a sudden attack below? I doubted it, because the only nine-one-one call had come from one of the commuters. No harm in checking, though. I wondered if the Henley PD had done that. Had they made sure to interview all the residents? I smiled at my arrogance. Good thing Virgil and his buddies on the force had me around.

I stood on the path for a while, for no good reason, the campus quiet and eerie. I looked south, toward the other

two dorms. My view of the wide Henley Boulevard, past
Paul Revere Hall, was blocked by equipment that should
have been familiar to me by now. This deserted morning
the dull yellow behemoths, badly in need of a hosing,
seemed animated, the sweeping arm of a cherry picker
waving at me, the sharp prongs of the forklift aimed
angrily at me.

I turned away.

I took one last look north, down the path where Jenn
had walked. A piece of paper, green or gray, stuck on a
bush, caught my eye. Something left behind during yesterday's attack? I'd learned what Virgil called Locard's
Exchange Principle, named after an early twentieth-
century forensic scientist—the theory that anyone who
enters a crime scene both takes something and leaves
something behind. But the police had searched the area
and surely would have found a piece of paper as large as
the one that I spotted halfway down the path.

Unless the gusty winds had sent it to this spot during the
night. In that case, it could have come from anywhere on
campus or across Main Street, for that matter, and was useless to the investigation.

What was wrong with me? There was no barrier keeping me from walking forward, to the bush and the paper,
except in my fearful mind. I finally stepped past the invisible obstruction onto the path, and walked a few steps.

Lacking binoculars and the courage to keep going, I
could only squint at the paper from about twenty feet away.
It looked like a bill. Money? I inched closer. Definitely
money. Closer still, on top of it now. A one-hundred-dollar
bill.

I squatted down for a better look. No doubt about it. A
one-hundred-dollar bill was entangled in the dry twigs of
the leafless bush.

I considered calling Virgil, but that seemed silly. Someone had lost one hundred dollars between yesterday after-

noon and this morning. Someone headed to or from the Coffee Filter on the other side of Main? A lot of money for a student to be carrying around. Did the fact that the bill was at the crime scene make it evidence?

My answer was to cover all bases. I took out my phone and clicked on my camera app, though doing so required removing my gloves. I hoped no one was watching as I took pictures of the bill from five different angles, plus one long shot to show the distance between the bush and the side wall of the Student Union. If caught in the act, I could always claim that I was on an art project photo shoot of flowerless, leafless twigs.

Before frostbite took over, I put on my gloves and snatched the bill. I stuffed it in my jacket pocket, not worrying about smudging at this point, and walked back down the path I'd come from. I could decide later what to do with the money. It might end up being fake money from a game. I wasn't going to remove my gloves again to examine it right now.

It felt good to move, and I took the long way to Ben Franklin Hall, walking around the fountain, behind the Administration Building, close to the back of the tower, but not too close. I stretched my neck and studied the crevices, cutouts, and layers of curved arches as they caught the sun and repeated themselves in shadows.

I resigned myself to the fact that neither the buildings nor their strange shadows would give up their stories. I'd have to dig out the secrets myself. I still had more than an hour before my calculus class, and I'd already sketched out the lesson and problems for the day. I had an idea where to start digging for stories.

I was the only one waiting at the door of the Emily Dickinson Library, stamping my feet to keep up my circulation. The door opened at ten to eight, moments before frostbite became a real threat. Donna Martin, our librarian, had taken pity on me and unlocked the dead bolts.

"Dr. Knowles, you must be freezing. You should have called in." An experienced librarian, but new to Henley College, Donna wasn't aware that such an act would have been anathema to our previous keeper of books and journals, who adhered to a strict schedule no matter what the circumstances.

"Thanks. You came just in time," I said, drawing much needed warm breaths.

"I heard what happened to Jenn Marshall. It's terrible," Donna said. She made a gesture to help remove my coat, but I wasn't ready to give up a single layer. "Jenn works in the stacks for us one day a week. Lovely girl, quiet. I know you know that. I hope she makes it through all right."

Once again, I voiced a "me, too," to a well-wisher.

I rubbed my hands, then shook them out, trying to recover the feel of my fingers. I wondered if Donna would be amenable to bending the rules enough to let me teach my classes here until the Franklin Hall heater was fixed.

We chatted a few minutes about whether there was anything Donna could do for Jenn (nothing I could think of) and how we needed better security during the day (I agreed), since times were changing for the worse in town and in the world (I uttered a neutral grunt).

"Anything special I can help you with this morning?" Donna asked. Chipper already, but then she'd been warm for a while.

I considered saying that I just wanted to browse, and find what I needed myself, but in the interest of time, I owned up to Donna. "I'd like to look through some old yearbooks. How far back do you keep them?"

Donna straightened to her full height, probably average, but everyone over five three looked tall to me. "We have every single one," she said. "The last ten years are in the corner"—she pointed to a small reading area at the back of the library—"older ones are in the stacks. What year are you interested in?"

I gave Donna the dates for the two years Kirsten was a student. If she was at all active—in music, sports, drama, or any of the dozens of clubs I assumed Henley supported back then—I'd find her picture and who knew what else about her. Maybe I'd come across a photo of her in a beret like the one Patty Hearst was often shown wearing.

I took a seat by a window in the main reading room, facing the west wing of the Administration Building. The tower, off center architecturally, was closer to this end of the building. I fought off the image of a woman falling? . . . jumping? . . . being pushed? . . . to her death.

Donna returned with four issues of Henley College's yearbook, *The Lighthouse*, one on either side of the dates I'd given her. More than I'd asked for. I liked that in a librarian. She also brought me a cup of hot chocolate, apologizing that they were out of tea. The day was looking up.

I turned to the indexes of the faux-leather-bound books and found Kirsten Packard listed in only one of them, as a sophomore member of two clubs—French and Music. Better than nothing. I paused a minute before flipping to the pages that contained the club photographs. I realized that, except for the poor-quality newspaper image I'd seen, I had no solid picture of what Kirsten looked like. In my mind, she was a rag doll falling from the tower, hitting the steps with a soft, bloodless thud, as if the only unhappy consequence of the trip was a bit of dirt in her thick yarn hair.

Now I was about to see the real Kirsten, as close as I would come to flesh and blood. I sipped the hot chocolate, finally warm enough to shed my coat and scarf. I checked out the French Club first. Kirsten Packard was third from right in the fourth and last row. Tall, then. I ran my finger up to row four and counted.

And started. If I didn't know better, I'd have identified her as Patty Hearst. Kirsten Packard wore the same gaunt,

haunted look that I'd seen in grainy photos of Hearst. Tall
and thin, straight hair slightly longer than shoulder length
with one side pulled over her ear, pointed chin, the begin-
nings of a smile that wouldn't go anywhere.

Yearbook photo shoots were usually completed before
the December holidays, which meant that Kirsten was still
five months or so from her fall from the tower. Did it take
her by surprise? A last-minute decision? A shocking betrayal
on the part of a friend? Or was this troubled look an indica-
tion that she'd always known how her life would end?

I blew out a breath and turned my gaze to the scene
outside the library window. The main entrance to the campus was through a checkpoint on Henley Boulevard
between the library and the Administration Building. My
view was of the guard post, busy now with faculty, commuter students, and—lately—construction workers, arriving to start their day.

I had only a few minutes before it was time to head for
Franklin Hall and my nine o'clock class. I left the French
Club page and turned to the Music Club photograph. I
would have loved a list of students and their instruments of
choice, but no such luck. It was a straight stand-in-rows
photo of all the members. All I could glean from the page
was that Kirsten was involved in music. She might have
played the drums in a marching band or sung soprano in
the Glee Club. Or she might have pounded away on the
carillon. There was no information here.

I decided to give five more minutes to the yearbook
project and turned to the pages of candid photos, collages
that had been put together to commemorate important moments, but weren't necessarily indexed. Each highlighted
event had its own colorful divider, in the middle section
of the yearbook. The Senior Ski Trip—happy, bundled-
up kids on the slopes and in the lodge. I couldn't find
Kirsten in the set. The Cotillion—dancing couples, with

men imported from nearby schools, no doubt. No Kirsten there either.

The last section—"Campus Life"—showed groups of students in the cafeteria, browsing in the bookstore, getting comfortable in their dorm rooms.

And there she was. In a photo of two young women in modest, tailored pajamas laughing as they pretended to make up their twin beds. One of the more dated photographs in the book. The caption read:

Sophomores Kirsten Packard and Wendy Carlson tidy up their room.

It would be a different picture if taken of today's Henley College roommates. They were more likely to be in sweatpants and a crop top than formal pajamas, and hardly likely to make their beds.

I looked again at Kirsten and Wendy. Both tall and thin with dark hair, the women might have been sisters. Did Wendy really have a more carefree look than Kirsten, or was I projecting what I knew of Kirsten's end?

I packed up and left the library, feeling as though I'd just met a new friend. Wendy Carlson, Kirsten's roommate, at last. All I had to do now was find her.

CHAPTER $\sqrt{7}$

Franklin Hall was even colder on Friday. Adding a layer of thermal underwear didn't seem to help, but at least I was getting some use out of my ski clothing. I liked the sport in theory, but in truth the roaring fires in the sheltered, comfortable lodges were the attraction for me.

Today I had the nasty thought of kidnapping the administrators who worked across campus and forcing them to trade their warm offices for our frosty ones. We'd been told in an email from Admin that the heat would return "shortly," but I wondered if anyone was even working on the problem. I considered making a trip to the lower floor to query Judy's allegedly hunky guy about when the building might be fit for humans. I decided I could give him one more day.

Judy and Ted were both solicitous when I arrived in the faculty lounge after my nine o'clock calculus class for what was becoming a routine steamy facial.

"Any news on Jenn?" Ted asked. "Any improvement?"

I rubbed my hands over the pots of boiling water and shook my head.

"I know how much you care about Jenn," Judy said, moving farther to the side of the hot plate so I'd have more space. "Do you think she knew she was in danger?" she asked.

"You mean, was she being stalked?" I asked, surprised at the thought.

Judy shrugged. "Or maybe someone she knew had a problem with her? I don't know. If she let someone get close enough to get the jump on her, she might have known him. It was broad daylight."

"What earthly difference does it make whether it was day or night?" Ted asked from his seat at the conference table. He lowered his horn rims and looked over them at Judy. "Haven't you ever heard of random acts of violence? It's the world we live in today."

"Touchy, touchy," Judy said, flipping her short bob, expressing my sentiments.

While never the life of the party, Ted was always pleasant and often greeted us with a brainteaser or brainy riddle. "Physics is all about puzzles," he'd say. "We deal with riddles like, what's the world made of? How do you cool a bottle of particles to zero degrees? What happens when matter and antimatter collide?"

As much as I didn't get all his jokes and puns, I missed the old Ted. I wished I had the nerve to ask him about his own college days and a certain roommate he'd neglected to mention to us. His silence left me with an uncomfortable question—why would he try to hide his closeness to Kirsten Packard's family?

Right now, though, I had a sad tale of my own to tell. Nothing compared to what the Marshalls were going through, but I shared it anyway.

"Wait till you hear about Kenny the Copyeditor," I said, and poured out my story.

"Is it too late for you to fix it?" Judy asked.

"It better not be. But it's going to take some time to sort out."

"Bummer," Judy said. "Who needs that kind of busy-work?"

Ted grunted. "Maybe that's just what she needs. Distractions can be the good guys."

Before I could ask Ted what on earth he meant, my cell phone rang. Virgil's number was on the screen. I felt a panicky twinge. I hoped he wasn't calling as a representative of the medical community.

"Can you be ready to view the security footage around three this afternoon?" he asked.

"You bet," I said, relaxing my grip on the phone. "Do you still want to come to campus?"

"If there's a place. It might be more comfortable for everyone if it's not at the station. They made copies of the videos for me, and I can take them anywhere."

"No problem. I'll find a room in another building. I'd invite you to Franklin, but our heater's out and it's bone-chilling cold in here."

"Thanks. Sorry about your inside weather, though. Can you round up the usual suspects?" he asked, then quickly added, "No comment, please, and don't tell Bruce about the slipup."

I zipped my lips, a spontaneous reaction. "Got it. I'll let you know where we can set up, ASAP."

"What's up?" Judy asked when I'd clicked off. "What do you need a room for?"

I explained the project and asked if she wanted to be one of the viewers.

"I'll have to pass. I'm completely booked all afternoon. Maybe if there's a second showing sometime?"

"I'm sure he can arrange that." I rattled off Virgil's cell number and she added it to her phone contacts.

"Is this that big guy who hangs around with Bruce?"

"The same. Tell him Sophie sent you."

From across the room, Ted chuckled. I was glad I could help change his mood. "I'm sure Randy wouldn't mind hosting the security viewing," he said. "He must have some empty practice rooms this month."

"Good idea, Ted. Thanks. I'll call the Music Department."

"Mind if I join you?" he asked.

Big surprise. I hadn't thought of inviting Ted. I almost reminded him that it was a useless project since everyone knew that random violent acts were the norm these days. Unless that was an oxymoron. Instead, I said, "We'd love to have you, Ted."

Anyone listening might have assumed we were planning a party instead of an electronic manhunt.

Partially warm at last, I left the lounge and braved the cold hallway and my arctic office where I needed to make a long list of phone calls.

A call to Randy Stephens's secretary got us a music room for our three o'clock video showing. No problem setting it up with a TV and DVD player.

"And your heat is on?" I asked, to be sure.

"Yeah, why wouldn't it be? It's in the teens out there."

"It's in the teens in here, too," I explained.

"Oh, sorry. I heard about your heater. Or lack of. Wish we could accommodate all your classes, but kids are in and out all day this month, practicing, and more practicing."

I thanked her, clicked off, and left a voice mail message giving Virgil directions to the music rooms in the Administration Building.

My next two calls also ended up in voice mails. One to Bruce, who'd gone off duty an hour or so ago, at nine AM, and was probably sleeping in his own bed by now; the second to Mr. and Mrs. Marshall, who shared a cell phone, inviting them to dinner at my house this evening.

I started to punch the number for Henley General to inquire about Jenn's condition, but figured if there was news to be had, it wouldn't come to me through a cold call to the reception desk. I had to trust Virgil, the Marshalls, and Jenn's roommate, Patty, to keep me in the loop.

My last item of business before my math history seminar was to track down Kirsten Packard's old roommate, Wendy Carlson. I had hopes that the newly renamed Alumni Office, updated from Alumnae Office to prepare for the first male graduates, would come through for me. I didn't expect to be scolded.

"Didn't you purchase the alumni directory?" an unnamed secretary asked.

"This is Professor Sophie Knowles," I said, thinking that would excuse me.

"Faculty can purchase the directory at a discount."

"Uh, I didn't get the notice this year." Or I may have tossed it, but she didn't need to know that. "Can you look up the address for me?" I spelled Wendy Carlson's name.

"If she wants to be found, yes. But not if she either didn't list her address or if she got married and changed her name. I can't promise anything if she didn't give us her maiden name."

Did people still call it that? Were there still maidens around?

"Okay, you're lucky," the alumni secretary said after a short time. "She's listed her business address and phone number." She rattled off the information and I typed it quickly onto a sticky note on my computer.

"Thanks, I appreciate this," I said. "One more thing. Can you tell me if she has an advanced degree?"

"None that she has listed. Just a B.S. with a physics major."

"Thanks. You've been very helpful." Trying to leave a good impression in case I needed her again.

"If you give me your campus address, I'll send you a form and you can purchase the alumni directory."

"I'm listed in the faculty directory," I said. I clicked off and had way too good a chuckle.

Wendy's business address was the Boston Public Library. From physics major to librarian? Why not?

Bruce was off this weekend. How handy. I had a sudden urge to visit our state capital.

It was Andrew Davies's turn to lead the seminar. His chosen topic: Archimedes, A Man Ahead of His Time. I'd emailed comments on his paper a week ago and hadn't seen it since, but I had good reason to believe he'd do an excellent job.

At least I didn't change his words and print the piece under his name, I thought, still in a huff over Kenny. The rogue copyeditor hadn't answered my urgent email request that he not send the altered crossword puzzle to press. The puzzle had been one of my better efforts, too, if I did say so, titled "No Exit." The main thread of clues was based on removing an "ex" from the answers. Who knew what was left of my bright idea? As soon as I had a minute, I'd email my editor and ask if she knew what was going on.

I headed for the seminar room and arrived in time to meet Andrew at the door.

"Dr. Knowles, can we start with a few words to, you know, send good vibes to Jenn?"

"Very nice thought, Andrew. Why don't you lead us?"

I took a seat in the back of the room and teared up with the rest of the students as Andrew said his few words about his friend and asked us all to remember her "whatever way we chose."

The rest of the hour was normal, as Andrew showed us why pi was often called "Archimedes' constant" and explained an invention known as the Archimedes screw. He showed a video of the screw, which operated as a pump, raising the water level through a helix-shaped tube. His

main visual was a collection of images of Archimedes on
postage stamps.

"If your country puts you on a stamp, you've really
made it," Andrew said, making me wonder if I still had
time.

Back in my office at noon, I sent a group email to students
I'd invited to the showing of the security footage, giving
them the time and the Music Department room number. I
added a note encouraging them to bring anyone else they
thought might be helpful.

I'd made plans to have lunch with Bruce at one o'clock
at my house. After my messy performance yesterday, I
wasn't ready to face Toi again so soon. I remembered how
thoughtful Toi and Bruce had been during my tea spill. I'd
be sure to have a little thank-you present in hand for my
next visit to Pan's restaurant. And a big thank-you for my
long-suffering boyfriend.

I needed to get one more thing off my mind before I left
the campus. I called up the number for Leila, my editor. I
reached her in her New York office and, with hardly any
intro, jumped right in.

"I need to talk to you about Kenny."

"Kenny who?" Leila asked.

I grunted. I'd blocked his last name from my mind.
"Kenny, the new copyeditor."

"We don't have a new copyeditor. Jamie is running a
little behind since we dumped a whole load on her when
Kate left on maternity leave. Is that what's wrong?"

"Jamie's still my copyeditor?"

"Of course. I thought you liked her."

"I do. I love her. So I'm not being shunted to Kenny
Something?"

"Sophie, we have no Kenny Anything."

I told Leila about the email from a person named Kenny who claimed to have made unapproved changes to my submission.

"It must have been a mistake, like a wrong number. I've done it. You know, hit send before I realized I had the wrong person in the 'To' slot."

I opened my email and searched for Kenny's note. "His last name is Simmons and the address is from your offices," I said. "And he's talking about a recently submitted cross-word puzzle, so I assumed—"

"Who knows why that happened? If you want, I'll forward you a copy of the most recent version you approved with Jamie. The theme is fabulous, by the way. Leaving off the 'exes.' 'Citing' for 'thrilling mention'? Loved it. Nice job, Sophie."

"Thanks." I hung up and tried to let go of Kenny Simmons. Leila clearly had.

Moments later, my computer dinged out an email notification. My message to Kenny last night had been bounced, the delivery status: action failed. How appropriate.

A lot of grief over nothing. And a waste of time, which I could have used searching on Google for events that occurred twenty-five years ago. I'd wanted to check on Fran's mention of a bank robbery, or maybe more than one, in Henley around the time of Kirsten's death. Never mind the wasted hours, I thought. I now had a way to find and, I hoped, talk to Kirsten Packard's roommate.

I clicked on the computer sticky note with Wendy's phone number at the BPL, as every Massachusetts native referred to the imposing main library in Boston. I debated, Sophie versus Sophie, whether to drive up tomorrow and catch her off guard, assuming she'd be working on a Saturday, or call ahead and risk her refusal to meet with me. Both Sophies agreed I should think about it more before deciding.

*   *   *

Lunch with Bruce was much less eventful than yesterday's great spill at Pan's. I'd picked up sandwiches while buying a pot roast for tonight's dinner. We talked about how awful it must be for the Marshalls, who were spending their days at the hospital even though Jenn's doctors were advising them not to expect any change.

Our conversation was too boring, apparently, because I chose to churn things up.

"Let's go to Boston for the weekend," I said. "You're off at noon tomorrow. We can drive up, stay till Sunday night or Monday morning."

"It's as cold in Boston as it is here," he said. "We might as well go to New Hampshire and do some skiing."

That was Bruce. If you're going to be cold, you might as well be really cold and linger outside in it.

"We can get symphony tickets," I said. To play into his likes, I added, "And walk along the Charles."

"You don't even want to walk through the campus parking lot in this weather." Bruce bit the end off a carrot. He chewed with a more thoughtful expression than required for the activity, then waved the carrot at me. "Something's up. What's in Boston?"

"I might want to check someone out."

Bruce gave me his "uh-oh" look, and I confessed, telling him all I knew about Wendy Carlson, including what color pj's she wore twenty-five years ago.

"You want to visit the roommate of the girl who jumped from the tower in the eighties?"

"Maybe."

"Maybe you want to visit. Or maybe it's her roommate?"

"Maybe she jumped." I waved my hand in an iffy motion. "Maybe she didn't jump."

Bruce took a long breath, trying to keep up. "You haven't spoken to her? The roommate?"

"No."

"You don't know if she's working tomorrow, or even if she still works at the BPL?"

"That's what's in the alumni directory."

"Which is always up to date, of course. Do you update your entry for your undergraduate degree every year?"

"Nuh-uh."

"For your grad school directory. Ever?"

I fiddled with the crust of my bread. "Sometimes."

"How about this. Write the roommate a letter and wait to see if she answers. She may not want to talk to you."

I'd been dismissing that possibility. I had a bright idea. "I'll call the BPL, see if she's working this weekend."

"And if she is?"

"I'll just show up."

"What about skiing?"

"Do I have to quote my grandmother again?" I asked.

Bruce smiled and we recited her one-liner together.

"Don't participate in any sport where there are ambulances waiting."

But our usual laughter didn't follow as the memory of real-life ambulances on our campus flooded the room.

CHAPTER $\sqrt{8}$

When Bruce left, our weekend plans were still unresolved. He knew not to push me when I was wallowing in indecision. It didn't hurt that he'd just returned from a New Year's Day ice climb in the Southwest, so if he were to be deprived of skiing in New Hampshire this weekend, it wouldn't be a big deal.

I'd sat with my jaw clenched as I'd watched the video of Bruce and his buddy doing the Ames Ice Hose climb near Telluride, Colorado. Each time Bruce slammed his axe into the ice, I was sure it wouldn't hold for the next step up the mountain. If he hadn't been sitting beside me, safe and whole, eating popcorn, smiling at the memory, I would never have caught my breath.

To me, ice was what went into iced tea and melted pretty quickly. It hadn't been easy, therefore, to watch Bruce thread a thick screw through an icicle, then pass a rope through the hole it made. Then lift himself with that rope.

"How can you do that?" I'd asked, not expecting an answer.

"It's probably just as well you can't hear the grunts and groans," Bruce had said.

He was right.

Now it came down to me. Boston or not? A different kind of adventure. I wasn't sure what to do other than start with a little fact-finding.

I checked the library hours online and saw that I had plenty of time to make a call before they closed at five. I punched the number for the BPL, tapping my fingers to speed the process. After a few rerouting steps, I reached a live operator.

"This is Dr. Sophie Knowles from Henley College. I'd like to find out if one of your employees will be working tomorrow." I hoped my voice carried the ring of authority and my credential would overpower any impropriety in the query.

"Is this regarding your research, Dr. Rawls?"

Rawls? I cleared my throat. What a good idea, using a fake name.

"Yes, I want to ensure continuity if I drop in tomorrow."

"And who is the researcher you've been working with?"

I realized I had no idea if Wendy Carlson was a researcher. With a bachelor's in physics, but no degree in library science according to the Alumni Office, she could be working anywhere in the BPL, from the map room to the computer center to the café. She could be a bookbinder for all I knew. I'd worked myself into a research corner, however, and I had to go with that.

"Wendy Carlson," I said, clenching my jaw, fiddling with a paper clip.

The wait was endless, until, "Yes, here it is. Ms. Carlson will be at her desk tomorrow from nine to four."

I said a quick thank-you, quitting while I was ahead, and

clicked off before she could ask the topic of my research. My creativity went only so far.

I let out my breath. I could now make an informed decision about a trip to Boston. I wondered what it would be.

Enjoying the warmth of my cottage, I was in no hurry to return to campus. I sat for a while on a comfortable chair in my office generating a short anacrostic around a quote from Einstein about pure mathematics.

Halfway through, I remembered that I hadn't retrieved my messages from my landline. I reached over to the phone on the corner of my desk and clicked the button.

"Hey," said Ariana from Florida. "You've absolutely got to come down here sometime. Oh, how about now? I got your message about the whacked-out heater in Franklin. Pleeeeeeeze, just get on a plane. Hey, get Bruce to fly you down." She'd trailed off, laughing.

I smiled, remembering a photo Ariana had sent from her phone the other day. She looked stunning, stretched out on the beach, on a lounge chair that happened to match her green and white swimsuit and complement her currently blond hair. I hadn't told her about Jenn's attack, and probably wouldn't until her vacation was over. No good would come of spreading bad news.

We all knew I wasn't about to leave my classes and fly to Florida, but it was nice to know that I now had two warm-weather alternatives to icy Franklin Hall—I'd been invited to Rwanda and to Florida.

The next message wasn't so welcome.

"This is Eric from Henley Savings Bank. Please call me at your earliest convenience regarding an issue with your credit card."

Now what? First Kenny, now Eric. Didn't the world know I was busy, looking into a twenty-five-year-old death of one student and a day-old attack on another? I let out an annoyed grunt and called my bank to make sure there was an Eric (unlike Kenny) and that the number he left was legitimate. Part of me was disappointed; I'd been hoping this was another error, as Leila, my editor, called it, or a stunt, as I called it.

I was shunted around to three different departments, placed on hold, and had not only music, but advice for putting my dollars to work for me—all piped into my ear before I reached Eric.

After making sure I was having a nice day, Eric asked, "Do you mind if I ask you a few questions, Ms. Knowles?"

"That's fine." I knew I sounded otherwise, though it was probably not Eric's fault that something had gone wrong in credit card land.

I gave Eric the last four digits of my social security number, the street where I grew up, and my mother's maiden name, though she wouldn't have liked that he called it that. "It's my only name," she'd say. "Margaret Stone." She was thrilled when I chose it as my puzzle-writer pseudonym.

"Thank you, Ms. Knowles. Do you have your credit card in your custody?"

"Yes," I said, drawing out the word, as I fished in my purse for my wallet, then inspected the card. "I do."

"Have you been out of the country recently?"

Not since college, but I didn't think Eric needed details of life in hostels across Europe more than twenty years ago. "No, I haven't left the country. Can you tell me what this is about?"

"We've flagged some charges to your card in the Philippines."

I stood and walked into the hallway. I paced a well-worn path between my bedroom and my kitchen. "Where did you say?" I asked, though I knew I'd heard him clearly.

"We have five hundred and fifty dollars in charges in three stores in Manila and Quezon City over the last week."

"I can't imagine how that happened. I've never been in

the Philippines. I hardly know where it is and I've never heard of Quezon City. I've been in Henley all week."

I spared Eric my litany of classes, puzzle deadlines, and the bigger issues of life and death that were already on my plate. I doubted he'd care how busy I was, but wasn't it his job to find out who had impersonated me in another country? Maybe that was asking too much.

"We understand," Eric said to my protestation of ignorance of the Philippines.

I wondered who were the "we" who understood, but I was too flustered to query Eric.

"Can you tell me the name of the person who made these charges?" I asked.

"I'm afraid not. But we're prepared to take care of this," he said. "The charges will be removed, but you need to come down in person to the bank and sign a form."

"Make an exasperating trip downtown and stand in line at the bank" wasn't on my to-do list.

"Can't you fax me the form?"

"I'm afraid not. You understand. We have to follow certain procedures to ensure that your—"

I interrupted Eric when a thought came to me. "I just remembered, my friend Judy had this happen to her once and she didn't need to appear in person. She was able to do everything online. I think they sent a pdf. Is there a way I can do that?"

"I'm afraid not. Every bank is different, Ms. Knowles. You'll also need to stop using your card immediately. Destroy it and we'll issue you a new one shortly. In the meantime, let me give you a temporary number that you can use until you receive your card in the mail."

"Okay, are you open tomorrow?" And don't say you're afraid not, I added to myself.

"From nine to one. And we close at five today. Can you hold, please?"

With great reluctance, I added "Make an exasperating

trip downtown and stand in line at the bank" to my to-do list for Saturday.

Grateful as I was that I wasn't going to have to pay for someone's Philippine souvenirs, I felt overwhelmed by the notifications I'd have to make. I thought of all my automatic billing sites—cable, video and magazine subscriptions, phone service, utility bills—and all the sites where I'd stored my credit card information—bookstores, clothing sites, gift registries.

I regretted every time I'd hit yes to "Do you want to save this information?" or checked off "Yes, remember me."

"Ms. Knowles?" Eric was back from "hold, please" land.

"Yes, I'm here."

"We're sorry for the inconvenience."

"Thanks."

"We also suggest you contact the Henley Police Department and file a report. They'll come out and interview you."

Great. Did homicide detectives handle credit card theft? Could I just ask Virgil to take care of it?

I thought about how this intrusion might have happened, all through the virtual world. My card had never left my wallet, which had never been out of my possession. How wonderful that we'd come so far technologically. A thief no longer had to be present to steal a credit card.

My cozy mood ruined, I ran my credit card through my shredder, piled on layers of wool, pulled on fleece-lined boots, and left for campus.

I wished I had time to pick up some popcorn for the video showing.

The Music Department was located in what was alternately called an interesting feature of the Administration Building or an architectural glitch. It was accessible only by descending a few steps from the third floor where a strange-looking door opened onto a hallway with a large auditorium on one side and a row of small rooms on the other. Attempts to match this pseudo-wing with its corresponding outside wall were hopeless. Arches and small turrets seemed to converge on that face and showed no simple connection to the labyrinth inside.

When I arrived a few minutes before three, most of the viewers had already taken seats on folding chairs in the small, windowless room Randy's secretary had prepared. Music stands, instrument cases, and boxes of sheet music had been pushed against the back wall. As I entered the room, I heard Randy congratulating Virgil for finding his way.

"Good directions," Virgil said, pointing to me, bringing me into their conversation. Not an easy trick, since Randy matched Virgil in height, both leaving me in the dust of five-foot-three. Randy and I shared hair color, however, each with a swatch of gray over brown, while Virgil's crop of dark hair was probably no different now from when he'd sat for his yearbook photo.

"Dr. Stephens—" Virgil began.

"It's Randy, please," Henley's First Musician said. Randy took a bow, as he often did for no apparent reason.

"Randy has a nice setup for us here," Virgil said. He pushed back his cuff and looked at his watch. "We'll wait a few more minutes before we start the show."

I nodded at the students I'd invited—Willa, Brent, Patty, Andrew, and Lauren—and five or six other students, apparently chosen by the group I now thought of as my regulars, those who had been at the hospital and in my home. I made my way to an empty seat at the front, between Ted and Andrew, each of whom took a turn leaning into me. Andrew said, "I hope this works and we see someone walking toward Jenn with, like, a baseball bat, or something." A second later, Ted said, "I don't know what they're expecting—that we'll see some guy carrying a golf club?"

One sports reference in each ear. It was almost more than I could handle. Both men had whispered, as if we were in church.

At three ten by my smartphone, Virgil thanked us all for coming and explained where the footage we were about to watch had come from and what time period it covered. We learned that it had already been gone over by the police downtown and by the three commuters who'd come upon the attack and rescued Jenn. The students had been unable to identify anyone who looked like the man they'd chased off. In fact, according to Virgil, the three young men agreed only on his clothing—"dark"—but not on any other physical characteristics.

"But I'd know him if I saw him again," each one had maintained.

I wondered if the cops' job was always this hard.

I was ready with the Notes app on my phone as the first images rolled, or pixelated, their way across the screen. I figured this camera site to be high up on the Clara Barton dorm, facing the front entrance. We saw students come and go, with long lapses in any activity. The screen showed a corner of the Student Union building, reminding me that I'd plucked a one-hundred-dollar bill near that spot. It was in the pocket of my jacket, now hanging from a hook at the back of the room. I typed a note to myself to talk to Virgil about it when this session was over. I probably should have dropped it off at lost and found in the Administration Building and been done with it. The chances that it was Jenn's were near zero, but maybe it had fallen from the wallet of a more financially comfortable student, who would be looking for it. Or, better yet, by Jenn's attacker who had left his prints all over it. I could dream.

Virgil spoke again before the next segment. "By the way, we've already cut some of the footage that has no movement at all. We could have queued up the rest so this wouldn't take so long, but I wanted to make sure we didn't miss anything. Remember, there might be someone at the edges who seems strange to you, or maybe you see someone who's been hanging around lately but doesn't belong. That's what we want to know."

I wondered if Virgil was telling us everything. Maybe he had a suspect in mind, a man he'd already identified, and we were here to confirm his suspicions. I looked left and right, at Ted and Andrew, and over my shoulder to Randy and several students whom I didn't recognize. Was it one of them Virgil was targeting? Surely not someone who'd been to Henley General and to my home. Virgil often quoted the rules of interrogation, how you never directly confronted the person you thought was guilty until you had incontrovertible evidence. First, you brought him over to your side, asking for cooperation, getting him to a point where he wanted to confess. Maybe Virgil was courting someone in this room. I pulled my sweater around me and faced front again.

We held our collective breath at the most intense part of the footage, time-stamped during the hour Jenn was attacked, when the three commuters, all male, exited the dorm and walked west. I didn't want to watch as the young men turned out of camera range, to where we all knew Jenn had been overpowered. I heard Andrew draw in his breath and hold it until the segment ended. I gave his shoulder a pat and was rewarded with a small smile and a thank-you nod.

Nothing useful came from the footage captured by the middle residence, Nathaniel Hawthorne Hall, which may or may not have meant that Jenn hadn't passed by there after she left Franklin Hall. The inadequacy of our camera system was never more apparent as we realized there were more hidden zones than areas covered by the system.

We saw a long shot of the fountain that graced the center of the campus. In good weather, the bench surrounding the water sprays would have been crowded with sun worshippers; today we watched a couple of hardy construction workers head that way carrying what was most likely lunch. The men sat facing the back of the Administration Building as if they were keeping watch over their equipment. If they'd been facing the other way, they might have seen Jenn and the thug who had beaten her.

The last footage came from a recording set up on the top floor of Paul Revere, the dorm closest to the Administration Building and Henley Boulevard. This camera was trained on the pedestrian entrance to the campus, which also happened to be the direction of the construction activity.

We watched the men split up into twos and threes, some climbing into the cabs to eat, some walking toward the campus coffee shop.

I heard giggles from female students in the row behind me when one of the workers entered the screen from the left. He walked to a car parked off to the right side and removed his heavy jacket, his muscles apparent through a tight-fitting long-sleeved T-shirt.

"Cute," said one coed, as Virgil would have labeled her.

"I don't know, he looks pretty old," another said.

"Not that old," said the first.

"I'll bet he's forty," said a new female voice.

"You have to admit he's cute." Back to coed number one.

When more than one student voiced the opinion that "Forty's not cute," I held my tongue. Except to ask under my breath "Who says?"

I straightened my shoulders and stretched my neck to minimize any wrinkles that might have formed lately. I watched the unsuspecting worker stuff his jacket in the trunk and pull out a different one, with the orange protector stripes across the back. He put on the second jacket as another man approached him and the two seemed to be arguing. Three other men, also in jackets with protector stripes, passed them indifferently and walked to the bottom of the screen, out of camera range.

"Wait a minute," Lauren said from a row farther back. "Can you rewind that?"

"It's not tape," Andrew said, ever the accurate engineer.

"Whatever," Lauren said, walking to the front for a better view. She hooked her wavy brown hair over her ears and steered her face to within a couple of inches of the screen. Virgil joined her and used the remote to go back in time. "There, see those guys?" she said to Virgil.

He stopped the DVD. The two combative men were now frozen in position, arms raised, necks straining toward each other. One of them was the jacket changer; the other man had an ordinary jacket and no hard hat. The image wasn't clear and it was difficult to distinguish all the similarly built and nearly identically dressed men from one another.

The audience leaned forward, staring at the time-frozen men, and became silent, waiting for Lauren to tell us why she'd singled out the men.

Virgil took a pen from his pocket and held it in front of the men, both firmly planted next to the cherry picker. "These two look familiar to you?" he asked Lauren.

Lauren nodded. "This might be nothing, but I think I saw them in the campus coffee shop yesterday." I swallowed. The day Jenn was attacked. "And they were fighting then, too."

"These were the guys?"

"Uh-huh. I think so."

"And they were fighting with each other? No one else involved?"

"Nuh-uh. I don't think so."

I noticed that Virgil's expectant look had collapsed into a polite smile. So had mine. I'd gotten excited when Lauren called out, hoping for something that could be directly connected to Jenn's attack.

"I think so" and "I don't think so" are the kiss of death in a lineup, I mused, as if we were even at that point, and a couple of guys fighting on a construction site wasn't exactly news.

Virgil started the video again. The men sprang to action, and this time one of them turned, face front. He looked familiar. Where had I seen him? Graying hair, clean shaven, older than most of the other workmen. I took a mental step back. Well, how about on the campus, working, carrying tools, carrying a lunch pail. That's where.

The men continued the argument for another few seconds, until a third man approached and broke it up.

"That's the foreman," Virgil said. "He couldn't make it today, but he's coming in to give us some names and addresses."

With nothing more to view, Virgil stepped to the center. He informed us that the footage from the Coffee Filter camera hadn't been processed yet, but he hoped we'd be available when it was ready. He thanked us for our time and handed out his business cards. If something occurred to us, we were to call him, "day or night."

I made a note of the offer, in case I needed to take him up on it.

CHAPTER $\sqrt{9}$

Security Footage, the movie, now over, students and faculty filed out of what had become an A/V room. I waited on the side, hoping to have a few minutes with Virgil before he left. A memory of our last conversation clicked in—the "money" thing, where he'd also heard that Jenn had purportedly uttered the word *money* as she drifted into unconsciousness.

I noticed for the first time the posters that lined the walls of the music room. Randy, or his staff, had mounted instructional photos of carillons, fully annotated, as if they were part of a music exhibit in a museum. I'd seen similar art on the walls of the hallway in this wing on my last visit, but at the time I hardly knew, or cared, how to spell *carillon*.

I studied a close-up of a bell labeled "the bourdon," described in the accompanying text as the largest bell in a carillon system, sounding the lowest note. Further documentation told me that a series of notes produced by a bell was called a "prime."

No way, I said to myself. Everyone knew "prime" referred to a number greater than one that had no positive divisors other than itself and one. I resolved to start a new project—making a prime number poster for the math floor of Franklin Hall. I was sure I could get help from someone in the department who was a better artist than I was.

Several photos showed carillonists in action. A man wearing a headset pounding on an extended keyboard made of long dowels, also called "batons," according to the caption. So many words for one item. I was glad math wasn't so complicated. An older woman with thick glasses standing at a two-level set of keys/dowels/batons, a complex set of wires and weights upright in front of her, looking like she was trapped in one of Ted's freshman physics labs. A duo—a man and a woman, side by side in a small glassed-in room, hitting the keys with four fists and four feet while visitors peered in from all sides.

"Do you play, Dr. Knowles?" Andrew's voice came as a surprise from behind me. I thought he'd left with the other students.

"No, but I do enjoy hearing others play."

From Andrew's somber expression, I sensed that he had more to say.

"How are you doing with all that's happened?" I asked him.

He held back tears. "I hope they get this guy. I know you're sort of connected to the police. Will you tell me if there's anything I can do to help?"

"Of course. I know what you're feeling, Andrew. Right now, it seems the best we can do is wait."

"I'm not good at that."

"I'm worse," I admitted, and got a smile from Andrew. Andrew moved on and I turned to my own thoughts. I pictured Jenn, my petite student, sitting on the bench, over-whelmed by the size of the instrument. I thought of how her instructor, Randy Stephens, had praised her talent and abilities to her parents. Had that been a true assessment, or a way to lift their spirits at a depressing time? I hoped someday I'd be able to attend a concert featuring Jenn Marshall and find out for myself.

I fingered the hundred-dollar bill in my pocket. Surely not Jenn's money, but—money that was part of the crime scene? Did Jenn simply see the hundred as she was crashing, and utter "money" in a battered fog? I thought it unlikely that she'd notice it, let alone feel it was important to mention to her rescuers.

While I waited for Virgil, I leaned against the wall and thumbed through my texts and emails. I had two more messages with "Delivery Status Notification" as subject. More rejections of my email to Kenny. Not that I needed them or cared. No longer a worry, the nonexistent Kenny was now just a nuisance until my service provider stopped trying to find him.

I switched to the list of notifications I was building, to stop automatic charges to my now-shredded credit card. It was taking more than one page of lines in my Notes app. I needed a secretary.

A booming voice broke into my concentration.

"Gaming?"

I looked up at Virgil. "Since when do you even know what that is?"

"I don't. Sounds good, though, huh?"

"Do you have a few minutes?" I asked Virgil.

He pointed to chairs in the middle row and ushered me to a seat. Since we were going nonverbal for the moment, I pulled the hundred-dollar bill from my pocket and handed it to him.

"Need a ticket fixed?" he asked.

"Funny. You're in a pretty good mood today. Hot date?"

"Uh, let's get to business," Virgil said.

Was that a flush on my friend's face? After the (roughly) trillions of times Bruce and I teased Virgil about his weekends, could this be the one where he really did have a date?

I studied his face. "Virgil? Is there something you want to tell me?"

"I thought you wanted to tell me something," he said, returning to his normal complexion.

Later, I told myself, and took out my phone. I queued up the shots I'd taken of the money-laden bush outside Clara Barton dorm. I handed the phone to Virgil.

"Sorry about the prints on the bill," I said. "I didn't have an evidence bag."

I let Virgil study the gifts I'd bestowed. He looked back and forth between the phone and the bill. I was impressed that Virgil, a self-proclaimed Luddite, knew how to flick the photos across the screen. He wasn't quite as adept at the motion as Fran's seven-year-old grandson, but I was impressed nonetheless.

"Hmmm," he said. It was never useful to try to interpret Virgil's partially verbal reactions. They were seldom very telling. I'd probably imagined the girlfriend lined up for the weekend.

"I found the money wrapped around a twig in the bushes near where Jenn was attacked," I explained.

"When?"

"This morning, on my way to class."

"You park over there now?"

Virgil knew me too well. "I needed some exercise."

"And I know all about gaming," he said, smiling.

"Is the bill something that would have been picked up yesterday by the guys who searched the crime scene?"

"If it was there at the time, I would assume so."

"So, it was probably dropped sometime last night," I

suggested. "Too late to be connected to the attack on Jenn. But it was windy yesterday. It could have been dropped during the attack"—I was getting better at using the word and not summoning the mental image—"and then blown away and then back again."

Virgil didn't say "far-fetched," but I figured it was on the tip of his tongue.

"Kind of a big bill for a college kid, huh?"

"Or a faculty member," I said.

Another smile. "Let me take it in anyway. No harm. I'll return it to you if there's nothing on it, and it will be yours to do what you want with it."

"Or you can keep it, in case I get a ticket someday."

Virgil happened to have a plastic baggie handy and inserted the bill. A little late to worry about contamination, I thought.

A bell rang, weaker than the Franklin Hall bell in my opinion, and students staggered in under the weight of large, unwieldy cases in the shape of violins or something in that family. Virgil and I headed out of the room, our business concluded anyway.

I'd left a message for Bruce about my credit card but hadn't had time to whine about it in person with anyone. Since Virgil was handy, I ran on about Eric's call and thieves these days. He understood it was just chatter, not a request for help. I knew what I had to do; I simply didn't want to take the time.

"Can you take my statement on the credit card theft?" I asked, for fun.

Virgil frowned. "Not unless there's a homicide involved. Is this bank guy, Eric, still alive?"

I admitted there was no murder one to investigate, and gave him a heads-up on Judy Donohue. "She's chair of the Biology Department. She wanted to be here today but couldn't make it. Judy's going to call you about looking at the footage some other time."

"Not a problem."

Just before the oddly situated portal was the half-open door to Randy's office, where what sounded like a late New Year's Eve party was in progress. We stopped and peeked in. I recognized members of the music faculty and a group of students, including Willa, who was having a busy day, apparently. Recorded carillon music was playing in the background; trays of champagne-filled glasses were making the rounds. One student carried a platter of hors d'oeuvres that produced a smelly cloud of butter and garlic.

"We got some of those gourmet frozen puffs and microwaved them," he said. "Would you like one?"

I declined on the basis of the oxymoronic description, "gourmet frozen." I was mildly surprised when Virgil, who wasn't all that fussy food-wise, waved away the offer with a polite "No, thanks."

Randy spotted us. "Come in, come in," he said, gesturing grandly.

"Randy found out this morning that he's been accepted into the World Carillon Guild," said Lorna Beckman, a music theory professor.

"It's a big deal," Willa explained. "He had to take a test and all."

"We surprised him when your movie was over," another instructor said, lifting a glass to the level of a toast.

"Congratulations," Virgil and I said, both reaching in to shake Randy's hand.

Randy, standing slightly in front of his faculty, took a bow. "Thank you, thank you. I'm now the official Henley College carillonist."

"It means international travel, with recitals all over the world," Lorna added.

"Come in and have some champagne with us," Randy said, flushed.

Pleased as I was for Randy, I wasn't in the mood for a party. Before I could respond, Virgil chimed in.

"I'd love to but I've been summoned to the station. I got dropped off." He pointed to me. "And I need a ride."

"Too bad" and "Come back later" and "We'll save some bubbly" came from among the revelers.

I put on my best disappointed look as the gang waved us off and the office door closed.

"You got dropped off?" I asked Virgil as we walked away.

"Uh-huh. Did you think I lied?"

"Only for a nanosecond."

"I'll bet you're less impressed now that you know I didn't lie."

"A little," I admitted.

We'd come to the weird door. Virgil opened it and we climbed the steps to the normal hallway.

"Strange building," he said.

"I agree."

We walked through the building greeting people with "Heys," mostly members of the administrative staff.

"My car's across campus," I said as we approached the exit.

Virgil shook his head. "I called in and a uniform is outside waiting for me."

"Then you did lie about my being your ride."

Virgil waved his hand. "I didn't say you were my ride. I pointed to you and said, 'I need a ride.' Whatever they assumed, they assumed."

I laughed. "I feel like I'm talking to Socrates."

"Was I wrong? Did you want to go to the party?" he asked.

"No way. This has been more fun," I said.

I considered telling Virgil about my recent discoveries about Kirsten Packard—locating, almost, Wendy Carlson, Kirsten's roommate of old, now a researcher at the BPL; the rumor of a Patty Hearst–like robbery scenario; the other set of roommates I'd unearthed: our own Dr. Ted Morrell of the Henley College Physics Department and Vincent Packard, former US attorney representing Massachusetts, and father of the long-deceased Kirsten.

Putting it all together, it seemed like a lot to talk about. A case worth reopening, perhaps. But Virgil had shown less than no interest—that would be negative interest—in a cold case.

Sure enough, when we exited Admin a patrol car was idling in wait.

"Anything else?" Virgil asked, as he prepared to enter the car.

"Nothing else," I said.

Bundled up again, I walked across campus, past the back of the tower, toward my car, parked as usual by the tennis courts. Another drawback of winter—it was already dark at just after five. There weren't many students around and most of the workers had left. A few stragglers in work clothes, carrying lunch pails, some with toolboxes, climbed into pickups and cars. A group of three workmen, walking much faster than I was, overtook me on the path just east of the fountain. One, a young man, turned and tipped his Yankees cap. I pegged him for a major risk taker, wearing a Yankees cap this close to Boston.

"Evening, ma'am," he said.

"Hey," I said, to be cool.

But no matter how I greeted him, we both knew I was old enough to be his mother. It was the same with most of my students, but they were, after all, students, not working adults. Different. Or so I told myself.

It felt strange knowing the construction workers were unaware that they'd been stared at, ogled, and suspected of a crime by a room full of faculty and students. Did that make us voyeurs? Did it make it better or worse that there had also been a cop in the room?

It took three more such greetings from young men to get me to my car, where a man, one of the workers, I assumed, but not so young, was standing by an old sedan. The car was parked three slots over from mine, with no vehicles in between. His hat was pulled low over his face, his arms were folded across his chest. I felt a wave of panic, though I couldn't pinpoint what was threatening about him. I looked around and was relieved to see a group of students, backpacks and duffel bags bouncing, coming toward us from the gym.

I hit the alarm button on my remote. A combination of loud sounds—a high-pitched *chirp, chirp, chirp* overlaid with a low pitched *blare, blare, blare*—filled the cold air around me. I looked up, feigning surprise and embarrassment, and waved as if to say "No problem, my mistake."

I ducked into my car.

I had no reason to fear the worker, except that it was dark, he was large, and I was alone. Was I a snob, thinking that blue-collar workers weren't to be trusted after dark? Would I have reacted the same way if the man had been in a suit and tie, or the male faculty "uniform" of decent pants and a sweater or sports coat?

I'd deal with my prejudices later. For now, I locked the doors manually.

The worker turned away and entered his own vehicle, but I caught a glimpse of his face through my side window, lit from a security lamp at the corner of the tennis court. I tried not to stare. I couldn't be positive, but he might have been one of the workers I'd seen on the video. One of the fighting duo. Not the jacket-changing man, however. The other man, older than the cute, young greeters I'd just crossed paths with. This man wore a cap, his hair in a gray or blond ponytail. Given the poor resolution on the video, it was hard to tell whether this was the same man. Video man might simply have had a thick, fuzzy collar, not a ponytail.

I drove off toward home, checking my rearview mirror often. Three times, I was sure the man was following me. Each time, I pulled off and let the suspicious car pass. Twice, I was clearly wrong, as the vehicles continued on their way with women or families on board; the third time I was sure I caught him. I turned quickly into a wide driveway in front of a convenience store and saw the car behind me slow down, then drive off, a man in a cap at the wheel. Big deal. How common was that profile at rush hour?

I tuned my car radio to news and weather to distract myself. The pending snowstorm took up more time than it should have. It was mid-January in Massachusetts. Snow wasn't news.

Nice, turning sour on an unsuspecting weather woman. I was rattled, embarrassed at my fear of a man who had done nothing to disturb me. He may have looked a little creepy, but he could simply have been tired. He'd put in a long day of hard work. Unlike me, going from desk to classroom to another desk to another classroom. Maybe he'd simply been waiting on campus for a coworker who didn't show up. My shame turned to anger at whoever it was who had turned our beautiful campus into a scary place.

But it wasn't all the fault of the thug who'd cast a shadow over the week by attacking my student. I was also the victim of my own imagination that wouldn't quit, and a mind that desperately wanted answers.

I remembered a quote my father had stuck in one of his math textbooks, something about having "a reverence for mathematics as an exalted and mysterious science."

Mathematics seemed the least mysterious of all at this moment.

* * *

Somewhat settled after the parking lot scenario and the drive home, I sat at my kitchen counter sifting through the best parts of day-old Thai food to share during Bruce's dinner break. I'd planned on preparing a New England pot roast dinner for the Marshalls. Instead, they'd opted for a hospital meal. They'd heard from the doctors that Jenn was stabilizing, meaning not getting any worse, and they wanted to be close by in case she woke up. I understood why they would grasp at any straw.

Whirr, whirr, whirr. Whirr, whirr, whirr.

I jumped. Not as settled in as I thought. I picked up my cell and greeted Bruce, calling from work.

"Turns out I can't take that dinner break," Bruce said when we talked around seven o'clock. "We're down two guys."

"No problem," I said, trying not to sound disappointed. "I have a ton of work."

I had a sudden urge to pack a bag and head for the airport. Except it would be too hard to choose: Florida or Rwanda? I dumped the food from Pan's in the sink, ran the disposal, and threw the plastic containers into the recycling bin. Then I grabbed a banana that was about an hour away from banana bread and went to my office.

A couple of hours later, I'd accomplished at least half of the ton of work I'd mentioned to Bruce, most having to do with canceling automatic charges to my credit card. My list for the next day, Saturday, had to include at least a call to the police station to report the fraud incident and a trip to the bank to sign whatever form Eric had talked about.

And, possibly, a journey to Boston.

About Boston—I thought of tossing a coin, or doing something equally silly, like when I was a kid. "If I can solve this puzzle in ten minutes," I'd say to my mother, "it means I should go to Dawn's birthday party. If it takes me longer, I'm supposed to go to the library with Cameron."

Margaret would shake her head. "You're just like your father," she'd say.

Which was what I wanted to hear.

While I was nibbling on a peanut-butter-filled pretzel and reviewing notes for Monday morning's class, Bruce called again.

"Meant to tell you, there's a big storm coming," he said. "Not great for skiing."

It hadn't occurred to me that Bruce was still considering a ski trip to New Hampshire.

"Too bad," I said.

"So, I might as well get some OT in while I can, if you don't mind. Unless you had your heart set on Boston? We could still catch an exhibit and stay over tomorrow night?"

"Not necessary. Take the overtime." I knew that once the snow started, if it did, MAstar's helicopters would be grounded and people would have to resort to slow-moving *ground transportation*, the term Bruce and his buddies used for ambulances. It made sense that Bruce should take the hours while he could.

"So you don't need to go and, you know, look for any-one?" Bruce asked.

I understood Bruce's reluctance to mention Kirsten or her roommate. Better not to remind me if I'd forgotten about the foolish errand.

"Nuh-uh." A white lie. I wasn't going to look for any-one. I knew where she was.

It wasn't entirely clear to me why I wasn't up front about my Boston plan to Bruce, except that I didn't want to be talked out of it. And maybe also I figured Bruce would tell Virgil and there'd be so much explaining and defending and hand-waving thrown in. Better not to bother the guys with my little excursion, which probably wouldn't amount to anything anyway.

"So, what'll you do tomorrow?" Bruce asked.

"Oh, just stuff."

"Class stuff?"

"Uh-huh."

"I'll get off whenever the storm hits and catch up with you. That sound okay?"

"Sounds perfect," I said.

I did a quick calculation. I could call the police station first and make an appointment for next week to report the credit card fraud, and be at the bank when it opened at nine, then zip onto I-95, over to I-93 and into Boston. With light Saturday traffic, I could easily be at the BPL by the time Wendy Carlson was ready for her coffee break. I doubted Wendy would give me more than an hour of her time, if that. If at all. Even if I did some shopping or made a quick visit to the Museum of Science, I could be home long before the storm hit and Bruce left his fair weather job.

I almost thanked Bruce for helping me make the Boston decision, but it would have been too hard to explain how he'd helped me choose between Boston and not Boston.

Later in the evening, I felt I'd spent enough time on cleanup work to restore my standing in the credit card world. I longed for the good old days when people simply saved up cash for a new couch or a ski outfit. I felt safe taking this position because I had no firsthand knowledge of those card-free years and there was no one within earshot who could contradict me.

I wished I'd spent time preparing myself for meeting, or thrusting myself upon, Wendy Carlson. There was so much I wanted to ask her, so many rumors to check out. I'd been eager to follow up on Fran's reference to a story about Kirsten Packard's alleged involvement in a bank robbery, à la Patty Hearst, but non-copyeditor Kenny and Philippines-liaison Eric had done me in for today.

I hoped I'd seen the end of nuisance distractions. What had Ted said about them? *Distractions can be the good guys.* Easy for him to say. I had too many other things to do.

CHAPTER $\sqrt{10}$

Saturday morning brought a new annoyance. When I opened my email client on my laptop, I had more than two thousand messages. How could that be? On average, I received about a hundred a day, including all my online groups, classwork, other business and personal contacts.

On closer inspection, I saw that I'd been spammed by ads, with multiple copies of each message that was trying to sell me a product. Dozens and dozens of identical ads from a car rental agency (hadn't used one in ages). Dozens more for golf clubs (what?). I scrolled past ads for eyeglass repair (no need for glasses yet), updated chess software (not my game), and gifts for the pets in my life (never owned one).

Not a single ad was from a site I'd patronized in the past. As if even those would have been welcome—but at least it would have made a little sense.

I'd come into my home office with a mug of coffee, half

dressed for my errands and my trip to Boston. I'd expected to take a quick look at my email and texts and be on my way by about eight AM. But I couldn't stand the thought of coming home to this mess in my inbox. I decided to clean it up and leave a little later.

Ring, ring. Ring, ring.

A call from Ariana on my landline. I was surprised she was up so early, unless she had an early morning swim date.

"Hey, Sophie," she said, the two words as full of concern as a whole sentence would be from someone else. "What's going on up there?"

"How did you know?" I asked.

"I'm having a morning swim with Chuck"—I smiled at my stellar powers of prediction, in spite of the gravity in her tone—"the guy I told you about, and his brother just got down here from North Easton. He said there was a mugging on the Henley campus a couple of days ago. And the victim was in the Math Department. And I said, no, I'd have known about it because my best friend—"

"I'm sorry. I should have told you," I admitted. "I didn't want to spoil your vacation."

"You know I'd drop everything, even Chuck, if I could help."

I assured Ariana that everything was under control and promised to text her immediately if I thought there was anything she could do. But before I clicked off, I shot a question to her.

"Do you remember twenty-five years ago, a suicide on the Henley campus? A student—"

"Sure," she said. "I was in college but it was all over the news."

"Maybe in Massachusetts," I said. "How come you never mentioned it?"

"I don't know. I'll bet I did. We weren't emailing and texting coast-to-coast every hour back then, remember. I might have put it in an actual letter with a lot of other stuff. Why is this coming up?"

"No particular reason."

"I doubt that, but I can't tickle it out of you over the phone, so this will be continued next week in person."

"Deal," I said.

"Are you sure you don't need me?" she asked.

"Positive," I said, clicking off.

I put in a call to my email provider, and while on hold, I sifted through the ads, trying to group like messages, using the Search function as much as possible. I isolated twenty different ads with close to one hundred replications each. I checked one more time to be sure I hadn't selected a real message, and hit delete.

One welcome notification was from my email provider, that "delivery has been aborted" and they would no longer attempt to send my reply to Kenny the elusive copyeditor. A relief, but I'd have preferred some closure, like learning what company Kenny worked for, if not the one I submitted to, and which puzzler he was trying to reach, so I could send that person my condolences.

Everything looked much better on my screen, so I hung up, still without a clue where this computer attack came from. I handled the real messages, and spent some time troubleshooting. I tried a help site, and even a chat room to try to determine how the spam storm arrived at my computer. About an hour and a half later, I still had no idea how to prevent further intrusions, other than take the precautions already built into my system. Next week I'd buy Ted, our Franklin Hall tech expert, a cruller, and see if he had any suggestions.

I clicked over to the weather report. Cute white smiley-faced snowflakes, each one different, of course, fell from a puffy blue cartoon cloud all over New England. They were due to land in Boston even later tonight than originally predicted. Great; I'd be in and out of the city, home midafternoon, well ahead of the storm's path, as long as I got moving soon.

Wanting to cross one more item off my nuisance list before I left, I called the Henley PD and poured out my fraud story to a man who identified himself as Bunyan. For the rest of the conversation I pictured a tall, strapping guy in a flannel shirt, with a forest of a beard, who could pick me up with one hand. Bunyan told me that an officer would be assigned to my case and would contact me soon. Check.

I finished dressing—a professional look with a long wool skirt, boots, and a jacket. I could hear Ariana as if she were standing in my bedroom and not thirteen hundred miles south: "Sure, that's a professional look. From the eighties," she'd have said, clicking her tongue. Ariana often commented on "the preppy look that should never have come back, twice." But it was exactly the way I pictured a BPL researcher. I'd soon see.

As I'd hoped, Eric wasn't working today. I didn't think I could handle a face-to-face with him. I was lucky to be called to the window of a woman who looked old enough to have been to the rodeo and back a few times.

Without a single "I'm afraid not," the woman whisked through some paperwork, asked for my signature, and told me to expect a new credit card in the mail in a few days. Meanwhile I could use the temporary number assigned to me. Even though I played around with the little inkless fingerprint pad on the counter—in the area of toys, online banking couldn't compete with brick-and-mortar facilities— I was out in ten minutes. My kind of errand.

I was ready to start the fun part of the day.

Weekend traffic was light along I-95, but heavier than I expected as I got to I-93, approaching Boston, and then close to impossible when I reached Copley Square. The big gray McKim building of the BPL finally came into view at

just after noon, not the best time to find someone at work.
I decided that a better idea might be for me to have lunch
first, especially since I'd had a meager breakfast of coffee
and half a muffin. I congratulated myself on coming up
with a completely acceptable stalling tactic.

The surrounding area with the centuries-old Trinity
Church and charming old hotels was familiar to me from
frequent visits. In recent years, I visited here for special
exhibits at the Museum of Fine Arts or the Museum of Science. And for shopping, when I was in the mood. Or, more
correctly, when Ariana was in the mood.

I parked in a large structure on Huntington Avenue,
under a shiny, less charming new hotel connected to Copley Place on one side and the Prudential Center on the
other. I did most of my shopping online these days, for
everything from toothpaste to kitchen spatulas to shoes,
but when I did want to step into the world of brick-and-
mortar stores, this was my favorite center. You could find
what you wanted here, whether your taste ran to a trinket
at Tiffany's and elegant dining at the Top of the Hub, or an
inexpensive scarf from a kiosk and a quick dessert at Ben
& Jerry's.

I entered the center's food court and chose a small,
counter version of the North End's Regina Pizzeria, another
"best of Boston" in my book. Sitting with a large cheese
and mushroom slice, I felt a little guilty. There I was eating
great pizza while Bruce and Virgil, my usual partners in
the activity, were both at work.

Thoughts of Jenn and the state she was in also intruded
on my enjoyment. I hoped Virgil and the HPD had made
some progress in the investigation. And that Jenn might be
waking up to sounds of relief from her worried parents.

I finished the last bite of crusty dough and the last sip of
lemon-flavored sparkling water and headed for the library.
Like a long thread of mozzarella that won't leave its moor-
ings on a slice of pizza, the thought that the fates of Kirsten

Packard and Jenn Marshall were connected wouldn't leave my mind.

I walked as far as I could indoors before stepping outside at the corner of Huntington Avenue and Dartmouth Street, not happy with the blast of bitter cold. I sketched out a memo in my head to the city's engineers—please work on a weatherproof underground tunnel or skywalk to get us citizens from the shopping center to the BPL. I was pretty sure no one else would want to spoil the look of the striking Romanesque architecture of the oldest public library in the country, but the mental exercise gave me something to do other than hop from one foot to the other while I waited at the crosswalk. I had just enough time to read the inspirational quote carved into the stately building: "The Commonwealth Requires the Education of the People as the Safeguard of Order and Liberty." An awesome example of the glory days of public buildings, when they were meant to inspire.

Across Dartmouth Street, a more modern building, a bank, favored passersby with a neon red crawl that told us the outside temperature was two degrees Fahrenheit. I shivered at the thought, and at the extra chill that passed through me once I knew the numbers. I took a freezing breath and started up the steps of the library, asking myself why I'd left my comfy cottage for this so-called interview with a woman I'd never met and who, most likely, didn't want to meet me.

By the time I reached the top step, snow had started to fall. Had the weather prediction I'd seen earlier been incorrect? Off by nearly half a day? I was shocked. What next? I mused, sorry no one was around to appreciate my sarcasm.

Inside the building, more architectural marvels awaited, with the grand ivory gray staircase, rich yellow sienna walls, and two giant marble lions. I felt I'd entered a temple, and in a way it was, a shrine to books and learning.

I spotted a small desk set apart in an alcove and headed that way to ask for Wendy Carlson. But as soon as I caught a glimpse of the woman on duty, I recognized her.

She'd stood to access a file cabinet behind her, a tall woman, with ramrod-straight posture. Her short hair, a shade between mine (medium-rare brown) and Bruce's (very well-done brown) was cropped, forming a neat helmet around her thin face. And—I whispered to the imaginary Ariana at my side—she was wearing a long black skirt, boots, a mock turtleneck, and a blazer. Very eighties.

A good sign, if I believed in signs.

I stalled, stopping at a bench, pretending to search for something in my briefcase while I watched two backpack-laden patrons interact with the woman. Even from a distance of thirty feet, I could tell there wasn't the same sparkle I'd seen in the eyes of the Henley sophomore making up her dorm room bed twenty-five years ago.

I wished I had a script, something that spelled out exactly what I wanted from Wendy. I told myself if I could simply hear Wendy's version of what had happened to precipitate her roommate's death, my curiosity would be satisfied. A few moments of commiseration, and I could be on my way, finished with the Kirsten Packard case. I might even be able to stop calling it a case. Bruce and especially Virgil would be so pleased. And Ted, I mused.

While Wendy served people in a short line at the desk, I sat on a marble bench and worked a quick game, similar to the hangman of my childhood, except with numbers. When she was free, I made my move and crossed the marble floor between us.

"Good afternoon," I said, winded. Probably not from the walk, but from reading the nameplate on the desk, which confirmed my guess. I'd found Wendy Carlson. "I'm

Sophie Knowles. I'm a professor at Henley College." *Your alma mater* hung in the air.

I was ready for anything, from a cold brush-off to a how-dare-you slap in the face. But I wasn't ready for what she said.

"Ted said you might be coming."

So much for surprising Wendy.

CHAPTER √11

It took a moment for me to adjust to Wendy Carlson's greeting.

"Ted Morrell?" I asked, floundering. "Ted said I might be coming?"

Wendy smiled, but not in a way that said she was glad to have bested me. "Yes, Dr. Ted Morrell of Henley College's Physics Department."

The same Ted who couldn't remember your name, I added silently. *The one who neglected to mention that he was roommates with Kirsten Packard's father. The one who claimed to have met Kirsten only once or twice.*

Wendy's calm, resigned look and clear, direct gaze disarmed me. Literally. My shoulders, stiff until that point, dropped so alarmingly that my purse slid off my shoulder to the right and crashed to the floor. Three Japanese pocket puzzles that I'd stuck in an outside compartment fell out and half rolled, half slid across the marble, then clanked to a stop. Red-faced as I was, the slapstick performance seemed to loosen Wendy a bit as she came from behind the desk, smiling, and helped me retrieve metal rings, loops, nuts, and bolts.

I struggled with apologies until all the pieces were back in my bag and we stood face-to-face, or my face to her neck.

"I wondered if you could spare a minute." I didn't think it necessary to tell her why.

Wendy nodded. "I almost didn't come in today, but I couldn't very well take an indefinite leave. Ted had no idea which day you might show up."

"That's a relief," I said.

Finally, a broad smile. "Ted was—is—very solicitous of Kirsten and her memory."

"I have no intention of spoiling it," I said, feeling a little guilty as I tried to push the image of Kirsten Packard–cum–Patty Hearst out of my mind.

Wendy picked up her phone, punched in a number, and arranged for a replacement on the desk.

"I'm just filling in here anyway," she told me, hanging up. "I'm usually up in Research, but our regular desk person lives in Attleboro and was afraid she'd get caught in the storm going home."

I gulped. Attleboro was just south of Henley. Should I also be worried? I looked out the main door and saw the flakes coming down heavier now, way ahead of the meteorologists' prediction. As if that mattered to the flakes. Any of them.

Wendy led me to her office on the third floor. Obviously proud of her place of employment, she couldn't help playing tour guide, allowing me a peek into the basilica-like Bates Hall, and a moment to admire a mural by John Singer Sargent.

"Imagine, this was the first place in the country where an ordinary citizen could borrow books and materials to take home," she reminded me. "It was a novel idea in the mid–eighteen hundreds."

"How does one go from physics to this?" I asked, when we reached her small office. I pointed to the piles of research books and notes that had taken over the space. Tiny as it was, the room had an air of elegance, with a high ceiling; rich, dark woodwork; and ornamental lighting. One wall was a floor-to-ceiling bookcase, with not an inch of empty shelving.

"This was what I needed, afterward," she said, her voice soft. I could understand that Wendy's life might be defined by *before* and *afterward* with respect to the terrible death of her roommate. "Especially back then, when you heard nothing above a whisper in a library, it offered a quiet retreat, with limitless resources to absorb my mind." Wendy spoke slowly, and I could see that she'd have a calming effect on anyone stressed out, looking for research assistance. "I applied for an internship and worked in a few of the branches while I got a master's in library science."

I shook my finger at her. "You have an MLS? You didn't update your entry in the alumni directory."

We both laughed, and I was amazed that I was joking so comfortably with a woman I'd known less than a half hour.

Wendy sat behind her desk, about the only option in the cramped room besides the one chair in front of it, which I took.

"What is it you'd like to know, Sophie? May I call you Sophie?"

I nodded. Wendy could call me whatever she pleased. I couldn't believe my luck, or whatever it was that had made Wendy Carlson so receptive to my sudden appearance. Well, not so sudden. Maybe Ted's warning had the opposite effect from what he'd intended, causing her to open up rather than keep me at bay. Or, maybe whatever Wendy said next was what Ted instructed her to say. In either case, I had nothing to lose.

"I'd love to hear you talk about that time at Henley, and what you think drove Kirsten to"—I threw up my hands, struggling to come up with a phrase that wouldn't sound offensive—"her death." I could have done better.

Wendy worked a strand of hair and gazed over my shoulder, at the past, I assumed.

"I met Kirsten my first day at Henley, at freshman orientation, and we really clicked. We were both fairly local, from western Mass. We wanted to room together, but it was the school's custom to pair one girl from a distance with one from nearby. We petitioned the Dean of Residents—I should say Kirsten petitioned; she was the brave one—and we got to share a room from the start. We were so different. She had . . . spirit. There was something about her that was so confident. She wouldn't let anyone define her."

"It must have been hard for her, being the daughter of someone prominent in the criminal justice system."

Wendy nodded. "I think that was a big factor in what she became in college. Kirsten was supposed to be the ideal, dutiful daughter, the poster girl for one campaign after another. By the time I met her, she was ready to break some rules. As soon as she left home, even though it was only half a state away, that's what she did. She'd stay out past curfew, sneaking back into the dorm with a bottle of wine." She smiled. "Or a guy. I loved her spark. Her daring. I was the opposite, yet she never looked down on me or called me the prude I was."

"I can tell you loved her," I said. I saw Wendy's eyes fill up. I stood, a twinge of guilt overtaking my desire to hear more. I couldn't bear the thought that I'd taken this lovely woman back to what was probably the worst day of her life. "I should go. I'm very sorry to have intruded on you."

Wendy let out a long sigh. "No, please stay. Will you let me get us some coffee? I didn't know it, but I have more to say."

I sat down again, part of me elated that I'd finally get

some answers, the other part fearful of what I might be awakening from a long sleep.

While Wendy was gone, I sneaked a look at my phone. I was amused by a text from Bruce, who hoped I was having a quiet, productive day. I scrolled through just-checking-in messages from Ariana and Fran, and came to—what?— another three hundred spam messages? I ignored them, except to note that they were from the same sites as this morning's deluge, and clicked over to weather. Not looking good. Nice of the weather gurus to catch up with what I could figure out by looking out the window.

Wendy was gone a long time for a coffee run. I wondered if she'd slipped out to call Ted and get some advice on how to deal with me. Or maybe she was calling BPL security to usher me out to the cold, snowy street.

"Sorry," she said, entering her office just as I was envisioning the Boston Police coming to arrest me for harassment. "I had to make a new pot."

I chose to believe her rather than my more dramatic imaginings.

She carried a small tray with two silver BPL travel mugs and packets of sweeteners and whiteners. I declined the extras, but wished I'd thought to bring a little dessert to share.

"I want you to know—" I began, planning to apologize again for stirring up a disturbing era in Wendy's life.

Wendy interrupted with a hand wave. "I'm glad you're here," she said.

"Thanks," I managed, and listened as Wendy started up again as if there'd been no interruption.

"What I didn't realize was that Kirsten's gumption, as inspiring as it was, and as much fun, would get her into trouble."

I gave Wendy a questioning look, not wanting to distract her by a verbal request for an explanation. I didn't need to.

"By the end of freshman year," Wendy continued, "Kirsten had fallen in with some rough types and I started to worry."

"Were they Henley students?" Not likely, since Henley was a women's college at the time, but I supposed there could have been some rough-type females around.

Wendy grimaced. "No, not students at all. The guys were dropouts from who knew where, who'd already been in jail or were on their way."

"Drugs?" I asked, trying to think back to the narcotic of choice twenty-five years ago.

"Not that I could tell. Some drinking, but mostly it was what I'd call petty crime. I told myself they were pranks. There were a couple of guys in particular who'd brag about stealing a fancy car and driving it to the city dump." She paused. "Maybe not so petty after all, huh? But no one seemed to get hurt. They always had wads of cash, and I knew it wasn't from their careers. One was a dishwasher, I remember. The others were more freelance, like construction and yard work."

"Were Kirsten's parents aware of these new friends?"

"Somehow—not from me, I assure you—they caught wind of what she was up to and made sure she stayed put at home for the summer. She called me two or three times a day to say how bored she was. Of course, I liked that."

"She counted on you to be there for her."

Wendy bit her lip. Not used to accepting compliments, I guessed. "All I know is that after the full schedule of political rallies and fund-raisers on the Cape, Kirsten came back to school sophomore year more ready than ever to live it up."

A small window behind Wendy was a constant reminder of the buildup of snow outside. It had accumulated on the roof of the newer wing of the library, and on the windowsill outside Wendy's office. I sipped my coffee, torn between making a dash for home and listening for as long as Wendy was willing to talk.

"Did you ever meet these friends of hers?" Was one of them in the tower with her that morning? Had they paired up to rob a bank? I had many questions. Doling them out one at a time was taxing.

"Once in a while Kirsten would invite me to hang out with them. I'm not sure why. We'd meet at a diner or, one time, at an old warehouse right here in Boston, down by the wharf, where there was a lot of merchandise that might have fallen from a truck, if you know what I mean."

"Did you ever confront Kirsten about the guys or about her choice of friends?"

Wendy shook her head. "I looked up to her. She even tried to fix me up with a couple of the guys." Wendy pressed her lips together and shook her head. "I knew Kirsten was trying to shake me out of my type, as she called it, which was clean shaven, law abiding, preferably pre-med. I just wasn't brave enough to step outside what I'd grown up with. Not even afterward." Wendy smiled. "I went to the junior prom with my cousin, who was an engineering student at Northeastern."

I sensed a tiny note of regret about how she'd spent her youth. And a touch of relief that she was still alive.

We'd been in sync in our sipping, and now we both sat for a few minutes with our coffee and our thoughts. I felt a great admiration for Wendy's studied, thoughtful temperament. She took a couple of business calls during our conversation and was in no hurry, either while dealing with customers on the phone, or while answering my questions.

Spending so much time with students in our faster and faster paced society, I'd become accustomed to rapid-fire Q and A; and quick, abbreviated messages.

CU, T2UL8R, LUV. Some days I gave in and used this new language; other days I missed longhand.

It was calming and refreshing to talk at what might be called an old-fashioned pace. If only the snow weren't speeding up, swirling madly outside the window.

We hadn't even come close to the question of how Kirsten died. How did she happen to be in the tower that morning? Was there anything to the rumors that she'd been pushed to her death? Did any of the guys Wendy met seem capable of murder?

Again, I held back.

"Did Kirsten play the carillon?" I asked. Very subtle, leading up to the tower, one step at a time.

"Not Kirsten. Me. I was the carillonist. I always loved it—the fact that you're high up in a tower and everyone down below can hear you. You have a captive audience, but still you're anonymous. Invisible. Not like a recital on a stage, which is just plain nerve-racking."

Wendy continued, talking about the carillon in the same beautiful terms that I'd heard Randy Stephens and our students talk about it. I thought of carillonist Jenn Marshall and wondered if there'd been any change in her condition. I hadn't had any messages from those who might know. Between the accumulating snow outside and my concerns about matters at home, suddenly I felt every mile of the distance between Henley and Boston.

"But you didn't come to hear about my music hobby. I should ask if there's anything else you wanted to know."

My response surprised me. "I guess my main question is why do you think Ted thought he needed to warn you that I might visit?"

Wendy's laugh was almost sad, and I knew it didn't come easily. "Apparently he has a high regard for your investigative skills. He didn't want to encourage you in any way."

"Why not? If there was something new to be discovered, wouldn't he be happy?"

"Ted was very close to Mr. Packard. He didn't want to see the family name dragged out again after all these years, and put through some press wringer."

"But if it turned out that someone had hurt Kirsten, wouldn't Ted, and whatever family is left, want to know?"

"Kirsten is dead. Nothing can change that."

Uh-oh, this sounded like Ted talking.

"Did the police ever question you?"

She nodded. "I told them what I knew."

"Including the names of the guys Kirsten was hanging out with?"

She frowned and lowered her eyes. I detected the slightest "no" gesture. "I didn't even know their real names. They had crazy nicknames. Like, 'Big Dog' was the guy who was always barking orders to the others. You could tell he wanted to be the leader, but he kind of lost out to this other guy they called 'Einstein.' Big Dog stopped coming around, but there was 'Ponytail,' because he had one, of course, real stringy and dirty, who was always there, and maybe some others, but those were the regulars. Especially Einstein and Ponytail."

"Even nicknames might have helped the police—"

"Nothing was going to bring Kirsten back," she interrupted, repeating the mantra, louder now.

I thought this would be a good time for me to pull back, lest I lose her. But Wendy went on.

"Why should I have sullied her name and ruined her family's life by listing every peccadillo, every shady friend she ever had? And it wasn't like I didn't have enough to worry about myself, with my physics and math classes."

I swallowed hard. Was I really hearing about a withholding of valuable information from the police? A cover-up?

Wendy sensed my discomfort, and, I felt, tried to return to script. "At the time, I believed that it was for the best," she said. "And the medical examiner ruled her death a suicide, so . . ."

Wendy trailed off, perhaps seeing the fallacy in her thinking, in the coaching Ted had most likely given her.

"And now? Do you still think it was for the best?"

"I don't know. I wish I'd spoken up."

I barely heard her. "What would you have said? Would you have given the police the names of Kirsten's friends?"

"I didn't know their names. I told you."

"Did Ted know about Kirsten's friends?"

Wendy seemed to be considering how to answer. I thought I'd help her out.

"I know Ted and Kirsten's father were close friends since college. Did Ted know about these shady friends?"

Wendy wrung her hands. "You'll have to ask Ted. . . . I think I've given you enough time."

What happened to "I'm glad you're here"? I pressed on. "Did you have suspicions about anything really serious, like the bank robberies that were rumored?"

Wendy stood up. My signal to leave. "I have nothing more to add." Should I take that as a "yes" to my question? That there had been more than pranks?

"Was it Ted who convinced you to hold everything back from the police? To protect the family?"

"I told you, I have nothing more to say." Wendy, now cold and withdrawn, looked down on me.

Resigned, I stood. I dug in the pocket of my purse, past the puzzle pieces, and handed her my card. "Will you call me if you want to talk again?"

She hesitated, then took my card without a word. She turned to the window, her back to me, facing a heavy snowfall.

I whispered my thanks and left.

CHAPTER $\sqrt{12}$

I left the library, realizing I'd blown it. I'd pushed too hard. Would Wendy have said more if I hadn't been so aggressive toward the end of our meeting? I wondered if I'd ever have a chance to talk to Wendy Carlson again.

She'd been warming up to me, possibly forgetting whatever formula Ted might have given her. Then, I'd all but accused her of obstruction of justice for not telling the police about the squirrelly men in Kirsten's life. She'd shut down.

But wasn't that exactly what she'd done twenty-five years ago—obstruct justice? Even if I had no business grilling her, didn't I now have an obligation to tell Virgil? I struggled with the dilemma. And with the weather.

Wind and snow whipped my face as I walked toward the parking structure where I'd left my car. Snow was coming down, fast and furious, piling up on the sidewalks and streets. It was one thing to admire the beautiful snowscape in Childe Hassam's *Boston Common at Twilight* at the MFA;

it was another to drive for an hour or more while your windshield wipers couldn't keep up with the whiteout.

It would be dumb to drive now, but frustrating not to be home. I needed to sit somewhere warm and think about what to do next. If I made a call to Virgil, I had only my word to back me up. Wendy could deny she'd ever mentioned that Kirsten had been hanging around with a group of losers who were capable of anything. She could claim she'd hardly talked to me, except for a casual chat between an alum and a Henley professor who happened to be in town. Could the HPD question Wendy twenty-five years later? Could she be prosecuted if they determined she'd impeded an investigation? She was only a teenager at the time. How about Ted, who'd been old enough to know better? I knew there was no statute of limitations on murder, but who said there was a murder involved?

Other than me, that is, more convinced than ever that Kirsten died at the hand of one or more of the rough types who lingered in Wendy's memory. Through her roommate, Kirsten had access to a key to the tower, if a key was even needed back then as it was now, and might have used it as a trysting place, only to meet her death instead.

I crossed Huntington, heading for a bagel shop at the edge of the shopping center nearest me, my mind still on Wendy. I realized I didn't know anything about her personal life. Had she ever married? Did she live alone? She didn't wear a ring, but that didn't mean much.

Whirr, whirr, whirr. Whirr, whirr, whirr.

No sooner had I turned my phone on but a call from Bruce was on tap. I could let it go to voice mail, but he wouldn't give up. My message icon told me I had ten voice mails already, and I knew that several would be from Bruce. If I didn't take a call from him soon, he'd worry. But if I clicked through, he'd hear the traffic noise and know I wasn't at home making soup for dinner. From my position at one of the busiest corners in Boston, could I convince him that the car horns he was hearing were from rush hour on Henley Boulevard?

"Hey," I said, all cheery and pretend warm.

The drivers of a fleet of cars and SUVs chose that moment to honk their horns to make a passage for a police car that flew screaming by me toward Copley Square. *Busted.*

"I knew it," Bruce said. "You're in Boston."

"How's your day?" I asked.

"Are you on the road?"

"No. I'm about to make a final decision."

"Stay there, please. It's worse down here than in Boston. We've got travelers' advisories all over the news."

"But you're off work and we could—"

"Never mind that. You need to get a room there. Promise."

I huffed and puffed. "Promise."

"How did it go with the roommate?" Bruce asked.

"Nothing special."

"No more information on the tower death?"

"No. It was good to meet her, though."

"Maybe you've done all you can. Just let Virge go after Jenn's attacker."

"Uh-huh. Right."

"You're not telling me everything, are you?"

"We can talk more when I see you. I'll text you when I have a room," I said, and the long-suffering Bruce let me off the hook.

"I'll give you a regular report on conditions down here," he said.

What a sweetie.

I knew Bruce was right about the folly of trying to drive home. The snow swirled around me as I entered the lobby of the shopping center and the door banged behind me, blown shut by the wind.

I took a seat on a bench in the center court area, surrounded by high-end stores, many of which were closing up for the night. Bruce and I chatted awhile, then I braced myself for a reluctant overnight stay.

An hour later, I was ordering soup and salad from room service, which sounded better to me than a cold bagel. Since January was not exactly tourist season in Boston, I had no trouble getting a room in one of the big Copley Place anchor hotels. I figured it wouldn't be so easy later, when there might be a crowd of workers realizing they couldn't drive home. I wondered where Wendy lived, whether I should invite her to be my roommate. LOL at that idea.

I'd picked up overnight essentials in the hotel gift shop and taken advantage of a luxurious terry robe, compliments of the hotel. I had my own coffee and tea setup, two double beds, and a pile of fluffy towels. The minibar was stocked with liquor (a waste) in a rack on the door and candy (tempting) on the shelves. Maybe forced confinement wasn't so bad after all. As long as I had Internet connectivity, which I did, for a small fee.

After my meal, my cleanup consisted of placing the tray on the floor outside the door. I could get used to this. I sipped tea, opened my laptop, and settled in. Nothing says "relax" like looking up bank robbery archives.

As I typed keywords into my search engine, I pitied anyone trying to profile me based on my browsing history. Today alone my searches ran from Archimedes to puzzles and games to bank robbery stats for Bristol County, with beading books (presents for Ariana) and fleece-lined boots (present for me) thrown in.

I was pleased to see that Henley and surrounding towns in Bristol County were singularly low in robberies. Occasionally a note had been passed to a teller, demanding all she had in her money drawer, but there had been nothing involving weapons or bodily harm to staff or customers. It gave me a warm feeling about my hometown.

Eventually, I realized that if Kirsten and her friends were planning to rob a bank, it would probably be in Boston, not small-town Henley or its neighbors. Boston wasn't called the Bank Robbery Capital of America without good reason.

There were more than three hundred robberies a year in Boston, though not all of them involved banks. Two of the robberies were legendary, making most lists of "Crimes of the Century"—the Brink's job in 1950, where eleven armed members of a gang, all of whom were eventually arrested, held up the Brink's building and stole millions of dollars in cash, checks, and securities; and the Gardner Museum heist in 1990, where two men posing as cops walked off with an estimated three hundred million dollars in art. In both cases, the spoils remain unrecovered.

I made a guess that the robbery I was looking for was smaller than either the Brink's or the Gardner job, both of which had been the subject of books, novels, feature films, and documentaries. For smaller efforts, I'd have to dig into police reports for the year Kirsten was a sophomore. It took a few minutes to call them up, but a Suffolk County website provided a long list of summaries for each year.

As I read through the paragraphs, I saw what excitement I'd been missing, focusing on differential equations instead of on the police blotter all these years. A seventy-year-old Chelsea, Massachusetts, man was turned in by his adult son who recognized him in surveillance photos of a local bank robbery. A Springfield woman fashionably dressed in a cloche hat, scarf, and dark glasses tossed an unknown green liquid at tellers and grabbed the cash available. A serial robber was caught after making off with loot from seven different banks in the greater Boston area, each time claiming he had a bomb strapped to his waist.

I must have been channeling my movie-loving boyfriend Bruce, whom I missed, because I kept thinking of the actors in Boston heist movies through the years, from Robert Mitchum in *The Friends of Eddie Coyle* to Ben Affleck in *The Town*.

Fascinating as the anecdotes were, I saw nothing that fit with what Wendy had told me, or with Judy's and Fran's reports on the gossip. I needed a story that included a woman not quite out of her teens. If the tale included the initials KP, so much the better.

On the fourth page of reports for Kirsten's sophomore year, I found what I was looking for. Two suspects—an armed man in his early twenties and an unarmed woman, possibly a teenager, according to witnesses—were being sought for questioning in a string of small robberies in Boston and a major heist at a bank in nearby Brockton. I clicked on the next page for "More" and saw a photo of a third man, who'd been caught fleeing the scene of the last, biggest robbery.

I peered at his grainy countenance. I cringed at the sight of his stringy ponytail, added twenty-five years, and shaved his face. My lying-in-wait man. I got up from my desk-table combo, nearly knocking my chair over, as if Wendy's "Ponytail" had just entered my hotel room. The long-ago robber was the man who'd been standing in the Henley College parking lot, watching me enter my car last night.

I slowed my breathing and went back for more.

The whole article was painfully brief, noting only that the man was being held for arraignment. So far, he hadn't given up his partners.

If this truly was a big heist, there should be follow-up stories. I searched using as many keywords as I could reasonably relate to the story. Nothing came up, even though I pleaded with my computer each time the pinwheel spun, trying to honor my request. What was wrong with Boston reporters?

Skimpy as the data was, I had no doubt who the man

was, and who his undisclosed partners had been. For better or worse, that's how my mind did its calculations.

I looked out the window at the still-falling snow. I wanted to flee to the safety of my blue and white Henley cottage, though I knew better than to head out in this storm. "If *we* can't fly, *you* shouldn't drive," Bruce always told me. I wished Bruce were with me now. I checked for the fourth time that the chain was pulled across my door, dragged the heavy desk chair over the carpet, and shoved it under the handle.

Foolish, I knew. My imagination was working overtime. I'd last seen the man in Henley, not Boston. I was actually safer here.

How come it didn't feel that way?

Reading my math journals in bed seemed to calm me, except that every time I heard a noise in the hallway or a rattling of the window, I jumped. I was happy that Bruce checked in with me often, but the ringtone startled me, also, and I set the phone to vibrate to avoid the sudden sound.

I hadn't told Bruce what I'd found in the police blotter. I debated calling Virgil. What could I tell them to get their attention? That I'd found an old police report and a newspaper photo of a bank robber from the eighties who looked like a man hanging around campus today? Oh, and that the eighties guy had a ponytail and so did the current guy. What a difference that made.

Maybe if I threw in my whole encounter with Wendy Carlson they'd see the connection I'd been trying to make all along. It couldn't be coincidence that, according to Wendy, a guy named Ponytail hung out with her and her roommate at a diner in Henley, and a look-alike, from his hair to his mug, showed up a quarter of a century later on the same campus.

All I had to do was figure out how the carillon played into the story, other than as a curse to those who climbed the tower. That, and questions like "Why did he come back?" I assumed Ponytail the Younger spent some time in jail for the Brockton robbery. Did he take the fall (I really had to cut back on TV talk) or had he given up the names of his two partners? A new, wild thought came to me. What if Ponytail had eventually ratted on his associates, and Kirsten, unable to face prison and the scandal for her family, had chosen suicide instead?

I rubbed my forehead, squeezing my eyes against a headache. Why did every tiny "answer" generate more questions, more possibilities?

I decided I'd call a meeting when I got home. Bruce, Virgil, and me. I could lay it out—Wendy's withheld knowledge and the bank robberies of the past, and my quasi-stalker in the present. Bruce and Virgil could point out all the holes and then I'd drop it, once and for all.

Sometimes for me, working out a problem, even if the solution wouldn't be implemented for a while, was satisfying. My mind at ease, I drifted off to sleep.

Tap, rattle.

Loud noises woke me.

Tap, rattle. "There goes the bride." *Tap, rattle.* "All dressed and wide." *Tap, rattle.* My doorknob shook.

Someone was trying to enter my room. I sat up, my heart pounding. I pictured the man with the ponytail trying to force his way in. I reached for the phone, then realized there wasn't some *one* outside my door; there was a whole choral group outside my door, many voices singing a parody of Wagner's "Bridal Chorus." My best guess was that they were from the wedding party I'd seen earlier on the ballroom floor. Unable to do the town on a stormy Saturday night, they'd taken the festivities indoors. And on my floor. Lucky me.

Eventually, the tapper and rattler of my door handle went away—*no, this is not the maid of honor's room*—and the loud group reveled their way down the hallway.

Fully awake now, my thoughts turned again to Wendy Carlson, who'd made a brief appearance in my dreams as a cowardly lion. I got up and walked to the window. A lovely view. I was too high up to see any sullying of the blanket of snow that covered the rooftops. The snowfall was softer now; maybe the storm had turned and headed east, to the ocean. I seemed to be able to see through the flakes to a dark but clear sky. I'd been so distracted when I checked in, I hadn't taken time to appreciate the panoramic view I had of Boston and points north.

I looked past downtown Boston to the streets of Cambridge and beyond, wondering where Wendy lived. Somewhere close by, I assumed. Who'd want to commute very far in Boston traffic, on roads carved out by meandering cattle four hundred years ago?

Tap, rattle.

One more isolated *tap, rattle* didn't frighten me. I was likely being bothered by a tipsy groomsman looking for ice. No one was deliberately trying to break into my room.

Was Wendy safe? What if Ponytail or Einstein, or whoever, had followed me from Henley, hoping to be led to Wendy? Maybe the third guy, the "Big Dog" who had allegedly disappeared, was still in the picture after all. And if Ted thought so much of my investigative skills, it was possible that the bad guys admired them also, and figured I could do what they hadn't been able to do all these years. Find the girl who'd sat in on their diner conversations. They probably didn't know her name any more than she knew theirs, and maybe they weren't Internet savvy. It was also possible that they simply hadn't seen her as a threat until now.

None of this could be connected directly to why Jenn was attacked. How could she be involved? Maybe she wasn't, as much as I wanted to make sense out of all the loose ends. Did Jenn know something that made her a target? What could that be? Kirsten, Wendy, the diner, the robberies—all of that belonged to a past before she was born.

I missed home. I wondered how the Marshalls, all of them, were getting along. I'd talked to Jenn's roommate, Patty, once today, during Wendy's coffee errand, and had some assurance that Jenn's parents were taken care of. A relative from Fitchburg had arrived with clothes and supplies to make their dorm stay a little more comfortable. I knew that neither of Jenn's parents had been to college; this was a tough way to experience campus life for the first time. I hoped they could bring themselves to trust in Jenn's safety in the future. I made a great effort to think of when, not if, Jenn woke up.

I wrestled with my responsibility to protect Wendy, especially if I was the reason she might be in danger. I couldn't fall back to sleep with her fate weighing on my mind. I checked my cell phone, down to 49 percent of its battery power, but still able to display the time. Eleven eleven. I liked the symmetry and decided to act on it.

I hit Virgil's name on my contacts screen. He might trust my instincts enough to have the police check on Wendy. He'd spent a lot of his career with the Boston PD and surely would still have friends here.

"Yo," Virgil said. Was that a spring in his voice, at this hour? I harkened back to his noncommittal answer regarding a date in his future.

I laughed, in spite of the disquiet building in me. "Yo, yourself. Did I wake you?"

"As if you'd care. What's up?"

I briefed Virgil on my last twenty-four hours, starting with the creepy appearance of a man at my car last evening, and then the same man showing up in a mug shot from twenty-five years ago. Of necessity, I confessed to tracking down Wendy Carlson, now a researcher at the BPL, and, in as few non-incriminating words as possible, told her story and expressed my reasons for concern for her safety.

"Ponytail is obviously out of jail, if he was ever in, and he may be after her. Can you get one of your old buddies to check on her?" I asked. "I don't know where she lives, but isn't that what you guys do?"

"Sure. And we bring cupcakes. They're the new donuts, you know."

Sometimes I thought Virgil stayed awake nights thinking up ways to aggravate me. "Virgil, this could be serious."

"I know that, Sophie. There have been some developments here."

"What? What developments?"

"Can you send me that mug shot? You probably know how to do that, right?"

"No problem. Check your email in five minutes." My heart beat faster. "What's happening there? What are the developments? Good ones or bad ones?"

I paced my small room with my phone. Were developments the same as breakthroughs? Was it a big clue? An arrest? And here I was miles away. It wasn't fair.

"As soon as I get a look at the picture, a car will be on its way to your new friend," Virgil said.

He clicked off, leaving me wondering not only what had developed in Henley, but why it had been so easy to convince Virgil to track down Wendy.

First things first. I opened my browser and easily found the last page I'd looked at, with the brief report and the photo of my other new friend, Ponytail. I clicked on the URL, copied it, and sent it to Virgil's email address.

I wanted to call Virgil back immediately and pump him

until he told me what was going on in my hometown. I wrote off that idea as futile and did the next best thing. I called his best friend and mine, Bruce.

While the line was ringing, I was aware that my battery might not last the night at the rate I was using it. I had a charger in my car, but did I really want to go down to the garage? Too scary. *A dark and stormy night* came to mind. I was sure a braver woman would just forge ahead, but not me. I wondered if the helpful guys who hung around the hotel door could be enlisted for the errand. This four-star hotel advertised many amenities and services—including hypoallergenic bedding, twenty-four-hour room service, same-day delivery for laundry, and free cable TV—but I doubted "phone charger retrieval" was among them.

My intention was to play it cool when Bruce answered, but I couldn't spare any voltage. I wished I had a display that would tell me whether the drainage was linear, or discrete, perhaps skipping 1 percent per minute, or if there were another more complex algorithm.

"Have you talked to Virgil lately?" I asked.

"What's up, Sophie?" Responding to a question with a question. My boyfriend was acting more like a cop every day.

"That's what I want to know."

I'd cornered myself into telling Bruce why I'd been communicating with Virgil. I launched into my whole story again, as I felt the battery slip away.

"Some guy was stalking you on campus?" Bruce's voice rose in pitch as he chose that one detail from my narrative.

"No, no, not at all. He was just there, near my car. It was a little strange to see him again in the robbery report, that's all."

Bruce groaned. "I'll be glad when you're home."

I didn't think it was a great idea to remind him that home was where the stalker was.

"I think the storm's abating," I said.

"It is. You should be able to head out first thing in the morning."

"Not a minute too soon. Are you sure you don't know anything about the development Virgil was talking about?"

"He mentioned a new homicide case." My gasp caused him to speed up and explain further. "Nothing to do with Jenn. Some guy was found on the edge of town, close to the airfield. Far away from campus."

I relaxed my jaw. I was aware that the murder of a stranger was not something I should take lightly, but I couldn't control my relief that neither Jenn nor anyone I knew was the victim.

Buzz buzz. Buzz buzz. Buzz buzz.

Call-waiting. "That's Virgil, Bruce. I'll call you back."

"I know where I stand."

"First in my heart," I said, and switched the call to Virgil.

"Did you get the article and photo I sent?" I asked.

"I did."

"Was it a help?"

"Big-time. It's all okay. Listen, Sophie, I'm sending a car there."

"To Wendy's? Great. Thanks."

"Not to Wendy's. The BPD already checked on Wendy and reported back. She's gone."

"She's gone?" Was nothing straightforward in Boston tonight?

"We sent a car to Newton Highlands, where Wendy Carlson lives. A neighbor says Wendy came home from work and an hour later she left the house with a full set of luggage, in a commercial town car, which is the only thing that will drive on a night like this."

"Wendy is—?"

"In the wind."

"Then why are you going to send another patrol car?"

"This car's for you. Get your things together."

"Wh—"

"It's all okay, Sophie. Just be ready to leave ASAP."

It was a good thing there was no *tap, rattle* at my door right then.

CHAPTER $\sqrt{13}$

Virgil was quiet, kindly giving me a moment to absorb the news of the missing Wendy, and his marching orders for me. I wished I were in the wind also, maybe in some alternate universe where the last few days could start over. I'd asked twice whether Virgil was sure the BPD had the right Wendy Carlson, not such an unusual name. He'd assured me the Wendy Carlson who'd been Kirsten Packard's roommate at Henley and now worked at the BPL was indeed the fugitive.

"Fugitive's a little drastic, isn't it?" I asked, loudly, still rattled.

"Sophie, you need to listen carefully," Virgil said.

"What happened to 'It's all okay'? You just said 'It's all okay.'"

"What's your room number there, Sophie?" Virgil's voice became softer and softer as mine went in the opposite direction.

"Fifteen ten," I said, finally coming down in volume.

"A BPD car is on the way to your hotel. An officer should arrive at your door in less than twenty minutes. Pack up. You probably don't have a lot of luggage." We both chuckled, to release a morsel of tension.

"They're going to take you to their station in Boston until the weather's okay to drive home. You'll ride to the police station with an officer; another will follow, driving your car."

"Why is this all necessary? What's going on, Virgil?" My moments of calm hadn't lasted long.

"Is it clear what's going to happen next?" Virgil's voice was firm.

"It's clear."

"And you can be ready when they get there?"

"Yes. And thanks. I'm not sure exactly why, but thanks."

I sat on my bed, hotel white, with deep maroon accents, waiting for the Boston police to pick me up. I faced the window and would have enjoyed the great view, the city lights, the sturdy brick buildings, but instead I envisioned Wendy down there, alone and running. Had I frightened her that badly? Had one of the Kirsten's unsavory friends contacted her? Threatened her? And, the worst thought, was it all my fault?

Then another possibility came to me. What if Wendy was not fleeing Kirsten's old friends? What if she was running from the police? She might have realized that she'd all but confessed to obstruction of justice and didn't want to face charges. I had no idea whether, given the coroner's ruling of suicide, there would even be any charges after all this time. Wendy would be smart enough to research that before making any drastic moves. And she had a world-class library at her disposal.

Virgil mentioned that Wendy lived in Newton Highlands, one of the more pricey neighborhoods in Suffolk County. On a librarian's salary. Was she bought off by the Packards? I stopped that train of thought. When did I become a conspiracy theorist? I had no right to judge her. It was never that simple; she might work three other jobs, or she might have inherited a house, just as I had. In truth, I knew nothing of Wendy's financial situation and had no reason to suspect her of any wrongdoing.

I blamed Virgil. If he'd only told me what was going on in Henley right now, I might not need to traipse through imaginary scenarios, sending Wendy swinging through the wind, first as victim, then as perpetrator, and back.

Tap, tap, tap. "Boston Police," I heard. A female voice.

I jumped from the bed and peered through the peep-hole, no small feat when the lens was about six feet off the floor. Two fresh-faced youngsters in uniforms, one male, one female, peered back, the man holding up his badge. As if I'd be able to tell the difference between a legitimate badge and a tin star from a party store.

I pushed the chair away, opened the door, and rejoiced that they hadn't drawn their guns.

Fifteen minutes later, I was in the backseat of a BPD patrol car. A first in my life. (But only because I'd slipped away from a party my junior year in college, just before a disturbing-the-peace bust.)

On the road to the Back Bay station, my chauffeur, Offi-cer O'Toole, would answer no questions. Not even "Why am I here?" or "Why can't I sit up front with you?" Once I reasoned that he was following protocol on the second question and probably didn't know the answer to the first any more than I did, I stopped badgering him and pre-tended to be interested in the history of Boston's finest.

Officer O'Toole, who appeared to be not much older than my freshmen, extolled the virtues of his department as if he were trying to recruit me. I flattered myself that he couldn't tell I was well over the age limit for entering the academy.

The patrol car bumped along the streets of the Back Bay, windshield wipers clacking, while, I hoped, the second officer at my hotel room door, Officer Babcock, followed in my car.

Through the grill between my driver and me, I heard all about the BPD's various programs. You name it, BPD had it: helping grieving families, special care for children, therapy for refugees, relief for victims of violence. What heading did my special care come under tonight? I wondered. And what had Virgil said to his buddies at the BPD to garner this much attention for me? Should I also map out what I wanted for my last meal?

"Not many people are aware that Boston is home to the first police department in the US," Officer O'Toole said, clearly proud of his employer. "Established in 1838."

"Wow," I replied.

"Yeah, there's some that say Philadelphia's department is older, but that's a bunch of fuzzy history. It's us."

"I believe you."

"You know, the first cops carried a six-foot-long blue and white pole to protect themselves. No other weapon. Plus some kind of noisemaker"—he pronounced it "kind-ah noise-mak-ah"—"that they used to call for assistance."

"For real?" I asked, rising to the occasion.

"Yeah, totally," Officer O'Toole said.

We pulled into a wide portal under one of the longest buildings I'd ever seen. Three flagpoles, banners down for the night, marked the entrance. I guessed they held flags for the country, the Commonwealth of Massachusetts, and the BPD. Impressive. Intimidating, also, I imagined, if one were to arrive here in handcuffs. I rubbed my wrists in sympathy.

Officer Babcock, a young woman with a ponytail like the one the real Ponytail sported, but much cleaner looking and prettier, pulled up beside us in my Honda.

I considered getting the jump on the two cops, climbing

into my car, and driving home. Then the fog cleared and I marched between them into the station.

I'd always wondered what it would be like at a big-city police station in the wee hours of a Sunday morning. (Not.) *Noisy* would cover it. *Chaotic* would also do. The scene was worse than what I'd experienced in an ER, since there usually weren't altercations between patients and staff in a hospital. Here, there were battles in every corner. A guy in a torn overcoat, clearly not his own, screamed that his wrists hurt from the cuffs; a heavily made-up woman yelled about her right to a glass of water. Phones rang, radios squawked.

The two young officers buffered me from the unhappy guests of the BPD. They took care of paperwork and got me settled in a room in an annex to the main building where, according to O'Toole, I'd be waiting "until the roads are good to go."

"Sorry the accommodations aren't four-star," Babcock said, when I refused a cup of BPD coffee on the grounds of, well, the grounds. "There's remodeling going on upstairs where the lounges are."

I didn't know if she was joking about "lounges" or not, but I did know that I wasn't being offered a choice, except in terms of a beverage. I asked for a bottle of water and assured her I was quite comfortable. Secretly, I missed the snuggly hotel robe and the mini fridge full of candy bars. What price safety?

I tried once more to get intel on my situation, but Babcock was no more forthcoming than O'Toole, my driver.

"Just try to take it easy," she told me. "We'll keep you safe."

"From what, exactly?" I asked, hopeful.

"I'm sure Detective Mitchell will explain everything when you get home."

"Thanks," I said, in my sweetest voice. No sense antagonizing the protector.

When she left, I took out my phone to call Bruce. Seventeen percent battery left, but who else would I be saving power for? Everyone I knew was in bed.

"Hey," he said. "Did they give you a vest?"

"Yes, and I'm packing heat." I lowered my voice in case what looked like a bullet hole in the upholstered wall was really the opening for a recording device.

That was about it for our police jokes. Bruce tried to convince me that he didn't know why I'd been escorted to a police station, but his answers to my question were evasive.

My final attempt fell as flat as all those before it.

"Is there any threat to me that I should know about?" I asked.

"You should know that you're in the best hands possible and nothing bad is going to happen."

I felt like I was in a courtroom, posing as a lawyer, struggling to ask the right question. Frustrated.

"Has something bad happened already?"

Bruce's pause gave me no comfort. "You just stay safe, okay?"

Not okay, but I signed off anyway.

I always read the signs and posters in a new environment, like an MBTA subway car or a theater lobby. The room I'd been assigned—dumped in—could have been either. There was no lock on the door and no obvious two-way mirror. The posters and flyers on a large bulletin board were surrounded by "Wanted" signs. Though they were much more interesting than ads for the Swan Boats or the next blockbuster movie, they seemed inappropriate for a friendly interview room. Maybe this was the make-do "lounge" while the others were being renovated.

I gazed at a photo gallery, rows of mean-looking guys and an occasional nasty girl, with labels like "Felony B& E," "Unarmed A&B," "Class A&B Drugs." Many of the photos were not the usual mug shot at all, but an image like the ones I'd seen while watching the security footage on campus. The smarter perps had their hats down over their eyes, as if they knew where the cameras were in that particular stairwell or elevator. Time stamps marked some of the photos. All together, the array was a more modern version of the old post office flyers with two standard poses and a ruler to indicate height.

There wasn't a lot to do in the windowless room. I couldn't even track the weather. I'd checked my mail in the hotel and didn't expect any new messages at this hour, except for the all-nighter students who might be writing to ask for an extension. There was always something a student wanted an extension for, no matter which term it was, or how far in advance assignments were posted. Over the years, excuses had evolved, from "I lost the folder" (paper, manila) to "I lost the folder" (virtual, on a thumb drive).

I turned to other flyers on the bulletin board and contemplated signing up for the next women's self-defense class or enrolling in gang-resistance education and training. A frayed pink sheet announced a citywide celebration last summer of partnerships between the BPD and community-based organizations. Free food, ice cream, and an inflatable slide were promised, as well as face painting and entertainment. I was sorry I had missed it.

I opened my laptop and searched for new math games. Very disappointing. The first game had poorly written instructions on how to prevent balls from traveling through a maze. I lost badly. I switched to brainteasers and skipped past the silly ones, like "count the number of Gs in this sentence."

I'd just helped an animated skateboarder successfully clear hurdles in his path by multiplying correctly and tim-

ing his jumps skillfully, when my cell phone rang. My screen
told me I had a call from an unknown wireless caller at an
unknown number. Ordinarily, I wouldn't have clicked to
answer it, especially with low battery power, but this was
no ordinary night.

"Hello," I said, as brightly as if I were in my den in the
middle of a sunny day and not in a snowed-in police station
in the middle of the night.

"Sophie?" a weak voice asked.

I sat up straight and looked around. "Wendy? Wendy,
where are you? Are you all right?"

"I'm okay. I can't . . . I just can't. . . ."

My screen went dark.

"Wendy? Wendy? You can't what, Wendy?"

How did my battery slip from 17 to 0 percent so quickly?

I slapped the phone against my thigh. Bruce would have
laughed and reminded me that I couldn't bring my battery
back to life without an actual, physical charger.

I rushed out of the room. I needed to get to my car,
which was . . . where? In an impound lot with the weekend's stash of cars that were classified as evidence? With a
fleet of stolen vehicles? Was my Honda next to an old
Chevy with a body in the trunk? Where were my keys?

I reviewed the logistics for how I'd gotten here. I'd last
seen my car when Officer Babcock parked it next to the
patrol car I'd ridden in with Officer O'Toole. Was my car
still under the station?

I started down the hall toward the front desk. Officer
O'Toole was at my side in seconds. "Can I get you something, Dr. Knowles?"

Hearing one of the officers use my name for the first
time, it occurred to me that they thought I was a medical
doctor, perhaps on assignment in Boston, one of the country's greatest medical centers, to track down a deadly virus.
I wouldn't have put it past Virgil to let them believe that,
figuring he'd get a better response than if he told them the

person who needed to be kept safe was a math teacher from Henley.

"I have to get to my car. My phone charger is in it and"—I held up my dead phone—"I need it." Wendy was waiting, I hoped. I knew it was unlikely that she'd allowed access through a callback, but she might have tried to reconnect when the line went dead, in which case a voice mail message could be waiting. Unless she'd been dragged away by captors, or changed her mind about talking to me. In any case, I had to give it a try.

"I'll get you a landline for the interview room," Officer O'Toole said.

"Isn't it possible to get my charger?" I pleaded. "The number I need to call is in my phone." Even if I knew Wendy's number, I couldn't imagine using a police department phone. I pictured Wendy seeing a call come in, the BPD caller ID in glowing letters on her screen. I doubted she'd pick up.

Officer O'Toole smiled and took my arm. "Let's go back to the room and I'll have a phone in there for you in no time."

I could see why the clients in the main foyer were yelling. There was no arguing with the guy. He was like a younger, thinner Virgil, already trained not to answer any question directly, but to push whatever agenda he had. And this time it was to not let me use my phone. I wondered why he hadn't taken it from me to begin with, if using it was the problem, but I wasn't about to bring that up.

I bit my lower lip and returned to my other "cell," the one that was a little room with no windows.

Officer O'Toole arrived at the door with a new bottle of water in one hand and an old-fashioned phone dripping wires in the other.

"Is there a reason I can't use my own cell phone?" I asked, not trying to hide my disappointment.

"You're going to find this will work fine," he said, plugging the phone into a wall outlet. He gave me a nervous smile.

He really was a mini Virgil, but I didn't have to make it easy for him. I could work with a less-than-confident demeanor, uniformed or not. "The number I need to call is in my cell phone," I said, waving the dark screen in front of him. I stopped short of singing "Hello?" with its new meaning of "Are you that dumb?"

Officer O'Toole took a chair, pulled it close to me, and sat down. *Uh-oh.* "Listen, Dr. Knowles. I'm also going to need your laptop."

I gave him my "I'm a teacher and I'm cross" look. "What?"

"Please don't make this hard for me. I'll have to take your phone and laptop." He cleared his throat. "Procedure."

"Procedure? Since two minutes ago?"

"I know. I should have done it already," he said, his voice near a whisper.

"What if I hadn't told you my phone was dead?"

"I . . . I . . ." By now Officer O'Toole was red-faced, and I thought I detected some twitching around his eyes.

He was young, yes, and probably just graduated from the academy. All the more reason he should know every little detail of procedure. His training couldn't have been more than a few weeks ago. In any case, I couldn't badger him further, any more than I could keep up my end when one of my students turned on the waterworks.

I handed over my equipment.

Officer O'Toole uttered a sincere "thank you" and walked out with all my means of connecting with the world, leaving me with a phone my mother would have been happy with.

I sat at the table, feeling helpless. I had only Wendy's work number. I hadn't thought to ask for her card when I gave her mine. Few people put personal numbers on their business cards, but she might have included her email address. In any case, I had nothing, since I'd been too preoccupied at the end of the meeting, not the most congenial part of our visit.

Now I imagined Wendy trying to call me back and getting my voice mail. I'd have bet a lot of money that what she had to say wasn't appropriate for a recording that anyone could eventually listen to. I could use the BPD phone to check for a message on my cell, now in police custody, but not if I was limited to only one call from the cops' landline, like prisoners.

My best option now was to call Virgil with the government-issue phone at my disposal. He should have a way to get Wendy's cell phone number. His tech guys might already have picked it off one of those amazing databases that movie cops worked with. In that case, I'd have to wrestle the information out of him for my own use. I needed a police procedure manual for times like this. So, apparently, did Officer O'Toole.

Not trusting my watch, I opened the door onto the hallway and located a clock on the wall. I shut the door quickly, in case Officer O'Toole was waiting to sneak in and claim more of my property. Either 1:28 or 1:31 in the morning, depending on which timepiece you trusted. If I had my phone or laptop, I'd know the exact time, I mused, still unhappy about being disconnected. It was a decent hour in Kigali, Rwanda; for revenge I could rack up long distance charges on the antique phone.

Just realizing how little sleep I'd had in the last two days sent waves of tiredness through me. I made a pillow with my arms on the table and put my head down, but I was too wired. Wendy might be out there, ready to flip on Ponytail or Einstein. Either that, or one of them, or their descendants, might have a gun aimed at her head. I dialed Virgil's number. If he was sound asleep, I reasoned, he wouldn't hear his phone, and no harm would have been done.

"Hey," Virgil said. Not even drowsy. "You safe?" he asked, though I was pretty sure he knew.

"Protected and served in Boston, but my phone battery died, and—"

"You're kidding," Virgil said. Snide. Maybe I had woken him up.

"It happens."

"That's why you're using the BPD phone?"

I whined out my story. "When I asked the teenaged officer to get my charger from my car, which, by the way, is also unavailable to me, he ended up taking my phone *and* my laptop. After the fact."

"He's young, huh?"

"Very."

"He probably isn't sure which category you fall in. And you intimidated him."

"Apparently I didn't intimidate him enough." I woke up to the urgency of the situation, though by now, it was almost moot. "I need you to make a call ASAP."

I briefed Virgil on Wendy's aborted call to me. "She's trying to reach me. She might be in trouble."

"Thanks, Sophie. That's good that she reached out to you. Let me see if the guys can work with that."

"You'll get her number for me, so I can call her back?" I asked. I could only dream.

"I'll call you if there's anything you need to know."

"That's pretty vague."

"It looks like the storm is fizzling already. Nothing like when Irene blew through here a couple of years ago, huh?"

Should I be sorry that today's storm hadn't reached Hurricane Irene proportions?

"I guess you'll fill me in when I get home," I said. Making a point.

"Gotta go," Virgil said.

"Wait," I said. "Can you call Bruce and tell him I no longer have a private phone? He's probably not on the BPD family and friends calling plan. And, besides, I'm assuming these calls are all recorded for quality assurance."

Virgil chuckled—I thought I heard an "I'll let Bruce know" in the laugh—and hung up.

Too tired for any further thinking, I dropped the heavy telephone receiver on its cradle and put my head down. I closed my eyes and tried not to think of this as a night spent in police custody in what my well-informed young wardens told me was the twenty-first largest city in the country. Good to know.

CHAPTER $\sqrt{14}$

It wasn't every day that I woke up to the sounds of dozens of armed men and women at a morning briefing. I hadn't noticed that my little room was next to a sort of assembly hall, to which all patrol officers reported before hitting the streets.

As I cleared my sleep-fogged head, I heard periodic eruptions of sounds, though it was hard to tell if they were cheers or groans.

It was 7:10 AM by my watch. No wonder I hurt all over. I'd slept almost six hours with only my arms as a pillow. I hadn't done that since my last cross-country flight a few years ago, when I'd used a tray table from the seat in front of me for support. I tried to remember how long it had taken for my back and neck to recover.

I needed a shower, a briefing of my own on events at home, decent coffee, my phone and charger, my laptop, a word with Bruce, and my car. Any sequence would do. Within minutes of lifting my head, Officer O'Toole, still on duty, entered the room, with as much sensitivity as he might use if he were infiltrating my private boudoir. He carried a cup of something that smelled vaguely like coffee, and a muffin wrapped in a napkin. The new face of the BPD. Where was Dunkin' Donuts when you needed it?

"Didn't want to wake you," Officer O'Toole said, in his now familiar near whisper. "I brought some breakfast."

"Thank you. That's very nice of you." I picked a walnut from the top of the muffin and ate it. Stale. Definitely not Dunkin' Donuts. "What's the weather like?" I asked. In other words, "Can we go now?"

"Storm's over. Gone east." Officer O'Toole made a wavy motion toward the Atlantic, which I took to mean that the snowstorm had dumped most of its contents over the ocean. "Turned out to be pretty lame. We're good to go. Well, not me. I'm going off shift. Officers Babcock and Galvan will be escorting you home."

I nearly growled. "Thanks, but I think I'll be fine, driving by myself."

This time, Officer O'Toole was ready for me.

"Sorry, ma'am. Our instructions are to escort you home and we're prepared to do that."

I growled for real. "Okay," I said, dismayed at my retreat into wimpiness in the face of law enforcement.

"How soon can you be ready?"

All I needed was a trip to the ladies' room. There was no packing to do—the cops had all my devices—except to shove the muffin in my purse for a hunger emergency. I'd be able to get rid of the coffee in the ladies' room sink.

"Five minutes," I said, feeling as if I'd been granted parole, but with an ankle bracelet.

Officer O'Toole gave a little bow and left. I frowned and saluted his back.

I was dismayed that I was using BPD resources for another convoy. Hard on the city's budget, and hard on my need for privacy. I hoped I'd never experience full witness protection protocol. Officer Babcock softened the blow a little by sharing with me that she'd be staying in Wrentham, a town near Henley, on a short break to visit family. Nice of her to make it sound like I was doing her a favor.

While Officer Galvan drove my car, I rode in the passenger seat of a patrol car with Officer Babcock, her brunette ponytail not as perky as last night. Or earlier this morning. I didn't even bother to ask if I could drive my own car to my own home. I assumed I was technically still in police custody and they weren't taking any chances on a malpractice suit if anything happened to me on I-95. Neither did I bother to ask for my phone and laptop. I'd seen Officer Galvan put them in my car. I'd have to carve out an hour later to check all emails, texts, and voice mails, as well as explain to Bruce why I hadn't been in contact. Unless his BFF, Virgil, had had time to carry out my request to let him know.

As expected, the highways were clear of snow, except for blackened mounds along the shoulders and medians. I resisted the urge to think of the storm as my personal nemesis, lasting just long enough to trap me in Boston while important things were happening at home—I was still hung up on Virgil's admission that there had been a "development."

The trip was quiet. Apparently, I'd already been exposed to all the BPD history my young escorts knew. I put my head back and napped on and off. It was a study a painter might title, *Sophie, Not on Coffee.*

I perked up when the Henley skyline, such as it was, came into view. Having just seen the real thing in Boston, the gold dome atop the Henley city hall looked second-rate. But it was my second-rate dome, and I was happy to see it.

I was surprised at what good time we'd made. Had the sirens been on the whole time I slept? I doubted it. Cop cars didn't need sirens to go fast, and my little Honda, especially when driven by a cop, could keep up with the best of them.

I'd become so acquiescent, I didn't even challenge Officer Babcock when she headed for the Henley PD instead of my lovely cottage, which had a shower and good coffee and real food. And my bed. But, I reminded myself, there was intel at Henley PD, and I could use a good dose of that, too.

Henley PD was significantly less chaotic than its Boston counterpart. I was sure it was partly due to the early hour. Who was ready for a fight or a crime before eight in the morning?

Within minutes of the BPD officers' signing me over to the HPD desk sergeant, and signing my property back to me, Virgil appeared, looking fresh, pressed, and ready to work. I assumed it was because his six hours of sleep had been in his own bed.

"Hey," he said, smiling as if glad to see me alive. "Let's get your car and grab some breakfast."

Music to my ears. It had been a long time since my room service soup and salad, and it had taken a lot of energy to be handed off from one law enforcement unit to another. I gave Virgil the small claim ticket for my car. "I'm in E-4," I said. "And that's all I know about the last twenty hours." Hint, hint.

"Got it," Virgil said, tapping the ticket on the palm of his hand.

"Any luck contacting Wendy?"

"Not yet."

"How about Bruce? Does he know I'm home? Maybe he can meet us?"

"He's, uh, busy this morning. We'll catch up with him after breakfast."

Something was funny. "That sounds like a cover story, Virgil. What's Bruce up to?"

Virgil laughed as he grabbed his coat from behind the front desk. "Too much going on here right now."

I dropped it. I couldn't be trusted to hear straight until I had coffee anyway.

"Can your guys get anything from my phone?" I asked Virgil. I had the idea that IT whizzes were able to trace numbers from any phone, with or without its charger, even if the number had been blocked by the caller. Surely the police department had as many techies as Henley's incoming freshman class.

"Might as well give it to them and we'll see," Virgil said.

I surrendered my phone to Virgil—grousing about how I'd just gotten it back, hadn't even plugged it in yet—and sat on a hard bench across from the tall wooden counter-cum-desk while he disappeared down a hallway. I had no desire to follow him now that I was this close to the building's exit sign. I nearly LOL'd when I opened my laptop and realized that, of course, my battery was dead.

The posters at the HPD weren't that different from those at the BPD, and, by now, I was ready for the more colorful ads of the MBTA. Henley's police station was the latest and last government facility to receive attention from the town council, with a planned relocation in the next year. The new building would finally join our new public library, courthouse, and city hall in a complex across town. For today, however, I was treated to the musty smell of the town's oldest public building.

I remembered Virgil's excitement and pride when he boasted to Bruce and me that the new station would have a Plexiglas shield in front of the reception desk (Yikes, we needed that?) and a public lobby with comfortable seating for visitors (I could hardly wait).

Virgil finally returned and we left the old building

through the shabby lobby. When we reached my Honda in stall E-4, Virgil, who had the keys, of course, stepped into the driver's side. I wondered if my car would remember me when I finally got to take the wheel and drive it home.

I had to smile when I realized that I now had my phone charger, but not my phone.

Louie's Dining Car was built like a black and chrome railroad car, with sleek lines and familiar art deco signage. On the inside, the red vinyl booths and the narrow black-and-white tile floor produced a dizzying effect, giving me the feeling that the waiter could shout an "all aboard" warning and drive us down the tracks at any moment.

Before nine on a Sunday morning, the few patrons who had gathered for breakfast seemed to have poured out of the Henley PD station, as we had. Not the office crowd, who were off for the weekend. My assessment of Louie's patrons might have been colored by the fact that I'd spent entirely too much time hanging out with cops this weekend and everyone looked like she or he was armed and dangerous.

Virgil and I were seated in a corner booth with a small jukebox at one end. I thought about declaring a hunger strike if Virgil didn't give me some answers soon. Luckily he didn't force my hand, since the diner coffee smelled rich and satisfying and the menu was something my mother would have felt at home with.

"They have blue-plate specials," I said, surprised. My mother's favorite restaurant fare—three courses that arrived on a dark blue plate with dividers, like those in foil-bottomed TV dinners. I thought the dish had gone the way of the green stamps and gas station tumblers my grandmother collected with each fill-up.

Without asking, our waitress arrived with a pot of coffee and filled each of the two thick white mugs on the table.

In honor of my ancestors, I ordered special number three—apple pancakes, scrambled eggs, and turkey sausage. Comfort food for a freezing cold day and an exhausted psyche.

"Ditto," Virgil told the gray-haired woman, who might have served my ancestors.

"Alone at last," I said to Virgil, my hands folded on the table, my head tilted, a "What have you got for me?" look on my face. I figured my tablemate already knew my questions.

Virgil smiled. Pleased that he could finally satisfy my legitimate curiosity? He reached into his jacket pocket, pulled out a sheet of paper, and handed it to me. A folded copy of the mug shot I'd emailed him from Boston. Though I'd been the one to send the photo, I recoiled. Ponytail was not a pleasant-looking man. I imagined him with his friends, including Kirsten and Wendy, in a diner, maybe even here in Louie's Dining Car, twenty-five years ago.

"You have more info on him?" I asked.

Virgil nodded, no longer smiling. "He's my homicide victim."

What? I shook my head to clear it. "Ponytail was murdered?"

I felt I was in a time warp, unable to keep track of the year I was living in. I checked my surroundings to confirm where I was. With a Henley cop, not a Boston cop. In a diner in my hometown, not in a hotel room searching the archives of bank robberies. Not snowed in. In fact, looking out the window at the streets of Henley, where you could hardly tell that an extra dump of snow had piled on top of the leftovers from two weeks ago.

Bruce had mentioned that Virgil was investigating a homicide unrelated to Jenn's mugging. Now I was hearing that Ponytail was the victim of that homicide. How much closer to Jenn's attacker could we get? They were practically on the same video footage together. Bruce couldn't have known, unless he'd spent the same inordinate amount of time I had thinking and acting as though I were on the payroll of the HPD.

I focused again on Virgil, who had already downed his first cup of coffee. "He's the guy on the video, fighting with another worker, right?" I said. "The old newspaper called him Ponytail, the bank robber. He's also my ponytailed campus stalker. And now he's—"

"Murdered," Virgil said, finishing my long summary, which provided no new, useful information to anyone. His voice was as low as I'd ever heard it. "He was shot a couple of times and dumped by the airfield."

I shivered and pulled my sweater up to my chin, forcing the crewneck into a turtleneck. I'd always thought of the Henley Airfield, in the northwestern part of town, as belonging to Bruce. MAstar, to be precise. I didn't like the idea of their beautiful open space being a dumping ground for killers. I sat back. More info to process.

Our waitress chose that moment to bring coffee refills, and, less than a minute later, our blue plates. "Here you go, honey," she said to me. "Here you go, Detective," she said to Virge. "Try not to eat hers, too, okay?" And she winked away.

I was ready to push my plate toward Virgil in case he did need a second helping of everything. But once the aroma of coffee, apple, and sausage reached my nose, hunger took over and I plunged in on my breakfast, adjusting to the news of Ponytail's death, thinking of not only his violent end, but his appearances in Henley across a span of a quarter century. What had he been doing in between?

Virgil swirled a line of ketchup over his scrambled eggs. His action started a tapestry in my head where Ponytail's killer was trailing blood, from the tower with Kirsten a long time ago, to the pathway with Jenn, a few days ago, and now to the airfield. Why Jenn was in the middle of the timeline, I didn't know. A random victim, was one guess.

Poor Jenn. Wrong place, wrong time. Either that or there really was something to my Curse of the Carillon theory.

Not too long ago, I would have been thrilled to have an iota of evidence of the Kirsten-Jenn connection. Now it seemed closer, but the gap might as well have been as wide as the icy chasms I'd watched Bruce clear on videos from his extreme sports vacations.

"Did the other man do it?" I asked, getting back to Virgil at last. "The worker Ponytail is fighting with on the video? Remember, Lauren saw them arguing in the cafeteria, too?"

"I remember. We don't know yet who killed him."

"Are you checking on that other guy? Fighting with the victim—I'd think he'd be your chief suspect." This from a highly decorated civilian.

I looked down to see that my mug was filled to the brim again. I guessed our waitress was used to clientele who required discretion; she'd learned to keep us happy without asking to look at pictures of summer vacation.

"We haven't ID'd that guy yet," Virgil said. "We have Pete Barker, the foreman, coming in this afternoon."

I loved that Virgil was being so forthcoming. I was about to thank him for filling me in, when an alarm sounded in my head.

Fortunately, I'd already had enough coffee and devoured most of my eggs and half my pancakes by the time I realized what Virgil hadn't told me yet.

"Ponytail's murder isn't the real reason you took me into custody."

"You weren't in custody. You were—"

"What are you not telling me, Virgil? Did you really think Ponytail's killer was coming after me? Why would you think that?"

Virgil made a show of chewing a hunk of sausage, washing it down with coffee.

"A lot's happened since you took off for the state capital."

"From the top, Virgil."

Virgil inhaled deeply. "I had this homicide. I had the mug shot you sent, from years ago. Then your friend came down to look at the video."

"My friend?" I asked, then remembered—Judy Donohue was planning to schedule a viewing session.

"Judy," we said together.

Virgil's plate was clean, so I pushed my sausage toward him. He stabbed it and chewed slowly. I was making heroic efforts to be patient.

"She recognized the other worker," he finally said. "The one Ponytail was fighting with."

"He changed his jacket on the video, right?"

Virgil nodded. "And the coeds swooned over him," he added.

I wanted to clue Virgil in that we didn't call them coeds anymore, unless he meant the male students, who were new on campus. And at the one rave I'd been to, I was sure I didn't see any swooning. Quite the opposite, as far as the amount of energy involved in the activity. "From where did Judy recognize him?"

"From the basement of Ben Franklin Hall. He was fixing your heater."

The guy who, allegedly, killed Ponytail was Judy's hunky guy? The buff guy downstairs in Franklin? More than strange. As far as I knew, construction workers didn't fix heaters.

"He was in our basement?" I tried to come up with a reason why he might have been anywhere in Franklin Hall. The crew had their own portables, and if he didn't like those, there were many closer men's rooms near the work site. "He was snooping?"

"Looks that way."

Another shiver ran through me as I conjured up the

image of my students and me blithely calculating the slopes of curves and discussing Archimedes while one floor below us a potential killer lurked.

"Now I have the two guys fighting on your campus," Virgil continued. "One is casing Franklin Hall, hypothetically, and the other was involved in a robbery twenty-five years ago, and turns up dead. I also have a student attacked on campus, a student who spends a lot of time in Franklin Hall." He pointed his fork, licked clean, at me. "And a professor who spends more than a lot of time in Franklin Hall." I drew in my breath. "And, may I add, said professor is nosy. So nosy, she pops off to Boston at the drop of a hat, in a snowstorm—"

"It wasn't snowing when I started out."

"I rest my case."

"You also know, according to Wendy Carlson, my informant, that the dead guy was associated with a student who died on campus that same twenty-five years ago."

"That's even more hypothetical."

"She named him."

" 'Ponytail,' you mean?"

"Yes, 'Ponytail.' "

Virgil shrugged and I knew I almost had him.

I needed a chart. I took out a pen and plucked a napkin from the dispenser. Virgil sat back and let me draw. The center of the napkin became the dividing line between "then" and "now." Under "then," I wrote a list of names: Kirsten, Wendy, and the two thugs, as I thought of them, Einstein and Ponytail. Under "now," I listed Wendy, Jenn, Ponytail, and the Unnamed Worker. Ted Morrell's name also belonged on both lists. I thought of our physics chair, Wendy's mentor, wondering how much he knew "then." But Fran Emerson, currently of Rwanda, had also been at Henley then, as well as other faculty. I decided to leave faculty off the list for now.

I drew connections: Kirsten, Einstein, and Ponytail

were connected by at least one robbery, and probably by other crimes, big and small. All three were connected to Wendy, at least personally if not as accomplice. The Unnamed Worker was connected to Ponytail, maybe through long-ago criminal pursuits, certainly through the fights on the "now" side of the line. It took only a minute to see the setup on the napkin as an equation. Kirsten plus Wendy plus Ponytail plus Einstein then, equals Wendy plus Ponytail plus Unknown Worker now.

"He has to be Einstein," I said.

"Huh?" Virgil asked.

"The guy fighting with Ponytail. He must be the other guy Wendy identified as Kirsten's friend. They called him Einstein."

Virgil moved his head side to side. I realized he couldn't commit to my conclusion, and strictly speaking, the "equals" sign in the equation I purported to solve was on shaky ground. An arrow might have been more appropriate, indicating travel from the eighties to the teens. Or, if I remembered my basic (and only) chemistry, a chemical reaction.

"I know it's not all wrapped up, but I feel like we're getting somewhere," I said to Virgil. I sat back and enjoyed the warmth of a refilled mug in my hands. "Do we know Ponytail's real name?" I asked.

"Not yet," Virgil said. "We—that is, the Henley PD, not you and I—are running his prints."

"If he was arrested for that robbery, he must be in the system, right? Don't they keep evidence forever?"

"Technically yes and yes, but the system doesn't always work on weekends. Or during the week, or . . . well, you know."

I was sorry I brought it up. Not that I wasn't sympathetic. But by now, I could practically replace Virgil in sounding off on the sad state of police forensics resources, especially compared to what TV crime dramas led the public to believe and to expect. To make his point at our last pizza night, Virgil had told Bruce and me about a medical examiner in the Midwest who had a backlog of eight hundred cases, all pending, thus hampering police investigations, depriving survivors of insurance benefits, and . . . He'd stopped only when the whistle blew for the start of a game on TV (my signal to retreat to my office).

"As I said, we have the construction foreman coming in later today, around four," Virgil continued. "We're hoping the video's good enough for him to give us ID on both men."

So the only question still was how the attack on Jenn Marshall fit into my equation.

"Once I sent you Ponytail's photo, you knew he was the dead man at the airfield, right?"

"Uh-huh."

"Then you knew he wasn't going after Wendy in Boston."

"Uh-huh."

I paused, my mind churning away as if I had a fifth-level brainteaser on my hands. "But maybe his killer would be after her. Is that what you were thinking? Wendy could be a loose end from the robbery or who knows what else?"

"Uh-huh."

"Maybe Unnamed Worker, aka Einstein, even killed Kirsten."

"Uh-huh."

"I'm still not clear on why you're protecting me. Why would Ponytail's killer come after me? What makes you think he knew I was—"

"Asking around?" Virgil suggested. "Snooping? What makes me think he might have known that?"

"That's it? Einstein knows I've been asking questions?"

Virgil blew out an unintentional whistle. "There's something else."

My heart raced as I thought of Jenn Marshall. Had she died? Had Ponytail's killer decided to finish his attack on

Jenn and gone after her in the hospital? Or was something wrong with Bruce? Had Bruce been in an accident? He had a dangerous job, dangerous hobbies. Had he gone off and hurt himself?

It was very strange that Bruce wasn't here. What was more important than being with me after my stressful night? Virgil had said Bruce was "busy," "tied up." With what? Before my mind could go off track even further, into heartbreaking realms, I looked Virgil in the eye.

"I'm waiting, Virgil." I picked up my fork and dipped a piece of pancake into a pool of maple syrup, hoping it might look like a threatening gesture—injury by a syrupy projectile.

"Your house was broken into last night."

I dropped my fork, sending a sticky trail across the table. Virgil mumbled what I assumed was an apology, and motioned for our waitress. She arrived with a wet and suspiciously stained piece of terry cloth and spread the syrup around before capturing most of it.

I watched, dumb for the moment, then annoyed. First Pan's and now Louie's Dining Car. Why did everyone give me bad news while I was eating out? I'd soon be blacklisted at every decent restaurant in Henley.

I heard Virgil's voice as if it were being filtered through all the ketchup, syrup, and whipped butter in the diner.

"Bruce says nothing was stolen, as far as he could tell, Sophie. Nothing even badly damaged. He's there now, putting things back together."

"Bruce is tied up, you said."

Virgil nodded and put his hand on mine. "Not literally tied up, Sophie. He's straightening things out at your house. He wanted to make sure you didn't walk into a . . . a mess. I can take you home anytime you want."

I nodded, letting the simple fact sink in. A break-in at my cottage. No one had been home; no one was hurt. I relaxed my shoulders. A break-in was nothing compared to an attack on someone I loved. Nothing to worry about.

Unless it was Ponytail's killer. And he'd been looking for me. Which thought apparently occurred to Virgil and prompted him to send out the cavalry to save me.

I repeated to myself: Nothing to worry about. Nothing to worry about.

CHAPTER $\sqrt{15}$

"Try to space out," Virgil said, as he drove my car toward my home.

Easy for him say. My home might even now be harboring an intruder. What if someone was there, hurting Bruce at this moment? How could I be sure the guy had left? Or that he wouldn't come back for regular visits?

"Are you spacing out?" Virgil asked.

"I'm trying."

I focused on the winter trees and their bare branches, which made beautiful shadows on the snow. I noticed the few places where the snow hadn't been trampled on, like the lawn of an elementary school, closed for the weekend. I imagined kids arriving later to build a snow fort or make snow angels. But not even all the angels, painted and sculpted, on display or in storage at the MFA could calm me down.

I tried preparing myself for the worst at my house— tables and chairs tipped over; dishes and vases in shatters;

drawers and lamps overturned; carpets, pillows, and draperies slashed. I was on my way to mirrors with threatening messages written in blood, when I felt the car lurch.

"Sorry," Virgil said, putting his hand on my arm. "I'm not used to this car."

His studied expression told me he'd purposely maneuvered the jerky right turn, to jolt me out of my panicked, horror-movie state. He could probably tell his "space-out" suggestion hadn't taken hold.

"Thanks," I said, and he grinned.

"Better?" he asked.

"Much."

I had to admit, things were falling into place, like a jigsaw puzzle in progress, and having a few pieces mesh was better than having them all upside down and scattered about. I couldn't help wishing that a prettier picture were taking shape.

"Is there any feedback on that hundred-dollar bill I found in the bushes?" I asked Virgil, thinking of loose puzzle pieces.

"Not yet."

"It's probably still thawing out," I offered, so Virgil wouldn't start up again about the underfunded, understaffed forensics lab in Henley. I'd read recently in a news magazine that police in a city in China were using a newly developed chemical illumination process that provided better quality fingerprints. I had no plans to mention it to Virgil and get him riled up about US crime labs, as justified as his complaints were.

"ETA one minute," Virgil said, as jargony as Bruce, turning onto my street with a smooth left turn.

I closed my eyes, counted to thirteen, my favorite prime number, and opened them to see my cottage, looking much the way I'd left it yesterday morning, except for a little more snow along the edges of the driveway. The outside was further enhanced by the presence of Bruce hurrying down the path to meet me. I barely let Virgil come to a full stop, then opened the car door and all but fell into Bruce's arms.

Virgil stayed in my car, adjusting the seat and rearview mirror to my position, tapping away on his phone, giving us a few minutes.

"Welcome home," Bruce said, holding tight.

I buried my face in his neck. Home had never looked so good. Never mind that the interior might look like a prehistoric ruin.

Prepared for disaster, I found instead a setting worthy of a magazine cover.

A vase of cut flowers, a fresh pot of coffee, and a pink box with my favorite éclairs warmed my kitchen, giving it the look of a staged home for a Realtor's open house. Bruce did his best to tempt me with the pastry, though he must have known that I'd already celebrated my arrival in Henley with a huge Louie's breakfast—part nutrition, part Virgil's stalling tactic, I now realized—while my house was being fingerprinted and put back together after my intruder.

The walk-through could have been worse. That's what I told myself as I picked a few books from the floor and deposited them on the desk in my office.

"Sorry," Bruce said. "I thought you wanted them there."

Virgil laughed. I gave Bruce a poke in the arm and a smile. I couldn't deny that the floor of my office often served as a resting place for books in transition from my briefcase to a shelf.

Bruce and Virgil trailed me as I moved chairs around and plugged my laptop in place and adjusted the lampshade next to it. I scooped up a few beads that had slipped off their wire, an unfinished key ring project. Little things, put right, seemed to make a difference, to restore order. The men formed a wall behind me, in case I fainted, I supposed, though I wasn't in the habit of swooning. If I were in a joking mood, I would have tested them by going slack and falling back into their arms, like the leaders of faculty retreats often had us do, "to build trust," they claimed. Some other time, maybe.

Our tour ended back in the kitchen, where the three of us sat at the table. I watched Bruce and Virgil eat éclairs while I pummeled them with a barrage of questions. Their answers were unsurprisingly guarded.

"What time did the break-in happen?" (*Sometime after dark*, from Virgil.)

"Did you know about it when I talked to you from Boston? (*Yes* from Virgil; a sheepish *Uh-huh* from Bruce.)

"Who discovered the break-in?" (*Celia* from Virgil; *Evelyn* from Bruce, leading me to conclude that it was one or both of the elderly sisters who lived directly west of me. They'd called the police and reported suspicious activity in my driveway. I was grateful and proud of the HPD for acknowledging the sisters, who were easily rattled and called for help often.)

"How did he get in?" (*Through the patio doors off your bedroom*, from Virgil; *A new super lock is already in place*, from Bruce.)

"How bad was it here before Bruce cleaned up?" (*I didn't see it*, from Virgil; *Not that bad, really*, from Bruce.)

"Do you think the guy was after me personally, to harm me, or did he want to shake me up by messing with my things?" (A shrug from each, then *Anybody's guess*, from Virgil.)

"Did the officers who responded lift any fingerprints?" (*Oh yeah*, from Virgil.)

"Do you think you'll get anything from the fingerprints?" (A shake of his head and *Probably not*, from Virgil.)

A wave of tiredness came over me. I put my head down, then raised it to speak. "If I say you both have to go so I can get some sleep, will you hold it against me?"

Bruce started off, and soon the faux Bellamy Brothers were belting out a song in my kitchen as they cleared the cups and plates. They danced toward the door. Not the reaction I'd expected when I paraphrased a favorite song of ours, but it was the best laugh I'd had in a long time.

"Will you let me know if anything develops?" I asked Virgil, at the door.

"Of course, I'll add another sheet of carbon paper when I type up my report."

"Good, I'll need to know about whether you can dig Wendy's number out of my phone, whether the hundred-dollar bill has any useful information stuck to it, and when you have complete IDs on the two workers."

Virgil pretended to be writing on his hand. "Anything else?"

"Not at the moment, but I'll see you at the station at four, when the foreman shows up to watch the video."

"You don't need to do that," Bruce said. He'd returned from another quick walk-through, during which he'd checked all the locks. "Don't set your alarm clock, okay? You should just sleep—"

"Bye, guys," I said, with gentle shoves, and closed the door.

Through the patio doors of my breakfast nook, I watched Bruce and Virgil walk slowly down the driveway, heads together, talking. I had no doubt about the topic. They stood at the end of the walkway for a few minutes, until an unmarked, but clearly identifiable, police sedan pulled up. Virgil talked to the occupant, then he and Bruce drove away in Bruce's car.

Progress, I thought. My posse was down to only one local unmarked car.

My first order of business: strip my bed. What if the intruder had sat on it, or even touched my pillows, perhaps leaning on one as he opened the drawer of my nightstand? It wasn't practical for me to divest my home of every piece of furniture and all my possessions, but I could cleanse key areas.

I pulled the drapes across my glass patio doors, hiding the entryway that had provided access to my intruder. I threw all the bed linens into the laundry area—sheets, blanket, spread, pillowcases, mattress cover, bed skirt, shams— and ran a couple washes using hot water, a setting I rarely chose. I couldn't guarantee that I wouldn't toss all the linens in the trash once they were clean, but this was a start.

I showered (after a serious spraying of the tile) and put on my warmest fleece robe. I grabbed a pillow from the closet (the crime scene ones were history), wrapped a clean blanket around myself, and flopped onto my bare mattress.

I started counting, but didn't get to thirteen.

I woke up to a phone call at two thirty in the afternoon. Judy Donohue apologized profusely when she realized I'd been sleeping. My foggy morning voice, no matter that it was midday, gave me away. I decided to spare her all the reasons for my disrupted schedule.

"No problem," I said. "I need to get moving anyway."

"You heard about the guy in the basement?" she asked.

"I did," I said, as we both made audible shuddering sounds.

"What if I'd . . . ?" Judy trailed off.

"Let's not go there," I said.

"Agreed. Are you going to the police station for a look at the new video footage this afternoon?"

"Yes. You, too?"

Judy cleared her throat. "Detective Mitchell invited me to, if I was free."

It wasn't clear why I needed to know this, until Judy asked, "Do you think you could pick me up?"

"Uh, sure." I untangled myself from the blanket and sat up against my headboard. It occurred to me that I hadn't cleaned the wood, and the intruder might have . . . I climbed out of bed, brushed off a chair by the patio doors, and sat there, facing the patches of snow where my garden should have been.

"You're probably wondering why I'm asking for a ride," Judy said.

"Sort of, but I'm happy to do it. Did your car die?" I knew all about battery problems.

"No, no. Can I ask you something?"

"Of course. What's up?"

Judy's pause was long enough to make me worry. I hoped I didn't have to add another friend-in-trouble to my list.

"What is it, Judy?"

"Okay. Is Detective Mitchell . . . Virgil . . . seeing anyone right now?"

What? Could Judy possibly mean what I thought she meant? Not literally, was Virgil at this moment looking a suspect in the eye, for example, but was Virgil *seeing* someone? As in *dating*?

My turn for a long pause, and Judy picked up on it.

"You don't have to tell me if you don't want to, Sophie. Or if you don't know, it's okay. It's just . . . I think I'm getting some signals, but I don't want to make a fool of myself."

It took great effort not to blurt out how shocked I was. To say that Virgil was not Judy's type would be like saying that Julia Child and Mahatma Gandhi would have little in common on a dinner date. Since her divorce about three years ago, Judy had dated only men who looked like fitness instructors, one of whom had, in fact, been her personal trainer.

Virgil, on the other hand—well, Virgil considered lumbering up my long driveway to be his exercise for the week.

"No," I managed. "Virgil's not seeing anyone." I thought

about his strangely chipper behavior lately. "But he's acting as though he's about to start."

"You're sure? I mean, you think I should trust these signals?"

"I'm sure," I said.

I heard a sigh. "Oh, good, then. You're probably a little surprised, huh?"

We both took a minute for a laugh. "A little. But I'm thrilled for both of you."

"It's not like we're engaged, Sophie."

"Yet," we both said, and laughed again.

"I'll pick you up in about an hour."

I'd realized, finally, that Judy wanted a ride to the station in case she and Virgil ended up leaving the HPD together. I was dumbstruck for a minute. Judy's and Virgil's paths had crossed many times through my association with both of them. Still, I'd never pictured them getting together. Also, I knew that in the same situation, I'd be taking my own car in case the evening didn't work out well—which wasn't the only clue that Judy was more adventurous than I could ever be.

The thought, once I got past the unexpectedness of it, really did thrill me. As far as Bruce and I knew, Virgil hadn't dated at all since his wife died a few years ago. His personal attention went to his son, who was now in college.

I clicked off with Judy, thoughts of double-dating for pizza night dancing in my head. My phone rang again immediately. Bruce this time.

"Hey. Have a good sleep?" he asked.

"Yes," I said, though now that I was awake, I felt all the unresolved issues of the last few days pile up on my shoulders. Jenn's attack. My computer and credit card problems. The short life of Kirsten Packard. The missing Wendy Carlson. The violation of my personal space. The murdered Ponytail. And someone who called himself Einstein, of all people.

"Who was on the phone? I heard you mention Virgil."

"You're not going to believe this. Judy Donohue asked me if—wait, how did you know . . . ?"

"I'm here. Walking toward you now," he said. "I didn't want to pop up in front of you and scare you."

"You're here?"

And there he was, in the doorway to my bedroom. How had I not seen the signs, like the pile of clean, dry, folded bedclothes on my vanity chair? And the extra blanket thrown across my bed.

"When did you get here?" I asked.

"I never really left," he said, as we hung up and faced each other. "I dropped Virge off at the station and slipped back in."

"I didn't hear you."

"I pulled your door shut and stayed at the other end of the house. I'd make a good spy."

Or a good intruder. I shook that image away and pointed to the clean laundry. "And you did all that?"

He looked proud of himself, as he should have. "I also stripped and washed the stuff on the guest bed. It's all made up so you can sleep there if you want until this bed's ready. In between, I've been watching *Top Gun* with the headphones on so I wouldn't disturb you."

"No wonder I slept so well," I said. "Thank you."

"You didn't think I was going to leave you here alone after all that's been going on?"

I gave him my biggest smile and my best hug. "I should have known better," I said.

CHAPTER $\sqrt{16}$

It wasn't until we were on our way to pick up Judy that I remembered to tell Bruce about her potential pending date with Virgil.

"Did Virgil say anything to you about it?" I asked.

Bruce zipped his lips.

I poked his arm. "C'mon. I told you what I know."

Bruce grinned at me from behind the wheel of my car. We'd taken my Honda, the better to fit another passenger. I gave him a look designed to elicit information, part coy, part threatening.

"I've been dying to tell you," he said, with a big smile. "It seems your girlfriend might have been putting out vibes to my buddy that she was available. He didn't want to make a fool of himself, though, so he asked me to ask you to ask her . . . Sound familiar?"

"Sounds like junior high. It also fits Judy. She's not shy, but she wouldn't want to fall on her face either."

"You had too many more important things going on the

last few days and I never got around to bringing it up with you."

"This is very important," I said, excited, happy to deal with an issue that wasn't life or death. "This means there's mutual interest." I punched the air with my fist. "I like it."

I felt like a schoolgirl who'd found her best friend a date for the prom. Not that I had any extra dates at the time.

Judy was ready and waiting, exiting her home as we pulled up. As usual she looked well put together. She was known for following the latest fashion trends but held to the old rule that a lady's shoes must always match her purse. Today both were a bright green, the perfect complement to her red blond hair. It was clear that her outfit was chosen with Virgil in mind. Her wool coat was a classic style, nothing a model would wear swinging down a runway. From under her coat, part of what I recognized as her newest sweater set was visible—conservative, but not my mother's sweater set. The shawl cardigan was short, with a draped front, and buttonless. My summary: up to date, but within Virgil's comfort zone.

"How do I look?" she asked, as she climbed into the backseat.

"You look terrific," I said, with the enthusiasm I felt.

"Perfect for an evening at a police station," Bruce said.

"I don't think that's what she wants to hear," I said.

Judy laughed. "It's exactly what I want to hear."

I couldn't remember seeing her in a better mood.

When we arrived, Pete Barker, the construction foreman for the Henley College carillon project, was in a private viewing session with Virgil and his investigative team. Barker was going over footage the rest of us had already seen, in particular, the Fighting Workers scene. I tried not to be too peeved that Virgil didn't invite civilians, that is, me, to the early showing. With any luck, Barker would come through and we'd soon know the names of the two men—the real names of Ponytail and the Unknown Worker, plus Unknown's nickname. I was rooting for "Einstein."

I used the waiting time at the HPD to clear up other nuisances of the week, making a side trip to the service desk to file the official report of credit card fraud first. While I waited my turn, I scanned the pamphlet rack— information on personal safety, vehicle theft, and managing disruptive behavior. I wondered if the last one applied to classrooms. I thought of my violated home—was it too late for me to read the one on crime prevention?

A small child in front of me dropped the pamphlet she was playing with. I sincerely hoped the child was at the police station for a happy reason, such as getting fingerprinted for security purposes, or visiting a relative on the force.

I picked up the pamphlet, since Mom had another toddler in her arms, and, when no one in the family wanted it back, I looked through it myself. "The Henley City Flag" was its title. I had no idea we had our own flag, let alone that the colors were continental blue and buff, that it was silk, and had to be exactly five feet in length and three and a half feet in width, or any proportion thereof. I amused myself by calculating other permitted sizes, from two and a half feet long by one and three-quarters feet wide on the low end. I stopped at twenty-five feet long by seventeen and a half feet wide on the high end.

I scanned a pamphlet on email scams, but none of the examples fit my problem. I didn't need a lecture about not handing over a few thousand of my dollars in order to collect untold millions from overseas. The leaflet did remind me that I still had to clear up my current email spam problem. When I checked earlier this afternoon, I found my inbox once again loaded with unwanted ads, in duplicate.

No sooner did I delete the offending emails than they were back. I'd thought of asking Ted if he could do something about it, but he'd been so contrary recently, I hated to ask him. I did have a host of student whiz kids, like Andrew Davies, whom I could call on. I'd take care of that tomorrow.

By the time Bruce came to collect me for another show of surveillance footage, I'd completed the forms for both my credit card fraud and my home break-in. I was ready for a movie.

The HPD interview room, our theater for the afternoon, was decidedly less attractive than the music room on campus. Peeling paint; cracked, stained linoleum; duct-taped furniture; water marks on the ceiling. A true fixer-upper. Except that the place was scheduled to be abandoned soon, sour odors and all. I was happier than ever that I'd contributed to the new building fund.

What made the room even less inviting was the fact that I'd been in this run-down facility only a few hours ago, undergoing transfer from one police department to another.

Bruce and I took two seats in the closer of two semi-circles that had formed around the video, with foreman Pete Barker, a short, balding man, in the center. I was glad to see a few different faculty members and one or two from the Admin staff who hadn't come to the first session.

I leaned over to Bruce. "Did you know that Henley has a city flag?" I asked.

"Sure," he said. "It's continental blue and buff, the official colors of the city."

I frowned at him. "Who are you? I don't even know you."

I was surprised when Andrew entered the room and took the seat next to me. I gave him a big smile, in preparation for asking a big favor soon.

"No one else wanted to come, but I want to do everything I can," Andrew said, in a sad tone, his mouth turned down. By "no one" I assumed he meant Willa, Lauren, Brent, and Patty, the students with whom he'd been traveling lately.

I gave him a pat on the back, realizing how much I'd missed contact with my students this weekend. Like most teachers, I seldom had a day "off" from them. There was always an email or text question to answer. *What are your office hours this week? Is there a book I can read that explains limits better than our textbook?* (Usually meaning better than I had done in class.) Or an invitation to an informal gathering. *We're getting together at the Mortarboard tonight. Come on over. Willa's playing classical guitar.* (Which could mean they'd discovered Peter, Paul and Mary.)

Hanging out with students, as we faculty all did to some extent, was a learning experience in itself. We had constant reminders that this was a generation who had never seen an airplane ticket, who watched TV shows almost anywhere but on a TV screen, and for whom partially exposed undergarments had always been a fashion standard.

I'd just gotten a quick update from Andrew on Jenn's condition (nothing changed) and on Mr. and Mrs. Marshall (up in the air about moving Jenn to a hospital nearer home) when a knock—*tap, tap, tap*—sounded from the table that held the A/V system. Virgil calling us to attention. Conversations came to a halt.

Virgil introduced foreman Pete Barker—a stocky man and the best-dressed guy in the room, with wool pants and a sharp, blue gray sports coat—then announced that we were about to watch new footage from the Coffee Filter and the bank next door to it, on Main Street. I almost raised my hand to ask what were the names Barker had come up with for his two employees who couldn't seem to get along. I looked at Bruce who apparently read my mind, maybe because I'd whined a lot in the last half hour about not being privy to the invitation-only session where Barker was to ID his workers. Bruce shook his head, ever so slightly, but I got the message and behaved.

I'd also been trying very hard to keep myself from studying the interaction between Virgil and Judy. Impossible. As we entered, I'd watched him take her coat. (Was that a broader grin than I'd ever seen on Virgil? A gleam in his eye?) Then he'd pulled out a chair for her. (Did she always tilt her head when she smiled? Flip her newly bobbed hair like that?) I guessed we wouldn't be driving Judy home.

Virgil briefed us on the video we'd already seen of activities on campus, and what we were about to see on the new footage from the Coffee Filter and the bank. I couldn't help thinking of all the segments of "Previously on . . ." at the start of episodes of serialized TV dramas.

The first DVD was queued up with footage from the Coffee Filter, from a camera pointing toward our campus. Unfortunately, the camera captured only a small section of the narrow pathway between the Clara Barton dorm and the Student Union building, the area I'd visited the day after Jenn's attack. The image fell short of including the bush from which I'd plucked a one-hundred-dollar bill.

"You can see part of the pathway where Jenn Marshall was walking that day," Virgil narrated. "Unlucky for us, neither this footage nor what we have from the bank shows the actual attack."

I sensed a collective sigh of relief. As much as we wanted to help, I didn't think any of us looked forward to watching the assault on our student and friend.

The video rolled on with its image of half of a well-trodden path, blackened old snow mounds on each side. We did learn that Jenn's attack had happened on the half of the path that was closer to the interior of the campus than to the street. Not much that we didn't already know from the commuters who came upon the struggle.

About three minutes in, finally, we saw some action. A lone figure, probably male, came into view, walking off college property and toward the camera—in the same direction Jenn had most likely been headed—approaching Main Street. The audience leaned forward. Was this the man who attacked Jenn? It was hard to tell if he was one of the workers we'd seen on the earlier video. I wanted it to be Einstein, but truthfully, there was no way to be sure. He wore a common jacket, muffler, and cap, and there wasn't much of a reference in the frame to gauge how tall he was. He was carrying some kind of bag, but it was impossible to identify what in particular he was toting, since the bag was slung over his shoulder with most of it on his back. It might have been Jenn's backpack. It might also have been his lunch or a set of golf clubs.

Virgil stopped the video. "You see this guy? Anyone recognize him? From anywhere?"

A disappointing chorus of "No" and "Nuh-uh" arose.

"Does he look like one of the workers?" Virgil asked, pressing for a lead. "Maybe you recognize the clothes he's wearing, the way he walks? Some gesture? Anything?"

The answer came in the form of shrugs and "I don't knows" and "no ideas," even from the boss of the site, Pete Barker.

Virgil continued. "He's walking away from where Jenn Marshall was attacked, during the right timeframe, but he's not running. Remember, our three witnesses claimed they chased the attacker along Main Street. As you'll see in a minute, the footage from the bank shows this same thing. The guy saunters along Main on the campus side, as if he had all the time in the world, until he just walks out of the frame. He's not running from anyone. So, either he's not the attacker, or . . ."

Virgil waited for someone to finish his sentence. I knew

the classroom trick to engage people (make sure they were awake) and decided to help him out.

"Or the commuter students didn't chase him as they claimed," I suggested.

Scattered "Hmms" filled the room.

"That could very well be," Virgil said. I suspected it wasn't a new idea to him. "Initially, we heard that one guy stayed back with the victim and called nine-one-one, and the other two chased the attacker around to Main Street. But this video could mean—"

"I don't blame them," Andrew interrupted, clearly animated. "They were probably scared to death."

"Why did they lie?" asked someone behind me.

"They'd be too embarrassed to admit they were afraid to chase the guy," Andrew, defender of commuters, said.

"Who could blame them?" came from Bruce, whose job it was, first as a soldier, then as a medevac pilot, to rush toward, not away from, danger. "The guy might have been armed."

Andrew leaned forward, caught Bruce's eye, and gave him a thumbs-up. I was proud of both men. Not that I didn't wish with all my heart that the attacker had been knocked to the ground and taken away in a police car.

We watched a segment of the footage from the bank, but it was more of the same. Whatever the man was carrying was now on the side away from the cameras. It was as if he knew where the cameras were, both on the Coffee Filter and the bank, and adjusted his silhouette accordingly. As if he'd cased the area before the attack, as a bank robber would do. As Einstein would do, I mused.

All in all, a frustrating session. All we'd done was out some guys who tried to help as much as they could without risking their lives. There was a good chance that they saved Jenn's life just by responding to what they saw. I, for one, was glad we didn't end up with three more students in the hospital.

* * *

When the show ended and the group was breaking up, I was torn: introduce myself to Pete Barker and ask him the names of the men in Thursday's video, or trust that Virgil would share the information.

Barker left the room so quickly, I didn't have a choice. I'd have to charm Virgil. The story of my life.

I was able to grab Andrew first and ask if he'd be willing to help with my email spam problem.

"Wow. Yeah, Dr. Knowles. I can come by anytime. Yeah."

"Maybe you can stay after the seminar tomorrow? I'll have the laptop in my office."

"Yeah. Thanks, Dr. Knowles," he said, as if I'd be, yeah, doing him a favor. Teaching—the pay wasn't very good, but you couldn't beat the benefits.

The room was clearing fast. When Judy and Bruce took off for their respective restrooms, I sidled up to Virgil.

"Hey, how did it go with Barker?" I asked.

"Good," Virgil said.

I didn't have time to waste. "Isn't it nice that my very good friend Judy could be here today?" I said. "She and I are tight"—I crossed my middle and index fingers—"like that, you know."

Virgil grinned, getting the subtext. "The late Mr. Pony-tail didn't work for Barker," he said.

"But—"

"According to Barker, he applied for a job, but"—Virgil showed his palms, in an as-we-know gesture—"he has a record, which is against Barker's hiring policy, especially for a job on a campus."

"Does he have the application?"

"No such luck. I guess it came out in an interview and the guy owned up to it and left."

"So we have to wait for something on his prints."

"Yes, *we* do."

"What about the other guy?"

"We got an ID from Barker and we're on it."

"Are his prints in the system maybe?"

An expected shrug from Virgil, as if to say, "See previous comments."

To me, there was no logic in requiring teachers at all levels to be fingerprinted, but not other citizens, like construction workers or their friends.

"Did Barker mention 'Einstein' as a nickname by any chance?" I asked, continuing my quest for information.

"He should be in for questioning by the end of the day."

I understood Virgil's need to follow protocol, but it didn't hurt to prod. "What if he's skipped town?" I asked.

Virgil shrugged. "I have an update on your cell phone," he said. "It's not looking good for digging out Wendy Carlson's number, but they have a few more tricks left."

Hardly a significant update. "Thanks. I appreciate your cooperation," I said, as if I were the cop.

He smiled, and I realized the gesture was meant for one of the people coming up behind me.

"Sorry I couldn't be more help," Judy said to Virgil.

"We always get something," Virgil said.

Was I hearing a double meaning from Virgil? Or was I too focused on the potential new relationship?

"Are you going to bring the commuters in again?" I asked.

"Have to," Virgil said.

"It's likely that they lied to the police," Bruce reminded us.

"Not a huge lie," Judy said.

"Still, you can't be sure what else was going on with them," Bruce said.

"You don't think one of them attacked Jenn?" I asked.

I heard a gasp from Judy. "Or all of them?" she asked.

"We just have to follow up and see what falls out," Virgil said.

"That's police talk for 'Who knows?' " Bruce said.

Tap, tap. Tap, tap.

A knock on the doorframe gave Virgil a pass on answering any further questions about the next steps in the process of finding who attacked Jenn and murdered Ponytail. And that was just in this century.

Tap, tap. Tap, tap.

A uniformed cop, with a young man in tow, wanted to use the room.

"We're done here," Virgil told him.

We carried our outer garments to the hallway, dumped them on a bench, and began dressing for the cold, one layer at a time.

"Anyone want to grab some dinner?" Virgil asked.

"I'm famished," Bruce said. Then, after a serious poke from me, which was hidden from no one, added, "I mean, I will be famished, but it's too early to eat right now."

I made a show of looking at my watch. "Yeah, me, too. Maybe another time. Judy, if you'd like to go, maybe Virgil can give you a ride home."

The four of us lost control of the charade at about the same time and our laughter caused heads to turn up and down the hallway.

We went our separate ways, two by two.

Bruce and I headed out the door of the police station. As soon as Virgil and Judy were out of earshot, Bruce turned to me.

"Hungry?" he asked.

"Famished."

Small clutches of people stood chatting outside the door to the station, in a small sheltered area off to the side. Who gathered to talk outdoors in the middle of January? *Aha*, smokers. I hardly remembered the days when I had to be concerned about the air I breathed in restaurants and on long airplane rides. No one in my inner circle smoked, though Fran admitted that her slightly gravelly voice came from her shady, smoking grad school days.

Though I was glad to have cleaner air everywhere, today I felt sorry for the people relegated to what looked like a bus stop or a carport, with a rickety metal canopy to shelter them from the freezing wind.

As Bruce and I walked by on our way to my car, I smiled at an older officer among the group. The short, well-dressed civilian he was talking to caught my eye also and waved, as if we knew each other.

We did.

I couldn't believe my luck. Pete Barker was a smoker, and apparently had friends among the HPD. It made sense that a guy in construction would have dealings with the police. Much the same as a college math professor would.

I gave Bruce a pleading look. He picked up on what I wanted, and I could tell he was wrestling with a response. He blew out a visible breath. "I'll warm up the car," my sweetie said.

I walked toward Barker and, to my surprise, he met me halfway. "Detective Mitchell said you might accost me," he said, with a wide grin. He kindly stomped out his cigarette in a patch of dirty ice and added, "I'm not at liberty to reveal information in an ongoing investigation." His follow-up guffaw told me he was deliberately mimicking Virgil.

I had a chance.

"I'm unarmed," I said, raising my arms and giving him my best smile—disarming, I hoped, even as my eyes watered from the frigid air. "Can you just tell me the name of the worker in the video?"

Barker's expression turned serious. Not a good sign. Up close I could see that he was older than I'd first thought, probably mid-fifties. "I really can't," he said, "but I know Mitchell will keep you informed as needed."

Good coaching job, Virgil. I hated to leave with nothing, my fingers and toes freezing in vain.

Barker closed up the lapels of his stylish wool coat and adjusted his hat, a modern version of the fedora I'd seen on my grandfather in photos. It was hard to reconcile his fashionable look with the ugly yellow monster equipment he worked with every day. The image shook something loose in my brain.

"How about a couple of tower questions, then?"

He gave me a quizzical look, his round face scrunching up a bit. "The carillon tower?"

I nodded. "When do you expect to finish the job?"

His loud laugh rang out again, causing smokers in the area to glance over at us. As long as no uniformed smoker rushed over to kill the conversation, I was happy.

"A simple question like that, huh? Don't you know you're never supposed to ask a contractor or a foreman when he's going to finish the job?" He leaned into me and I caught a whiff of smokers' breath. "What are you, from the budget office?" He laughed again.

There was one good thing about blushing—a fleeting wave of warmth crossed my icy face. "No. I didn't mean to—"

He waved his hand, cigarette smoke trailing. "No worries. We are really close to done and will probably be out of everyone's hair by the end of next week."

"Then the tower will be open to everyone?"

"Pretty much. You'll still need a key after hours."

"That would be key cards, right?"

"Yeah, we changed the old lock and key system right at the beginning of the project. They're planning tours and concerts like they had back then, too. Lotta traffic. But you'd know that."

I decided not to admit how little I knew. "Who has key cards now?"

"Just the teachers. The kids who go up to practice have

to sign them in and out. Not too many. Stephens, the head of music, would know exactly."

I wondered how easy it would be to get a list from Randy Stephens or his very cooperative secretary. I wondered why I'd need it. I was flailing again.

"Do your workers have key cards?"

"No way. Just me. They have to get it from me on an as-needed basis. Too much delicate stuff up there, you know. You don't necessarily want the bricklayers spreading their lunch out on the keys. Do they call them keys? They're a heck of a lot bigger than the old ivories on a piano."

I apologized for detaining him and keeping him from his compatriots in the smoking section, and thanked him for talking to me.

"Anytime," he said.

I hoped it wasn't an empty gesture on his part. I might have to take him up on the offer.

Snow flurries, unpredicted as far as I knew, melted on my face as I walked to my idling car.

"Get anything from him?" Bruce asked.

"I'm not sure," I said, which was the absolute truth.

CHAPTER $\sqrt{17}$

The somewhat pretentiously named Inn at Henley was our best bet for a quiet dinner on a Sunday evening. Its nautical theme was soothing, except for the live fish tank in the entryway. After passing the innocent crabs and lobsters, unaware of their fate, I invariably ended up ordering a shrimp salad. Wherever shrimp were fighting for their lives, it wasn't in front of me.

"Where do you think Virgil and Judy are having dinner?" I asked Bruce.

"Virge mentioned driving to Boston if the weather held out."

Sheltered and warm at a table by the fire, snacking on an appetizer plate of fried calamari and stuffed Greek olives, I could barely recall the snowstorm that had stranded me in the Commonwealth's capital.

"The food court in the mall at the Pru is good," I said, evoking a sympathetic look from Bruce.

He reached across the table for my hand. "I was worried about you, Sophie. I *am* worried about you."

"I'm fine. It's been a good day." I spread my hands across my place setting. "I haven't knocked anything over." I returned Bruce's smile. "We . . . Virgil, that is . . . has a little more info on the two workers; I signed off on both the nuisance police forms; Andrew is going to fix my email spam problem tomorrow; nothing new has been taken from me for twenty-four hours; and"—I took Bruce's hand—"we're together for a wonderful dinner."

Bruce squeezed my hand, but I could tell he wasn't sold. "I still think it's a good idea if I skip my shift tonight. Until they catch this guy—"

I shook my head. We'd been over this in the car on the way to the restaurant. I was weary of the topic and of being constantly under surveillance. "They've probably picked up Einstein by now," I said. "And, if not, my house is the last place he'd choose to hang around."

"There could be more than one guy. Your unnamed worker—"

"He has a name now. It's just that Virgil won't tell us. I wish I'd been able to get it from Barker."

"He was probably told to keep quiet about it for now."

"Protocol," we both said, but only I grimaced.

"I should have been able to drag it out of him," I said. "I wish I'd at least asked him if he'd heard the nickname 'Einstein.' "

"Okay." Bruce would neither confirm nor deny my ability to drag things out of people. He was ready to pick up the thread of my theory. "Your named-but-unknown-to-us worker could be someone entirely different from the guy they called Einstein twenty-five years ago. You have no clue that Kirsten and Wendy's friend is back in town."

"Ponytail was. And they hung out together," I said.

"Twenty-five years ago."

Bruce was right, technically. I had no proof, but I

couldn't let go of the theory that Einstein was back, working on the carillon project, and that he'd probably thrown Kirsten off the Admin tower long ago, attacked Jenn last week, murdered Ponytail, and invaded my home. For all I knew he'd also stolen my credit card identity and hacked my email, though I didn't peg him for a tech-savvy guy. I hoped someday I could abandon all these connections, true or not, and get back to where the name Einstein would conjure up only Albert, undoubtedly the most influential physicist of the twentieth century, and not a thug whose crimes, in my mind, reached back to the early carillon days on the Henley campus.

Bruce gave me his most serious look. "Sophie, Einstein or no Einstein, maybe this guy knows you've been asking questions. Maybe somehow he knows you went to Boston and saw Wendy Carlson and he thinks you know more than you do about those old bank robberies. I need you to be careful and let me be there for you."

I did my best to express how much that meant to me. Then, so we could enjoy our dinners, which were due to arrive, I agreed that Bruce could call in sick and stay with me if there was no unmarked police car in front of my house. I loved how we compromised.

Getting my hands under control to meet my no-spill objective for the evening was easier than taming the thoughts and questions in my head. I wondered where Wendy Carlson was at the moment. Fleeing? Hiding? On her way to Henley to correct the error she'd made all those years ago? I'd lost hope that Virgil's techs could retrieve her number from my cell phone. Maybe I'd put Andrew on the case.

I'd forgotten to ask Virgil again about the hundred-dollar bill he was having tested. Since I was the one who'd found it, I felt I should get a heads-up on the results. What else was there to worry about or close the loop on? I was afraid I'd forgotten something important.

How rude would it be for me to take out my notepad

now and make a checklist? Bummer that it would have to be paper and pen since my smartphone, with its Notes app, was still in the hands of the HPD.

"Bring it on," Bruce said.

"Huh?" Had I been talking out loud? Or was he addressing our efficient young waitress, who'd served our aromatic fish dinners.

"I know you're making a pie chart or spreadsheet in your head, so"—he opened his palms and wiggled his fingers—"tell me where you are in this puzzle. What's the status?"

"Really?"

"Uh-huh."

"You're the greatest."

"I know."

I dug into my shrimp salad. Bruce, unaffected by the crustaceans' struggles in the tank at the entrance to the inn, had ordered lobster Newburg with extra cayenne pepper, and seemed to enjoy his first taste.

"There's Jenn's backpack," I said, buttering a piece of French bread. "Where is it? You know how on TV they're always finding purses and wallets in Dumpsters after they've been stolen and stripped of cash and credit cards? I wonder if the police looked for it?"

"There aren't a lot of dumping places along that stretch of Main," Bruce reminded me. "The closest one might be the one behind the campus coffee shop."

"The Mortarboard," I said, picturing an area of campus I seldom strolled. "The Dumpster is not right on the street; it's set back, on the campus."

"I can't see the guy heading back onto Henley grounds to dump his load. He wouldn't risk that."

"Good point," I said. "And he didn't cross Main, at least not while he was in camera range, so maybe he just took it to his vehicle. Assuming he had a vehicle."

"A backpack takes longer to look through than a purse

or a wallet. My guess is he took it home and went through it at his leisure."

"Well, the police know where he lives now."

"If—"

"I know, if the guy on the video is even the worker Barker ID'd. If, if, if. But I have to start somewhere."

I took a sip of lime water and a calming breath. During that short break, I looked around at the other patrons in the crowded dining room. Too many of the guests at adjacent tables were looking in our direction. It was tempting to feel flattered that they found our conversation more interesting than their own, but I suspected one or two of them might have nine-one-one on standby. From snippets of our chatter, they might reasonably assume we were about to accuse Albert Einstein of robbing a bank and fleeing with a backpack containing one hundred dollars.

"What are the other loose ends around the attack and the murder?" Bruce asked.

I motioned for him to lower his voice. "I think we're scaring people," I said.

"Good thing I don't have my flight suit on, huh?" he said, in an only slightly lower tone. He followed with a near whisper, "There's that bill you found. Do you think it fell out of Jenn's backpack?"

I shook my head. "I can't imagine that Jenn would be carrying that much cash."

"Didn't you tell me she said something about money to the commuters who found her?"

"Yes, but she could have just meant that the guy took her money—maybe she was worried about her checkbook and what little cash there might have been in the backpack—not necessarily that there was this other money, the hundred-dollar bill. Besides it's a little hard to take everything those commuter guys said literally."

"Because they may have lied about chasing the bad guy? I wouldn't be so hard on them."

"What would you have done?" I asked.

"That's different. It's my job."

"It's your DNA."

I saw no point in reminding Bruce how it took a certain kind of person to embrace jobs like his and Virgil's in the first place.

"The other option," I began, "is that Jenn's attacker lost the bill in the struggle, and his prints are on it, and that would be one more data point."

"You're thinking they're Einstein's."

"Uh-huh," I said, stabbing a shrimp in as gentle a way as possible, not to further frighten our neighbors, which now included a toddler at the next table. I gave the little girl my kindest smile, and hoped her parents would be reassured.

"And that would put him at the scene of the crime."

I nodded. "Do you think Virgil's job is always as hard as this?"

"I know it is."

"So I should cut him some slack if he doesn't act like I'm his partner?"

"You said it," Bruce replied, laughing and soaking up creamy sauce with bread.

"I'll think about it."

I thought the day demanded dessert and warned Bruce that if he declined to order his own, it had better not be because he thought he'd get some of mine. I was in a good mood, but not that good.

Rring, rring. Rring, rring.

Bruce's ringtone was the closest he could find to an old-time teacher's bell, to balance out the sound of helicopter blades on my cell phone, he'd claimed.

The call came as I was halfway through a dessert called triple chocolate dazzle—a brownie with chocolate ice cream and hot fudge sauce. Despite my warning that I wouldn't share, I pushed my plate to Bruce, who'd already polished off a sweet-smelling praline delight. I was suffering from what my mother would call "your eyes are bigger than your stomach" syndrome.

"No kidding," Bruce was saying into his phone. Then, after a pause, "Wow," then a final "Good news. Thanks."

All this, while I waved my arms and mouthed, "Who is it?" twice and, "What is it?" three times. And to the absent Virgil, I mouthed, "Where's *my* phone?"

Bruce clicked off.

"Virge got a work call, so his dinner with Judy was cut short."

"She'd better get used to it if she wants to see him," I said. "He called you just to say that? That was 'good news'?"

"Not exactly."

I gave him a look that would have withered his flight suit, and he quickly caved.

"Jenn's awake," he said, a broad smile crossing his face and lighting up the whole room.

I nearly sailed over the blue green tablecloth to hug him, probably the effect of the Inn at Henley's nautical theme.

"Virgil says her parents are going to take her home as soon as she gets clearance, so if anyone would like to visit, now would be the time. Interested?"

I caught our waitress's eye. "Check, please."

The light snow had continued to accumulate while we were at dinner, and now formed soft piles on the edges of the sidewalk. Bruce was dressed for fall, not winter. In my judgment, a sports jacket didn't qualify as cold weather garb. Still, his arm around me provided extra warmth as we turned into the lot where we'd parked my Honda.

"ETA to Henley General ten minutes," Bruce said, sliding behind the wheel of the car.

I was beyond excited that Jenn was awake. A huge smile formed every time I thought about it on the trip from the Inn. It hadn't been easy to convince Bruce to drop me off at the hospital and take off for his shift in my car. I was sure someone in the group would drive me home. As part of the deal, I had to accept Bruce's smartphone, since mine was still with the HPD and Bruce would be well connected at the MAstar trailer.

"It's not wired to the Bat Phone, is it?" I asked, as I took the device from Bruce. "Am I going to get a call to rescue a cat from a tree in the middle of the night?"

"You'd be surprised how seldom that happens."

What Bruce didn't know was that I was ready to make almost any deal as long as I got to see Jenn Marshall awake and functioning.

I arrived at the hospital and found Jenn's student friends in the waiting room. Patty threw her arms around me, surprisingly not a first for a roommate of one of my majors, but usually the emotion was related to a rejuvenated GPA.

"The Marshalls are in with Jenn," Patty said. "They've been in there awhile even though the doctors said they could have only a few minutes."

"Maybe she got a boost of energy when she saw her parents," Lauren said. "I hope so. I tweeted some other friends that she's awake, and I'm getting lots of retweets and woots."

"Glad to hear it," I said.

"The doctors still won't let anyone else see her, though," Andrew added. "Maybe tomorrow."

Willa and Lauren donned their many layers of outer clothing. "Yeah, they wouldn't even let Professor Morrell in, so he left," Lauren said.

I found it curious that Ted would come. I suppose he found out the same way the students did, through Patty, who had essentially lived with the Marshalls these last few days.

"You have to be a cop to get in there now," Willa grumbled. "We're leaving."

"But we'll be back if Jenn wants, you know, company later," Lauren said, as Willa dragged her by the elbow.

"Has Detective Mitchell been here already?" I asked, addressing Andrew and Patty.

"Yeah, and they let him in right away, even before her parents got in," Andrew said.

"I'm sure that's procedure," I said. Pretty sure. I'd been present on occasions when Virgil got a call from a hospital that a crime victim or witness or suspect was physically able to talk. Virgil would drop everything—including Judy this evening, apparently—to get there before the person was "tainted" by other visitors, in his words.

"He wouldn't tell us what Jenn said," Andrew noted. "But we asked someone coming out of the wing—I think, maybe, like a male nurse—if he'd heard anything. He said he could see through the window that the detective showed Jenn something."

A bit removed from firsthand information, but we might as well go with it, I decided.

"He thought it might have been a photo," Patty said.

"The guy also said Detective Mitchell looked disappointed, so I'll bet Jenn didn't recognize the picture," Andrew added.

The mug shot of Ponytail was my guess. As far as I knew, we didn't have a good likeness of the other worker, unless Virgil's techs had been able to pull one off the web. The other worker, my Einstein, didn't have a record, or Barker wouldn't have hired him, and the videos didn't even come close to being useful for an ID by anyone who wasn't familiar with him to begin with.

"Did the Marshalls tell you anything about how Jenn is doing?" I asked Andrew. Patty had excused herself for a trip to the vending machine. After my triple chocolate dazzle, I could easily pass on candy, or anything else that came out of a machine.

"Yeah, Mr. Marshall came out and talked to us, which was very nice of him," Andrew said.

"I'm sure they both appreciate your concern," I said, thinking that Andrew was giving Los Angeles a very good name for compassionate youth.

"She'll need a ton of therapy," he said. "The best things I heard are that she has temporary dysfunction with no long-term complications. Not that I understand that completely, but I like the sound of it."

"Me, too," I said. I figured doctors were slow to use phrases like "full recovery" and this was as good as we were going to get.

"They've assigned a case manager in Fitchburg who'll coordinate everything," Andrew continued. "Physical, speech, neurology, and on and on. Even a vocational counselor to advise her about coming back to school and all."

I wondered how soon Jenn would be fit to be moved to her hometown. I knew it wasn't the most important thing, but I hoped she'd be able to help Virgil find her attacker first. Only Jenn might eventually be able to tell us if the second worker was the guilty party, and possibly give us a clue about why he might have chosen her to batter, her backpack to steal. Unless she'd blocked out the memory, which would be the second best thing to happen.

"I just hope they find the guy," Andrew said, summing up my thoughts. He put his backpack down, letting it rest between his legs.

"I can't believe she might not come back this spring." Patty had returned with chips, candy bars, sodas. Apparently, the vending machine was out of hard-boiled eggs and bags of granola. She unloaded everything onto a small table. "Help yourself," she told Andrew and me. "I guess I should just be more grateful, huh? I mean, I thought she was going to die"—Patty held back tears—"but I want her all the way back, you know what I mean?"

Andrew nodded and picked up a bag of chips with sea salt.

We sat for about ten minutes with our own thoughts, Patty and Andrew snacking while I felt a bit guilty, having enjoyed a full meal at the Inn.

I watched as doctors and nurses with unidentifiable titles passed by. How did you tell who was who these days—doctors, nurses, paradoctors, and paranurses. I saw only one woman and one man in white coats. Most of the employees wore cotton pants in a dull shade of blue and a tunic top in a matching shade or a print, with hearts, flowers, kittens, or butterflies. The most popular design I noticed was a yellow and green short-sleeved shirt with images of dogs on skateboards. We could have been in Hawaii.

Rring, rring. Rring, rring.

The phone startled me. I wasn't as used to Bruce's ringtone as I thought. I walked away from Patty and Andrew and clicked on.

"Hey, Sophie." Judy Donohue's voice. "I was so glad to hear about Jenn. Whew, huh? Have you seen her?"

"No, not yet. I'm getting bits and pieces that say she might be able to go home in a week or so."

"*Home* home, or back to school?"

"To Fitchburg, most likely."

"Any word about returning to school?"

"No. How'd you find me at this number, by the way?"

"Virgil gave me Bruce's number. He said he had your phone and you had Bruce's. I didn't ask why."

"Long story."

"Listen, I have Virgil's car."

"You have Virgil's car?" I parroted.

"Long story."

We both laughed.

"I can pick you up at the hospital," Judy said.

"Thanks, but you don't have to do that. Patty, Jenn's roommate, has a car. She'll be able to take me home."

"I was hoping to talk to you," Judy said.

"Another long story?"

"All good," Judy said.

"What's convenient for you?" I asked.

"I can be there in ten or fifteen."

"That will work. I doubt that I'll get in to see Jenn tonight anyway. I'll wait for you at the main entrance so you won't have to park."

I clicked off, with a smile. Jenn was awake and Judy had a good story to tell me.

CHAPTER $\sqrt{18}$

I assured Andrew and Patty that I was all set for a ride home from the hospital with Judy and sent them on their way.

Andrew issued a parting reminder over his shoulder. "See you tomorrow, Dr. Knowles. Don't forget, I'm going to work on your email problem after our seminar. Be thinking of an appropriate e-punishment for the hacker."

"Done," I said. My evil twin had already decided to find a way to spam the culprit with ads for the puzzle magazines that featured my submissions.

I gathered my cumbersome winter wear, ready to locate the correct color-coded line to the hospital's exit. Halfway into my heavy jacket, I saw Mr. and Mrs. Marshall walking toward me, from the other side of the glass-topped double doors of the waiting room.

A cautiously optimistic smile adorned each of their faces, one that said there was hope for their family. Mrs. Marshall pushed through the door and approached me with her arms open and gave me a tearful hug, a surprise, since I hadn't felt that we'd connected over the past few days.

Mr. Marshall waited his turn then said, "Dr. Knowles, we're glad to see you. Andrew and the girls said you'd get here as soon as you could."

"She wants to talk to you," Mrs. Marshall said, stepping back and taking a deep, audible breath. She dabbed at her eyes and smoothed her skirt, the same one I'd seen the first day of Jenn's hospital stay. "Do you mind going in? The doctor says she should be okay for another few minutes, then she has to take a pill and, I guess, that puts her to sleep."

"But just sleep, that's all," Mr. Marshall said. I understood that he meant "not another coma."

I did my best not to knock them over on my way to Jenn's room.

It was all I could do to maintain a smile at the sight of my heavily bandaged and bruised student. Jenn was surrounded by lifelines of tubes and blipping green lines that made it difficult for me to believe she'd be leaving the hospital anytime soon. I tried to adjust my breathing to avoid large doses of whatever foul-smelling chemicals were nearby. I hoped they weren't being pumped through Jenn, or any other patient. I had great admiration for Jenn's parents, keeping up their spirits in the face of the sights, sounds, and smells in the tiny room, for their daughter's sake.

A large female medical professional with a matching set of blue scrubs glanced at me where I was standing a foot or so inside the room. She turned away, continued fiddling with apparatus, and said, "You can have five minutes."

"Thanks," I said, stepping in.

"Don't agitate her," she added in a tone as serious as a military command.

Did I look like an agitator? I wore a simple mauve

sweater with a matching scarf—calming, I thought. "I'll be very careful," I answered, glad, in a way, that Jenn was in the hands of someone as protective of her as her family and friends were.

I hoped my five minutes started only when the woman finally left the room, leaving in her wake a scowl, aimed at me.

I tiptoed to the head of the bed. Jenn was flat on her back, sleeping, I thought. Close up, the bruises looked even more lethal. Her white bandage was thicker than any I'd ever seen, with the possible exception of one on Bruce's head after an ice-climbing incident (he never acknowledged "accidents").

I'd read strange stories of people waking up from a coma. They came back to flood my brain. A young German man who woke up unable to speak anything but fluent French, which his parents claimed he'd had only a cursory knowledge of before his accident; a middle-aged woman, shy and reclusive all her life, who woke from a coma as chatty, outgoing, and the life of the party; a car mechanic who became so agitated and confused when he emerged from his coma that he had to be restrained. I shivered and pulled my sweater around me. I looked down at Jenn and hoped her recovery would be the most normal on record.

More than ever, I wanted to find the person who did this to my student. Whether his name was Einstein or Dillinger, I wanted him in custody.

I hesitated to wake her now. I'd forgotten to ask the Marshalls if Jenn had said anything other than she wanted to speak to me. I wouldn't have been surprised if they'd imagined she'd said anything at all, eager as they'd been to make contact with their daughter.

I bent over her, to be sure she was breathing. She snapped up, almost knocking our foreheads together. I let out a little (I hoped) yelp.

"Sorry," Jenn said (possibly) in a muffled voice.

"That's okay," I said. "I'm so glad to see you."

"Sorry," she said again.

I took her hand, the one without the needle, and stumbled over a few words I intended to be soothing. "You're doing so well." "It's wonderful to have you back." "We've missed you." I wished it hadn't felt so much like a funeral.

As desperately as I wanted to ask Jenn cop-type questions, I couldn't bring myself to agitate someone in such a fragile state, and wouldn't have, even if I hadn't been warned by the large nurse-like person. I decided instead to talk about positive things like school and her future.

"All your friends and teachers are waiting to welcome you back," I began. "I've been thinking about how to make it easy for you to finish the Intersession and get your full credit, working from home. Once you're up to it, you can do a book report for the math history seminar. I have a new book on mathematics as a language that I think you'd find interesting, and another one that's a biography of Blaise Pascal's sister, Gilberte. Remember, she's the one who—"

"Sorry," Jenn whispered for a third time.

I leaned in. "Am I talking too much?" I asked.

She shook her head, which for her was to turn her neck about fifteen degrees to each side. She raised her untethered arm to her bandages and multicolored face.

"Why are you sorry, Jenn? You don't think this is your fault, do you?"

"Money," she said.

Money? Again? Maybe the commuters were right about some things.

"Tell me about money," I said.

"Took some." Two consecutive words seemed to drain her energy. Tears formed in her eyes.

"I know. He took your money. But please, please, Jenn, don't worry about that. We'll make sure—"

"Wrong," she said, her head now moving faster, back and forth, in a decisive "no."

"Jenn, I don't know what you're talking about," I said. "Are you telling me I'm wrong? That the man who beat you didn't take your money?" I was confused, and aware that Jenn was becoming excited. I saw full on tears now. I took a risk. "Do you know who attacked you? Or why? Does it have to do with your money?"

I'd kept my voice low and smooth, I thought, but still Jenn's body tensed. Her fingers clenched, her feet wiggled under the thin white blanket, and her head rolled as much as forty-five degrees, back and forth.

"Jenn, please calm down," I begged, looking for a button to call a nurse.

Before I could figure out how to get help, Mr. and Mrs. Marshall came through the doorway. I hadn't realized they'd been standing in the hallway, close to the threshold probably the whole time of my visit.

"That's enough, please, Dr. Knowles," Mrs. Marshall said. The large lady in blue was on their heels, summoned by them (possibly); it was time for me to leave (certainly), and I did.

The lady ushered the Marshalls out a minute later. We reconvened in the waiting room.

"I was telling Jenn she doesn't need to worry about school at all," I told them.

"Why was she so upset then?" Mrs. Marshall asked.

"I don't know." Only a small lie, since I wasn't absolutely sure. I wasn't about to tell them their daughter seemed worried about money.

"That's not good for her," Mr. Marshall added.

"She's not supposed to get excited," Mrs. Marshall said, her voice as strained as when Jenn was first hospitalized.

"She shouldn't be moving around like that," Mr. Marshall said, shaking his head. He might as well have pointed a scolding finger at me.

"I know, and I don't know what upset her. I was simply telling her that I would take care of the logistics for finishing her classes this term."

"You can do that?" Mr. Marshall asked, his attention drawn away from his censuring.

I nodded. "And even if she's still in Fitchburg at the beginning of the spring term, I can talk to the dean. I'm sure we'll be able to arrange something. Maybe a special project that she can do on her own. We'll get creative."

I felt confident that the administration would be willing to cooperate with anything that put things right for a student who was attacked on our campus going about her business in the middle of the day. It was the least we could do. Besides reevaluating our network of security cameras.

The Marshalls thanked me as I donned my outerwear. The expressions on their faces were somewhere between pleasant and neutral, but I noticed they stood solidly, shoulder to shoulder in the doorway, between me and their daughter.

I walked the red line to the hospital exit as quickly as I could. I'd lost track of time and now realized Judy must have been circling the hospital entrance looking for me.

As I rushed along the hallway, I revisited the few words Jenn had spoken.

Sorry (three times). *Money. Took some. Wrong.*

Not quite haiku, but adding *snowy day* might make the difference. My first thought had been that Jenn was worried that the mugger took her money, which was a "wrong" thing to do. Now, due to her apparent turmoil and three apologies—from guilt?—I had to admit another possibility. The only other thing that made sense was that it was Jenn who *took*—I couldn't bring myself to say "stole"— money. She knew she was wrong and now she was sorry. But what money? Whose money? Einstein's? Was that why he attacked her, because she took his money?

No reasonable scenario came to mind. Except one that was so ridiculous it brought a smile to my face: Jenn, all in black, with a team of questionable characters, à la Patty Hearst and Kirsten Packard, robbing a bank, frightening a teller, forcing him to hand over a pile of money. My mind did strange things when I hadn't had enough sleep. Possibly even when I had.

I wondered if Jenn's parents knew more than they were saying. They might have been ready to cut my visit short even if Jenn hadn't become restive.

Rring, rring. Rring, rring.

Judy calling. I hoped her dinner with Virgil, brief as it was, had put her in a forgiving mood.

"Sorry," I said, echoing Jenn. I checked the signage on the walls, thought back to my trip into Jenn's wing, and calculated that I had one long hallway and two short ones before I'd be at the exit, where all colors met. "I should be at the entrance in five minutes."

"No problem. Are you sure you're ready to leave?" Judy asked.

"More than ready."

Eager as I was to talk about the few minutes I'd spent with Jenn and the Marshalls, I let Judy lead the conversation on the way to my house in Virgil's Camry.

"I like him," Judy said.

"He's a likable guy," I said. "Most of the time."

Judy laughed. "Except when he's not reading you into an investigation?"

"Hmmm. I hope you didn't waste too much of your first date talking about me," I said.

Judy laughed and gave away no secrets.

When we pulled up in front of my house behind an unmarked police car, I knew the answer to one of my questions: No, the police had not yet found Einstein. No, he wasn't in custody, pouring out a confession to crimes old and new. Wouldn't it have been great if he'd been picked up on a lesser charge, like shoplifting, or driving without a license—the way that Al Capone had been nabbed, only for cheating on his taxes—but then Einstein would blurt out all his other crimes, from robbery to murder.

I came out of my reverie. "Do you want to come in for coffee?" I asked Judy.

"No, thanks. I'm going to return Virgil's car."

I looked at my watch. Eight o'clock. "Do you think he'll be home? He's been known to work late."

"I have a key," she said.

"Good for you," I said, smiling, thinking, *fast work*. It still boggled my mind that truffles-and-champagne Judy Donohue and pizza-and-beer Virgil Mitchell were dating. It also occurred to me that someone at this moment might be marveling at the partnership of stay-at-home-and-do-puzzles Sophie Knowles and Yosemite-is-an-easy-winter-climb Bruce Granville.

As I unbuckled my seat belt, Judy let out a little gasp. "Sophie, I never asked you how Jenn is. What's happening to me? I'm reverting to sixteen years old. Talking about me, me, me. I can't believe it. Tell me, how is she?"

"I would have stopped you if there were anything big to report. I had less than five minutes with Jenn," I said, taking the easy way out.

It was too late to tell Judy how the words Jenn spoke were still running around in my head and that I had conflicting theories about what they might mean. I didn't have the energy to bring her up to speed on my trip to Boston. She didn't know that I'd found Kirsten Packard's physics major roommate, Wendy Carlson. She didn't know I'd found out that Ted had lied when he claimed he hardly remembered Kirsten and couldn't remember her roommate's name. I couldn't tell her one thing without dragging every other little thing along. I didn't miss the irony that I now had more interesting tidbits of information than the self-proclaimed mistress of gossip.

"Is she awake and talking?" Judy asked.

"Not really, just mumbling."

"Poor kid," she said.

"I told her and her parents we'd work something out so she doesn't have to drop her Intersession classes, and then we'll see where she is when the spring semester begins."

"That's nice. You should talk to Claire in the dean's office. She helped us with that last year when Mona Farrell had her ski accident."

"Good to know. Thanks."

"I'll bet Jenn and her parents were thrilled that you were there."

"Oh yeah," I said.

I waved good-bye to Judy and hello to the cops and went into my well-protected home.

The police car notwithstanding, I went through my house, room by room, closet by closet. Nice that I could laugh as I asked myself a critical question: What was my plan if there was someone behind the shower curtain or my rocker or inside a kitchen cabinet? Scream? Offer a cup of coffee? At least I should carry my portable phone so I could hit nine-one-one immediately. And a weapon would be useful. My father's old metal slide rule was handy, hanging in its leather case on the wall above my computer. Nothing to worry about.

I almost shouted, "Clear!" when I'd finished the tour of my cottage. I could now turn to the mountain of catch-up work waiting for me. Check my email; review notes for both of tomorrow's classes; finish a summer-themed crossword puzzle for a magazine editor who was waiting for it; follow up on the changes I'd had to make for paying bills with my credit card; answer dozens of legitimate emails from students, or friends in Africa and Florida.

The thought of Florida brought images of my BFF,

Ariana, who was due back home next week and would be on my case about how far I'd gotten (not) on my beading project for the class I was taking at her shop. Maybe that's why I hadn't called her for a couple of days. At the moment I couldn't even have said for sure where the half-finished hair clip was. I'd stuck it in one of my "miscellaneous" drawers before my guests arrived the other night. I might never see it again.

I also needed a spreadsheet for the logistics of the last couple of days. I took time to tick off a few reminders: I now had my cell phone charger, but not my cell phone, which was still in the hands of the HPD. Bruce's car was in front of my house from his cleanup and visit. Bruce had my car but not his phone, which was in my hands. Virgil's car was on its way to him through Judy, who'd driven me home with it, but I was out of that loop.

All set. I could go to work.

What I really wanted to tackle first were all the threads of Kirsten Packard's death in the distant past and Jenn Marshall's attack in the recent past. I was haunted by the idea that Jenn had stolen Einstein's money and he beat her up to get it back. It wasn't the Jenn I knew, but it would explain the worried, preoccupied state she seemed to be in lately. I'd attributed her mood to fatigue, but it could just as likely have been guilt.

I recalled seeing or hearing about Jenn's new laptop and smartphone. Patty Reynolds would probably be able to tell us if her roommate had made any other out-of-the-ordinary purchases recently. I hated the road I was traveling with these thoughts, but I saw no way to avoid it.

I turned to something simple, like setting up an example for using the disc method to calculate a volume of revolution around an axis. Then the weekend caught up with me. The total number of hours of sleep I'd had since Thursday night didn't add up to double digits, and for most of them,

I'd been sitting in a chair or riding in a car going at highway speed.

I exchanged my sweater for a robe and stumbled down the hall to my guest room, hitting the up arrow on the thermostat on the way. I fell into a bed that was fully outfitted, thanks to Bruce. I dozed off, Jenn's words swimming in my head. In my dreams I was pummeled from all directions by car keys, belonging to me, Bruce, Virgil, Judy, and cops in two counties of the Commonwealth. I kept warding them all off, muttering about a man named Kenny, who was pretending to be a copyeditor. If Andrew found my email scammer without too much effort, I'd put him to work on finding Kenny. My evil twin had some ideas for him as well.

Clang, clang. Clang, clang. Bells ringing.

I woke up at ten o'clock to the sound of my alarm clock. What? I smashed down on the button to turn it off. I couldn't remember the last time I'd set the clock in the guest room, or when any guest had done so. I picked up the vexing clock and checked the back panel. Sure enough, the alarm had been set for ten PM. Either Bruce had done it accidently when he reassembled the items on my nightstand earlier today, or my intruder was the playful type and wanted to rattle me.

I sat up and resigned myself to the fact that I might never again sleep for more than two hours at a stretch. I adjusted my robe around me and wondered also if I'd ever again wear nightclothes to bed. Who was it who'd said "Sleep is overrated"? Maybe I could convince myself it was true.

I tried to recall what I'd been doing before I fell asleep. Trying to solve a puzzle. What else was new?

Clang, clang. Clang, clang. The bells again.

Apparently, I'd hit the snooze button instead of the off button. I could fiddle with the tiny switches in the back or

I could stop this nonsense once and for all by throwing the clock across the room. I chose the reasonable route and, not surprising, triggered the bells again.

But this time the ring set off something in my head. Not the equation for the volume of revolution, but everything else. I felt as though I'd been awakened by a large carillon bell, perhaps the more than eighteen-ton bourdon that was pictured in the Music Department's photo gallery. The bell resided at the Rockefeller Chapel at the University of Chicago, but all thirty-seven thousand pounds of it might as well have been stuck in the corridor outside my guestroom.

The pieces came together like the notes on carillon sheet music. With a little help from the HPD, I'd be able to follow the tune from Kirsten, Ponytail, Einstein, and *money*, all the way to Jenn and *money* and *sorry* and *wrong*.

Usually I was elated when I saw the pieces of a puzzle fall together. This time my pleasure was greatly reduced by the fact that my solution involved accusing my lovely, bright student of theft. For the first time that I could remember, I hoped my logic had led me down the wrong path.

CHAPTER $\sqrt{19}$

As much as I hated to interrupt a date that might still be in progress, I couldn't wait to call Virgil with my newest, definitive theory. I worked out as tight a sequence of events as I could for such a complex story, so my call wouldn't take too long. Besides, first dates were usually short, I reasoned.

I sat on the couch in my den and rehearsed, as if I were writing a newspaper account:

Twenty-five years ago, Kirsten Packard, using her roommate Wendy's key, hides money from a bank robbery inside the carillon tower. Ponytail and Einstein don't know exactly where, and probably kill her trying to find out. After her death, a wall is erected; the tower is sealed. Ponytail and Einstein can't get back in to look for the money.

In the present day, with the tower about to be reopened, Einstein takes a job on the project, but, with no key card of his own, he can't hang around in the tower long enough to search for the money.

Jenn stumbles upon the money during a practice ses-

sion. *Jenn* (I winced) *has been taking money from the stash. Ponytail and Einstein follow her, and Einstein attacks her to get her key card, then kills Ponytail so he'll have the treasure all to himself.*

There it was. It couldn't have been neater. Why hadn't this obvious narrative occurred to me days ago? Was I losing my touch? My reputation as an expert puzzler was at stake. The most likely explanation was that I'd been blinded by my tendency to think my students could do no wrong. Jenn Marshall wasn't the first of my math majors to stray from perfection, but each time, it caught me by surprise.

At first, I didn't even want to think about how Ted would react when we caught Einstein and he confessed to pushing Kirsten to her death. But if Ted knew about that possibility from the start, it would have given him yet another reason to cover it up—to protect Wendy from being Einstein's next victim. No wonder he was upset with my nosing around.

My theory in place, I played devil's advocate with myself, trying also to anticipate Virgil's cross-examination.

The biggest question was, what had Ponytail and Einstein been doing for twenty-five years? No more news-making pranks or bank robberies? I thought it unlikely that they would have been model citizens all this time.

I decided to let Virgil help me with those little details. It was his job, after all. I slid Bruce's phone on and tapped Virgil's name.

"Hey, Sophie."

"How come you knew it was me and not Bruce?"

"Bruce knows I'm busy right now."

I felt my face flush. "Oh, Virgil, I'm sorry. I'm ruining your date." I didn't add what I was thinking—that it was all the more lamentable since dates were in short supply for him. "I can call you tomorrow."

"No, no, just kidding. Besides, I warned Judy that my job wasn't nine to five, Monday to Friday."

"And what was her response?"

"She warned me back that she might be keeping biology experiments in my fridge."

I heard Judy's laugh in the background and my face reddened again. I wasn't accustomed to hearing Virgil in such a sharing mood about his personal life. It was going to take a while for me to get used to it. For now, I'd have to deal with a lot of blushing.

"Sounds like you're very compatible," I said.

"What's up?" Virgil asked, back to work.

"I know why Einstein attacked Jenn," I said.

A big sigh from Virgil, then, "If he attacked Jenn."

"We have three crimes, Virgil—Jenn's attack, my break-in, and Ponytail's murder. Don't you think they're related?"

"Let's look at this in a way you'll understand, Sophie. It's not like getting a box with five hundred jigsaw pieces, where you know they all belong to the same picture. The real world doesn't work that way."

How dare he? Of course it does.

"Hear me out," I said. As quickly as possible, I gave Virgil the rundown, starting with Jenn's whispered admission to me in the hospital. "What do you think?" I asked, nearly breathless.

"Jenn actually admitted taking money from a stash in the tower?"

I repeated Jenn's words. "Doesn't that sound like an admission?"

"I have to admit, it's closer than I got."

"You mean you figured that out already?"

"I was working on it. Couldn't get anything out of the girl, though."

"Glad I could help," I said, with only the slightest touch of sarcasm.

Virgil laughed.

"Not to poke holes in my own theory, but it does seem

weird that Ponytail and Einstein would have stayed around all this time, just waiting for the tower to be opened. What if it never reopened? What if someone started looking into Kirsten's death again." Like me, I thought.

"Well, in fact, they were very busy," Virgil said.

"Huh?"

"We ran Einstein's real name—"

"Which Barker gave you and neither of you will tell me."

"And it turns out he and Ponytail lived in New Hampshire, Rhode Island, and Connecticut for a while, and maybe Vermont, both of them under at least three different names."

"Circling the state where the cash-filled tower was."

"Ponytail was charged a few times with theft. Some jewelry, some money. He did a little time in minimum-security prisons in each state. Einstein was brought in twice, but never charged."

"Then you know Ponytail's real name, too?"

"We've given the press both names now, so it can be revealed."

There was no use announcing my pique at being lumped in with the press. I waited, like the general public.

"They're cousins," Virgil continued. "Einstein's parents adopted Ponytail after his mother died and his father split."

"Which might be why Ponytail never turned on his partner. Double loyalty," I guessed. Until his benefactor murdered him, I noted.

"That and they probably had an agreement that one of them at least would be able to keep a clean record," Virgil said. "I've seen it before. Makes it handy. One of them wouldn't have his mug on file when it came to casing a target or getting a legit job."

"Waiting till the tower opened up," I offered.

"Maybe not that specific, but, yeah, if there's a big enough stash up there. Their birth names are Harold, that's

Einstein, and Gabriel, with the ponytail. Last name, War-nocky," Virgil said.

By now learning the "real" names of the fighting duo on the security video was anticlimactic. I realized I'd grown quite fond of the guys' nicknames. They seemed to suit my image of the men—poor, deceased Ponytail, like a meek, bushy-tailed animal being led around by one of the smart-est guys in the world, who, it turned out, was his cousin.

"Einstein killed his cousin," I said, processing the new data.

"Looks that way."

"And now they both have records," I said, moving from my den to my office. "Once Einstein's caught, that is."

I took a seat at my desk, my laptop open in front of me. I opened a new document and started a list.

"The first thing we need to do is make a thorough search of the tower," I said to Virgil as I typed "1. Search tower."

Virgil laughed. "See me saluting," he said.

"It's going to be open to the public very soon, Virgil. You should get there first thing in the morning."

"Hold on," Virgil said. "My date is calling me."

"But—"

"Gotta go. I'll be around tomorrow."

I was at the keyboard, typing "2. Find Wendy. In danger from E.?" when I heard a soft *click*.

Detective Virgil Mitchell had (almost) hung up on me. What did he mean he'd "be around tomorrow"? Was that his way of agreeing to the search of the tower? Or was he putting me off?

I was worried about Wendy Carlson. Virgil didn't men-tion whether they were able to trace her call to me in Bos-ton. And Einstein (a much snappier moniker than Harold Warnocky, which relegated him to the far end of the alpha-bet) was still on the loose with one, if not two, murders on his résumé, and not much to lose. If Virgil had been more hospitable, I'd have been able to ask him about the status of all three—my smartphone, Wendy, and Einstein.

I'd have to speak to Judy about teaching her new boy-friend some manners. Unless she'd been the one who'd bro-ken the connection.

Eleven PM. A snack was in order. Too bad I hadn't thought of taking the rest of my chocolate delight to go instead of passing it on to Bruce. I rummaged in my fridge and came up with bits of Brie and Jarlsberg cheeses, a few crackers, and a handful of grapes. Too healthy, so I added a cup of hot chocolate to the menu, plus two cookies from my emer-gency supply. I kept them primarily for Virgil, who loved my peanut butter cookies. If I were out of them the next time he checked in my cabinet, it would serve him right for hanging up on me.

I carried my laptop and the ad hoc feast into the den and settled in my favorite curl-up place on the couch.

This time the rampant spam in my inbox didn't bother me; Andrew would be on it soon. I ran through legitimate emails and texts from Fran (missing me, worried about calling in the middle of the night again), Ariana (missing the snow, had had enough winter sun, hoping I was beading a lot), and students (missing Jenn, wanting to know when they could visit).

It took about an hour to get my materials in order for my nine o'clock calculus class and finish a biography of the Bernoulli brothers, Jacob and Johann, the subjects of my eleven o'clock seminar, to be led by freshman Brent Riggs. Both Ted and I were courting Brent as a major for our respective Physics and Math Departments, and I suspected Brent had chosen his topic accordingly, to include notables in both fields. What freshman was going to play favorites among his professors?

I wanted to run my Kirsten-Einstein-Jenn theory by Bruce and took a chance that he was on a midnight movie break at the MAstar trailer. I called the company's land-line. The one that was not the Bat Phone.

"Miss your cell phone?" I asked, between nibbles of cheese and sips of warm chocolate.

"Nope. We're watching *The Hurt Locker*."

"Isn't that a little heavier than your usual fare? A bomb defuser who loves his job?"

"We're running down the list of Best War Movies of all time."

"What's next?"

"*MASH*."

"That's more like it," I said, knowing the MAstar crew usually liked a little humor with their battle stories. Who could blame them, since most of the pilots and flight nurses were either military veterans or retired firefighters whose own stories often hit the height of seriousness.

"What are you up to?" Bruce asked.

"Snacking." I crunched down noisily on a rice cracker to prove it.

"That's it?"

"Well, I do have a theory to run by you."

"Imagine my surprise."

"But it can wait till the movie's over."

"Nah, I know how it ends."

"Imagine my surprise."

"Touché."

I wondered if I should evaluate my tendency to get involved in circular repartee. Did it make me a shallow person? That was a meditation topic for another time.

I recited my story to Bruce, adding details I'd learned from Virgil about Ponytail and Einstein, the Warnocky cousins. He had some questions, as I'd hoped. There was nothing better than a thoroughly vetted theory.

"Once the tower opened, Einstein could have gone up anytime he wanted, and taken his cousin with him," Bruce said.

"I talked to Barker, remember? The Henley construction foreman in the smoking section outside HPD. He told me he has the only key card outside the Music Department. He lets the workers into the tower as needed."

"They could have smashed their way in at night," was Bruce's suggestion.

"You watch too many action movies. They couldn't very well leave a wreck in their wake and not attract attention. And if they couldn't find the money, they would have blown their chances. Or maybe they did go up once or twice and manage to get in quietly but—mission not accomplished. So they staked the tower out at night and saw Jenn go up."

"Why didn't they follow Jenn into the tower in real time and get the money on the spot?" Bruce asked.

"Same reason as above. It would attract attention, and what if it was a false lead and Jenn didn't know where the money was? Another blown chance," I said.

"Sounds like you've thought this through pretty well."

I gave a vigorous nod, though no one was around to witness it. "The question is, how did Einstein know that Jenn did find the stash on that particular trip last Thursday?"

"Wait, are you poking holes in your own theory now?" Bruce asked.

"I like to stay objective," I said, picking the last crumbs of cracker from the plate. I pulled an afghan over my legs and stuck another pillow behind me on the couch. This might be my bed for the next two-hour sleeping segment, I mused.

"I'm thinking that Einstein attacked Jenn and then killed Ponytail, which implies he was successful in getting the money finally, and didn't need Ponytail's help anymore," I said. "The fact that he took a chance attacking her means somehow he was sure she had the money in her backpack."

"Maybe he saw her go up into the tower that day and come down right away, no chance to practice," Bruce offered.

"Good thinking," I said. "Plus, there was that one bill

that fell out at the scene. Maybe there was another one, or more, before that."

"Like he saw her leave a trail of bills."

"Uh-huh. HPD still has the one I found, in their lab."

"So to speak."

"Meaning?" I asked.

"Their facility for forensics leaves a lot to be desired. It's very hard for small departments like Henley to get the resources for any kind of timely reporting, even on things as simple as fingerprints."

"You sound like Virgil. But I get it."

I made the mistake of giving in to a yawn and Bruce picked up on it.

"Are you near a bed?"

"Close enough," I said.

"Do me a huge favor and get some rest. The problems will all be there in the morning."

It sounded like something my mother would say. I didn't find it comforting when she said it either.

CHAPTER $\sqrt{20}$

I thought I'd earned a good night's sleep, overrated as it might be.

I'd done my part in creating a reasonable theory that tied up crimes spanning twenty-five years. Now if Jenn would continue to recover, and the HPD would simply bring in Einstein and make sure Wendy Carlson was safe, I could get on with my math classes and differential equations research, with puzzling, beading, and lots of quality time with Bruce on the side.

Surely that wasn't too much to ask.

After a quick check out the window to wave to my protectors in the unmarked car, I took a normal shower and changed into my usual winter nightwear. Feeling somewhat human, I slipped into the guest bed—tomorrow I'd restore my bedroom to its pre-intruder state—at a little before one o'clock in the morning, not even bothering to read before turning out the light and hitting the pillow.

* * *

Clang, clang. Clang, clang.

This time the alarm went off according to plan. After six solid hours of sleep, I was ready to face the day. If all went well, I'd soon know who'd been bombarding my email inbox with junk. My cyberlife would be pleasant again.

I grabbed a cup of coffee and toast and called it breakfast, eating at my counter, watching local news. There was no mention of the Henley campus, but the murder of one Gabriel Warnocky earned a few minutes of attention. The sight of his unpleasant expression and stringy ponytail brought a bitter taste to my mouth, and I added a spoonful of apricot marmalade to my toast.

"A career criminal," Ponytail was called, with no connection to the area. In other words, citizens of Henley should not be worried about this small blip in the city's crime stats. The implication was that Ponytail committed his crimes elsewhere, his body inconsiderately dumped in Henley. The upbeat news lady almost made me cheer.

Back in my bedroom, which still seemed unclean to me, I donned wool pants and three layers of upper wear. I was in as good a mood as possible, given the five to ten extra pounds of attire necessary to weather the outdoors. As I laced up my short black boots, unfashionable according to Ariana, I missed her and my sandals.

I drove along Henley Boulevard and turned into the southwest entrance to campus at eight fifteen, an hour later than my customary arrival time, but more rested than I'd been in several days.

Morty Dodd, one of the regular security staff, greeted me. "Morning, Professor Knowles. Lots of action here already today."

"Really?"

He pointed toward the fountain. "There's a bunch of cop cars over in back of Admin."

I felt my pulse quicken. *Not another incident.* I couldn't stand the idea of another crime or insult to me or my campus.

"What happened?" I asked, shutting my eyes for a moment, shielding myself against the answer.

"Dunno, but they drove in about an hour ago and they're still buzzing around back there. Us guards are the last to know."

"I'll see what I can find out," I said. I shifted to drive and rolled away toward the tennis court parking area. Once I passed the west wing of Admin, I was able to see two HPD cars between the fountain and the wing. Not exactly "a bunch of cop cars" as Morty had reported, and I didn't see cops "buzzing around" either, but the position of the vehicles directly at the rear entrance to the tower was ominous.

Until I thought of my conversation with Virgil. The HPD was here to search the tower for a stash of money. I wished I could have given back that extra hour of sleep and been here to greet them.

I parked quickly in the one available spot in what we considered the Ben Franklin lot, and walked back toward the action. I was glad for my extra layers of clothing this morning. Temperatures had plummeted, according to the weather lady on the morning news, and I felt every additional lost degree.

The wind and freezing air triggered a hope that the Franklin Hall heater was fixed by now, and not by Einstein. The thought of Harold Warnocky, aka Einstein, aka murderous fugitive from justice, skulking around our basement last week sent an extra chill through me. What if Judy, who'd reported seeing the "hunky guy," or one of the students had engaged him in conversation and he'd become agitated and had struck out at them in some way? He'd shot Ponytail—allegedly, I added, in deference to the letter of the law—so it was conceivable that he carried a gun on a regular basis.

I wondered if the HPD had searched the grounds for him. Maybe they'd find him in the tower. Which was where I was headed. Smart.

My eyes watered and my cheeks burned from the cold. I pulled one thickness of my knit scarf over my nose, leaving just enough of an opening to breathe, and continued on until I reached the yellow and black tape that warned of construction hazards. I figured our PR representatives convinced the cops that the message was just as effective in keeping people away. Another dose of crime scene tape so soon after the last one wouldn't be good for our image.

Since it was only a warning, not a "Keep Out—This Means You" sign, I slipped under the stiff plastic and walked as close as I could to the tower entrance, where a uniformed officer stood guard. Perhaps it was the stately shape of the tower that inspired him to stand as stiff as a royal guard, arms straight by his side, an imaginary rifle perched against his shoulder.

"Hey, good morning," I said to the tall, lean young man, as if I were reporting to work on the project. I tried to present a purposeful demeanor, someone with a right to proceed into the tower. A musician, perhaps, ready for an early morning practice session. Or the cleaning lady, hired to polish the enormous bells and dust the keyboard.

"Morning," the officer said, moving his body toward the center of the opening, the better to block it from my meager frame.

I looked past him—stopping only to read his name, Dillon—and at the yawning cave-like opening. I knew the main tower entrance was through the front of Admin, up the grand set of steps that led to the vestibule of the building, but off to the left. I guessed the cops had chosen to use this rear entrance to the tower rather than park their vehicles out front. I commended them for not appearing to commandeer the whole building, which faced Henley Boulevard, the wide commuters' thoroughfare.

"Is Detective Mitchell here yet, Officer Dillon?" I asked.

He looked at his watch. "Should be here any minute," he answered.

I tilted my head even farther to the side, past his shoulders, toward the sepulchral mouth of the tower entrance.

"Okay if I go in?" I asked, hoping he drew his own conclusion, that once Detective Mitchell arrived I'd be going in anyway.

"Hmm, uh," he said, relaxing his posture, frowning. Considering the reasonableness of my request, I hoped.

I shifted my weight from one foot to the other to emphasize how cold it was and how inhumane it would be to leave a lady outside in these hostile weather conditions. Especially since she clearly was here to meet the detective in charge. It wouldn't be good for Officer Dillon if he were reported as being uncooperative.

"I guess it would be okay," the accommodating officer said, stepping aside.

"Great, thanks," I said, and hurried by him before he could reconsider.

Once through the opening, I needed a good minute to adjust to the darkness. And to the sour, dank odor. It was going to take an enormous dose of air freshener to prepare this venue for concerts, no matter how much structural retrofitting had been done.

I remembered reading FAQ in memos distributed by the administration when the tower work started. One hundred seventy-six feet tall with a belfry at the top. I recalled phrases such as "a beautifully appointed lobby," "historical artifacts," and "newly refurbished practice rooms." Not that I could see any of that at the moment.

Andrew—along with Jenn, before her recent troubles—was excited about a complete schedule of concerts, six days a week when school was in session, and tours of four levels of the tower, which would include the Henley College Carillonist's (that would be Randy Stephens's) studio, and a carillon library.

Was I in the right tower? I couldn't connect any of the buzz and brightness of the memos and brochures with the hollow aboveground crypt, a monument to mustiness, that I'd wheedled my way into.

In the dark, I nearly tripped over the first step, only two or three inches off the stone floor. I braced myself, slamming my hands against the wall, and decided I'd have to throw away my gloves at the first opportunity.

Was the passageway this unpleasant when Wendy Carlson climbed the steps twenty-five years ago to play an instrument that gave out such beautiful sounds? When Kirsten Packard climbed them? Had it been in her plans that she'd never walk down them that last time?

The stone steps spiraled up, making it difficult to see past a couple of feet. I climbed farther, turning corner after corner, hoping a ray of light might seep through the thick, damp wall. I could hear nothing but a whooshing of the wind (*please—wind, and not bats' wings*) and an occasional tapping or rummaging sound.

If the two police cars had arrived fully loaded, there could be as many as seven officers upstairs, the eighth being my manipulable young friend who was stationed at the doorway, though not too effectively, as I could attest. For all practical purposes, I was surrounded by cops. Why did I feel completely alone and unsafe? I had probably climbed the equivalent of only one normal flight of stairs up from the guard and the sunlight. Still, I wouldn't have been surprised if I heard a loud clank and the turning of a giant key, locking me in the tower forever.

If I were going to turn back, now would be the time.

I forged ahead, rounded one more corner, and finally heard muffled voices. I considered yelling for help. Maybe one of the cops would come down and escort me the rest of the way. I was saved from embarrassment by a shaft of light through a window in what I guessed was the belfry. I climbed the steps leading to it, expecting eventually to see the practice room.

Creak, creak, creak.

I jumped at the sound of a door opening just behind me.

A voice, low and menacing, nearly knocked me off the step.

"I thought you'd never get here."

I turned to see Virgil. Did everyone expect me these days? From the BPL to the Henley College tower, I seemed to show up on a cue that I didn't know about.

I bent over to catch my breath.

"I'd have been here a lot earlier if I'd gotten the memo you distributed to all the badged officers in the HPD," I said.

"You did okay anyway. Didn't mean to scare you, by the way," he said. Unconvincing. My judgment was that he enjoyed my little gasp of fear ever so slightly.

"I walked right by this door. How did I miss it?" I asked him and myself.

"Maybe because it's the same color as the wall?" Virgil said, ushering me into a brightly lit room, the lobby described in the administrative memos and in the shiny brochures we approved at faculty senate meetings.

The room was warm enough for me to lower my scarf to a fashionable level around my neck. Although the temperature wasn't so comfortable that I could remove any layers of clothing, it was clearly okay for Virgil, who'd draped his coat over a chair. I was tempted to throw it over my shoulders, but with my knit hat and bulky jacket, I looked enough like a waif as it was.

I saw immediately that the room had two entrances. The normal one from the front tower entrance, at the top of the steps facing Henley Boulevard—the one Virgil had used—and the slimy back entry that I'd so wisely chosen. What I'd done was like climbing to the top of the Empire State Building, then realizing there was a bank of elevators.

The ordinary visitor here for a tour or a concert wouldn't—shouldn't—see the innards I'd just passed through. Why hadn't the guard sent me to the nice part of the tower? Maybe he thought I knew what I was doing. Wrong.

And which portals did Jenn use, entering and leaving? I wondered.

I followed Virgil into the lobby, also a museum of sorts. Wood and glass display cases in the center of the room housed yellowed pages of sheet music and black-and-white photographs of the original construction of the Administration Building, tower included, almost one hundred years ago. At one end of the rounded enclosure was a stained glass window depicting what looked like a gathering of gods and muses, perhaps those especially assigned to music. Upright cases against the wall held small instruments and parts of instruments with documentation I felt sure was interesting. A blowup of a schematic showed how the bells in the tower were connected to the keyboard by a system of wires, springs, and levers. The drawing looked like something Ted's physics students might have left behind in a Franklin Hall classroom. Fascinating, but for another time.

I looked at Virgil, big, quiet, and eminently straight-faced. I'd half expected him to toss me back down to the lanky Queen's guard at the mouth of the cave. Virgil and I were the only people in the room; I assumed the crew of officers was searching other floors. Virgil waited me out. I knew I couldn't win; I had to ask.

"Did you get it back?"

He dug in his pocket. "Your phone? Yup, here it is." He handed it to me. "Fully charged."

How could I not be grateful? "Thanks. Were they able to retrieve anything?" I paused a beat. "Would you tell me if you found Wendy?"

Virgil laughed. We were both in good humor for so early in the morning. "No, and maybe."

"Back to the money. Any clues?"

"None here and none on that bill you found in the bushes."

"It doesn't have some magic logo that says this bill was taken from XYZ bank, on such and such a date?"

"Nope. And that makes me think that the rest of the loot, if there is any more, will likewise be clean."

"That's disappointing," I said.

Virgil pointed to floors above us. "We haven't given up on finding anything yet. The guys are up there now, going slow, trying to be as careful as possible." He waved his hand around the newly polished room, floors and walls gleaming, not a speck of dust or a chip of wood in sight. "It'd be a shame to have to knock out what just got put up."

"I'll say," came from another voice. Foreman Pete Barker, the smoker, had walked in from the true, clean, and unscary entrance and come up behind me.

This morning Barker was dressed as expected. Unlike the natty clothes he'd worn to the police station, today's outfit comprised jeans and a down vest, accessorized with a bright orange hardhat that he carried. A fine dusting of plaster and a few paint stains on his thick shoes showed evidence of Barker's being a worker as well as a boss.

"You've done a great job," I said.

"Thanks. But, hey, if the uniforms mess it up, I wouldn't mind starting all over again here with another contract."

"That doesn't seem quite fair," I said, loyal to the college's budget office.

Barker shook his index finger at me and smiled. "But it wouldn't be my fault, would it?"

He moved on and I entertained a new thought. As foreman, Barker had the only key among the construction people. What if he'd already found the money, by chance? Or, what if he was one of the gang who met Kirsten and Wendy, Einstein and Ponytail, in the diner in the old days. I considered nicknames. "Smoky"? "Sharpy," for the way he dressed during off-hours? Or, one that would fit me also—"Shorty." Could Barker have killed Ponytail? Maybe he caught the rejected Ponytail where he shouldn't be and— Nah, for now I was sticking to my original theory and pinning it all on Einstein.

I realized that Virgil was talking to me. I abandoned thoughts of Barker, who'd moved on himself.

"Of course, the easiest thing would be if Jenn Marshall told us where she was getting the money," Virgil said. I hoped I hadn't missed something important.

"*If* she was getting money," I said.

I liked how careful I could be when the reputation of one of my students was at stake.

"Any chance that you can talk to Jenn again?" Virgil asked.

"If you can keep her parents at bay."

"I can call them in. There's always a form or two that can be dug up for them to fill out."

"So that's what all the forms are for."

"You didn't hear it from me," Virgil said.

"I'll be happy to give it a shot." I cleared my throat. "Before that, I have a couple of requests."

"You're bargaining with me? An officer of the law?"

"Not exactly."

"Shoot."

"I think we should get footage from the west entrance to the campus. There's a camera on the guardhouse between the library and Admin, the vehicle entrance. We don't know for sure that Jenn went to the tower after leaving Franklin Hall, but there's a high probability. If we get the footage for Thursday, it might show Jenn going to the tower right after our seminar that ended at noon. Then we might also see Einstein following her to the passage on the northeast side."

"Good idea."

"Also, we should get her bank records. If she's been taking cash from here, she can't be hiding it all under her mattress."

Unless she spent it all. I thought of Jenn's new backpack. I knew they could be pricey these days. I remembered Patty, her roommate, mentioning a couple of other new things. A laptop? A smartphone?

"All done," Virgil said.

"You already have her banking information?" I hoped my wording didn't sound too much like "You mean you thought of that, too?"

"Now and then we get it right."

"Then I should get another request. I asked for two."

Virgil gave out a loud guffaw, which echoed in the room, once again empty except for us.

I gathered that I'd pushed my luck far enough.

Just as well. I had to get to class. That was, after all, my primary job.

CHAPTER $\sqrt{21}$

As I finished my conversation with Virgil, Barker came back into the room and offered to take me on a tour of the upper floors of the tower.

"There's a great view from up there," he said. "You can see the whole city, down to the Cape, and Boston if you try really hard."

I didn't want to one-up Barker and tell him that I'd seen that view from much higher up. On one of our first dates, Bruce rented a helicopter and took me for a ride over Henley and surrounding cities. How to impress a girl.

Circling over the campus had been the most interesting—looking down on the complex architecture of Admin; marveling at the way the Nathaniel Hawthorne dorm seemed nestled within the other two, like a perfectly designed puzzle; swooping over the fall trees and the smooth, lush lawn. From the air, the campus seemed like a fortress that could withstand any storm. I hoped it would be none the worse for wear from the present crisis.

"And those big bronze bells, they're something else,"
Barker continued. "You gotta see them." He pointed
straight up, to the belfry. Without waiting for my response,
Barker went on, with great enthusiasm and arm waving.
"Fifty-three of them installed in that pretty cramped area,"
he said, shaking his head at the marvel.

I followed Barker's gestures to a beautifully finished
spiral stairway that led to the next level. The polished steps
and handrails seemed more suited to a home in an affluent
suburb than to a bell tower, especially considering my first
tower-climbing experience of a few minutes ago. I realized
also that to me, the Henley Tower, the belfry in particular,
had become the place where Kirsten Packard died. I wel-
comed the idea of replacing that association with something more uplifting.

It did seem odd that a man holding a hardhat was helping me with that.

"The new library is right below that," Barker said.
"There's music books—of course, right?—but there's also
pictures along one wall that show you how the bells are
cast in the foundry. Would you believe it takes a temperature of two thousand degrees?"

As cold as I'd been lately, I didn't think I'd mind working there.

"The bells, they're enormous," Barker continued,
spreading his arms to indicate enormity. "I'm telling you,
you could hide a person in that big one."

"Is that where the HPD officers are now? In the belfry?"
I asked, wondering why I hadn't seen a uniform since I left
my guard friend at the entrance.

I hesitated to mention "searching" in case Barker didn't
know the purpose of the current police activity. He might
guess that they were looking for something, but perhaps
not the specifics. Was it possible that Virgil was able to get
his cooperation, even identifying the workers on the video,

without telling the foreman the details of the investigation into a member of his crew?

"The cops aren't done yet, but the practice rooms are free. Didn't you ever wonder how they could practice on that big thing without the whole city hearing them?"

"As a matter of fact, I did," I said.

Barker placed his hardhat on the floor—and not on the glass case near him, I noticed. He leaned against the wall and crossed his ankles, thick with leather work boots. I had the feeling that he didn't have a lot of people to talk to on a regular basis. Or maybe he didn't want to waste the time of his workers in conversation. Whereas I was just a teacher with all the free time in the world. I figured I could be accommodating, since he'd probably need a cigarette break soon anyway. And I did want to know more about the carillon.

"Well, it turns out the practice keyboards have no bells; they just make their own sounds close enough to what the bells will sound like. The real bells won't be used until the tower's opened and the concerts start."

"Fascinating," I said, meaning it, but having a hard time imagining this burly construction worker caring about musical bells. If he was so open-minded, maybe I could interest him in mathematics.

I wished I had a better feel for where Barker stood in the investigation. Was he the helpful foreman he seemed to be, innocently involved in our exciting new construction, working with the police to provide information on his workers? Or was his enthusiasm due to having stumbled upon a cash treasure trove that he counted as his just deserts for years of hard work? There was also that earlier notion I'd entertained, that Barker, aka Smoky (in my mind only), had come back to Henley after twenty-five years, like Einstein and Ponytail, to claim the spoils of a robbery.

While I tossed the possibilities around in my mind, the

unsuspecting Barker talked on about his newfound love of all things carillon.

"Oh yeah, there's this other neat thing, too—on the anniversary of the Chernobyl disaster every year, carillon-ists all around the world play the same melodies. Like a memorial. Quite a thing."

"It sounds as though you've enjoyed this project," I said.

"Oh yeah. You gotta get up to the belfry sometime."

It was hard to refuse the opportunity, especially one that would take me close to cops on a mission, but a glance at my watch told me I had to leave for class. If Fran were around, I'd have been tempted to get her to sit in for me, since I wasn't the presenter anyway. But my teacher con-science won out over my tower curiosity. "I have a class in about ten minutes; otherwise I'd love to."

"Rain check?" he said, handing me his card.

"Sure."

Barker pointed an index-finger gun at me. "Okay, I'm going to hold you to it."

"Okay yourself," I said, and proceeded to bundle up again, now adding "flirting" to possible motives for Bark-er's interest in aspects of the tower that had nothing to do with construction.

Barker headed out through the nasty stairway. He called over his shoulder, "You know, maybe there's something to this going-to-college thing."

"We can always use more math majors," I responded.

Left alone, I had a choice of where to exit the tower. I could follow Barker, back down the spooky way I'd ascended, and end up closer to Ben Franklin Hall, with a straight shot to my classroom. Or I could exit through the decent stairway that Virgil had pointed out, the one that led to the front entrance of Admin. Less scary, but giving me a much longer walk on this below-freezing morning.

It didn't take too long to decide on the bright and airy route, ice notwithstanding. I rushed down the tower steps and came out on Henley Boulevard, then hurried down the outside steps and along the street, heavy with commuter traffic, to the vehicle entrance to the campus. Shivering all the way.

I thought it only right that I stop long enough to give our campus gatekeeper, Morty Dodd, a brief report on the intriguing police presence on our campus this morning. Morty seemed happy that I remembered my promise, which reminded me how easy it was to please some people.

"Sorry I have to rush," I said, doing my usual foot-stomping dance to keep circulation going. "But I have a class in a couple of minutes."

"Hold on, Professor Knowles," he said.

Morty picked up his cell phone and hit a contact number. "Jake, get over here, okay? We got a lady that needs a ride."

Before I could figure out what Morty was up to, I heard a rumbling sound. A motorcycle? A snowmobile? A yellow construction vehicle come to life? I turned to see what we all called the security golf cart. A low-riding four-wheeler, white with blue and gold racing stripes and the college seal, and a canvas canopy over the otherwise open frame. Better than full-body exposure.

I climbed in, and Jake whisked me away to the parking lot and deposited me next to my car, where I picked up my briefcase. He tipped his hat and drove off while I stood a moment and waved at him and Morty, who'd stepped out of his box to watch our journey.

I walked the few steps to the entrance to Franklin Hall, counting the blessings of my job.

Heat!

Franklin Hall was mercifully toasty this morning. A real maintenance person must have visited our building over the weekend, not the fake hunky guy who'd fooled

Judy Donohue in spite of her credentials as chair of the Biology Department. I dropped multiple layers of clothing and headed for the classroom, sans gloves, sans scarf, sans shivers.

Only two minutes late, I presided over a lackluster calculus class for the next fifty minutes, reviewing volume of revolution exercises and laying the groundwork for the next homework assignments. I promised that tomorrow's topic of problem-solving strategies would be both fascinating and useful to their lives as a whole.

"Like how to get a date?" one male student asked.

"You wish," said the female seated closest to him.

I passed on commenting, following one of my rules: *Whenever possible, let the students do the work for you.*

At the back of my mind the whole time was the real-life problem of the three women who dominated my life of late—Jenn Marshall, Kirsten Packard, and Wendy Carlson. How could the trio have consumed so much of my attention lately, when I'd known nothing about two of them until last week, and the third had given me no cause for concern for a year and a half?

I couldn't wait to visit Jenn in the hospital this afternoon. At the request of an HPD homicide detective, no less. I wished Virgil had issued me a temporary badge, in case Mr. and Mrs. Marshall or the large nurse who attended Jenn tried to interfere. I supposed I could make myself a fake document, perhaps call it a "certificate of civilian authority." Perhaps not. I'd have to make do with my erect posture and confident manner. *Lots of luck*, I said to myself.

My free hour was nearly as uninspiring as my calculus class. Both Judy Donohue and Ted Morrell were missing. There'd been one good outcome from the lack of heat last week—it had forced us all to the lounge and to close contact around the pots of boiling water on the hot plate. Now with our offices at normal temperatures, for the most part our routine would go back to chatting while we filled our mugs, then returning to desks in our private quarters. Which is what I did now.

It was just as well that Judy, a TMI kind of person, didn't show, since I wasn't sure I was ready to hear about her date with Virgil.

My email inbox was crammed with spam again, but I knew help was on the way via Andrew this afternoon. I wrote quick replies to the legitimate messages.

To Bruce:
So glad to hear you're off tonight. Better still, that you're going to cook for me! xoxoxoxox (smiley face emoticon).

To Ariana:
So sorry to hear about your latest date (sad face emoticon). *Will have your favorite gingerbread and vanilla ice cream to welcome you home* (smiley face emoticon).

To Fran:
So glad to hear about your newest student and her love of puzzles. Will send a package off soon (smiley face emoticon).

To several students:
So glad you're enjoying the history of math seminar (smiley face emoticon), or *So sorry you're finding calculus harder than you expected* (sad face emoticon).

Before heading out for the seminar room, now fit for human occupation, I needed a couple of relaxing minutes with a puzzle. I pulled out the metal pieces that had recently fallen out of my purse, clanking to the floor of the BPL at Wendy Carlson's feet. I sorted through the rings and curvy loops that made up three pocket puzzles and put them in piles on my desk. One puzzle was especially challenging, the size and shape of a napkin ring if I could ever complete it.

Tap, tap. "Ready for class, Dr. Knowles?"

Andrew Davies at my door. Saved from another fruitless (but relaxing) attempt to complete the puzzle.

"Are you still up for checking out my email problem?" I asked as we walked down the hall.

"Can't wait," he said.

"Neither can I."

"I know I'll crack it."

I liked his spirit.

Brent Riggs was front and center for the presentation today. The subjects: the Bernoulli family—the brothers Jacob and Johann, and Johann's son, Daniel. A politically correct choice on the part of an astute freshman who knew he was being subtly recruited by both Ted and me for our respective departments. Jacob and Johann were known for important contributions to math; Daniel was a noted physicist. Brent was leaving all his options open.

Brent and the Swiss Bernoulli family were the reasons I wasn't surprised to see Ted in attendance today, already seated in the circle of chairs. I took a seat next to him and found myself once again, as with the security footage viewing, sitting between Professor Ted and Student Andrew.

"What a family," Brent began, explaining that there were several other Bernoulli offspring who were also noted mathematicians and scientists.

Brent began with the intriguing enmity between the brothers. He talked about the professional jealousy and personality differences that marked their relationship. At least one didn't murder the other, I mused, unable to brush off nagging thoughts of the Warnocky cousins, Harold and Gabriel.

"I did a lot of reading and I think it was Johann's fault," Brent said. "He didn't get along with his own son, Daniel, either."

And thus a more than three-hundred-year-old mystery was solved by a Henley freshman. I looked over and caught Ted's eye. I felt we were both asking, which lucky department will claim him? A humorous moment in the little competition in Franklin Hall.

The dynamic between the Mathematics Department and the Physics Department wasn't exactly adversarial, but there was always a little tug of war for students who showed interest in both. Math and physics were closely related, often interchangeable in subject matter. The two disciplines attracted students with similar habits and styles of thinking, distinctly different from the mental requirements of biology and chemistry.

Everyone in Franklin Hall, including the seminar students, was aware of the friendly competition.

When Brent walked us through the (Daniel) Bernoulli principle and its applications to thermodynamics, Ted clapped loudly. When our young seminar leader talked about the (Johann) Bernoulli rule to evaluate limits or the (Jacob) Bernoulli sequence of rational numbers, I clapped as hard as I could.

The students clapped and laughed with us equally.

Brent, probably having the best time of all, asked for a short break to set up a demonstration.

Most of us remained in the room since the classrooms were slightly warmer than the hallways. I also felt that some of the students were afraid the heat might go off at any moment and chose to soak up the Btu's while they were available. Who could blame them?

I hadn't noticed the entrance of Lauren Hughes, the sociology major who'd have majored in math if she had a different head. She came up now and knelt in front of the three of us—Ted, me, Andrew.

"This is so cool," she said. She looked at me and offered a defense of her presence. "I came to hear Brent. We're sort of together. He said it would be okay?"

"Absolutely," I said. "We're glad to have you."

Lauren thanked me and glanced at Andrew, but still addressing me, said, "Andrew says he's going to help you with an email problem?"

Uh-oh, I thought.

"Oh?" Ted asked.

I'd hoped Andrew would have kept my request confidential, though I hadn't explicitly asked him to. I shouldn't have been surprised. Students talked. (Didn't we all?) And Andrew was a dramatic sort who'd want to make the most of his professor's special request for his talents.

I looked at Ted, who was giving me a questioning look. I hadn't wanted to hurt his feelings. He'd always been the go-to guy for Franklin Hall computer problems but, first, he'd been grumpy lately, and second, I wasn't sure this kind of job, which required an understanding of hacking, was within his skill set.

I mumbled something to Lauren about how nice Andrew had been to offer his assistance, hoping Ted would interpret the comment to mean it wasn't my idea. Then I mumbled something to Ted about how busy he'd seemed lately.

What a wimp I was when it came to situations like this. How was I going to handle the challenge of talking to Jenn this afternoon?

Brent called us to attention for demonstrations of Bernoulli's principle of air flow. First up: He deftly opened the sides of an envelope by blowing over an open edge. We clapped. Next, he held the short end of an eight-and-a-half-by-eleven piece of paper to his lips, blew across the surface, and—*ta da* (he would have said if his mouth weren't otherwise engaged)—the whole sheet rose and floated on the air. We clapped again as the sheet of paper flapped in the breeze until Brent ran out of breath.

"Fluid mechanics," Ted said, the way an ordinary person might say, "Good show."

Brent used his laptop to show a video with other marvels of physical motion like the boomerang and the curve ball.

I waited for the math.

I listened with mild interest to Brent's discussion of applications of the Bernoulli principle to the wings of airplanes and perked up when he showed a small ball could be held in place in the interior of an upside-down funnel.

Our knowledgeable presenter, who seemed to sense my "Where's the math?" question, admitted to all that he couldn't quite handle the equations that would describe the demonstrations he'd shown.

"All the more reason to major in math," Andrew said. More points for Andrew, erasing the bad marks I'd given him earlier for spreading the news of my email problem.

When the seminar ended and we got up to leave, I couldn't resist a little teasing. "Will we see you here tomorrow, too, Ted?" I asked. "The subject is Pierre de Fermat."

He laughed. At least he wasn't irreparably ticked off at me for choosing another fixer for my computer. "I don't think so. Fermat's too pure a mathematician for me. But I'll be back later in the week when Monica talks about Caroline Herschel." He turned to Monica, who was gathering her belongings. "As long as you promise not to whine about how she did all the work and her brother got credit for it," he said.

"I won't have to, Dr. Morrell. Caroline did her own calculations of the positions of heavenly bodies. And she discovered eight comets all by herself."

Ted tipped an imaginary hat to Monica. So did I.

By the time I finished settling a few matters for individual students—Can I have an extension on Wednesday's homework? How many references do I need for the Intersession paper? Did you read my seminar proposal yet?—Andrew was waiting outside my office. He sat on the floor cross-legged, his back against the locked door, his laptop open, supported by his knees.

I thought he might be studying a hacking manual, but as I got closer I heard carillon bells. Andrew was listening to a carillon and choir concert from France.

"I didn't want to play it too loud," he said. "But isn't it awesome?"

"Awesome," I said.

Clicking away, Andrew found an audio file of "God Save the Queen" played by a carillonist at the Peace Tower in Ottawa.

"Sometimes I think I should have majored in music," he said, smiling.

"Bite your tongue," I said, smiling back.

I leaned against the wall, but upright, grown-up style, and watched Andrew's laptop screen as he tuned in on different videos. A young woman in a dark blue hoodie played movie themes at a carillon on a Midwest campus; an old man in suspenders played rousing hymns at a church in Belgium. Before I knew it, students from my seminar and other classes in the building had gathered around and Andrew raised the volume.

It might have been fewer than ten minutes, but as we made brief virtual visits to carillons in England, Poland, France, and universities across the United States, we were united in the special way that comes from sharing music.

I resolved to find a way to have more carillon music in my life.

In my office, I showed Andrew my little email problem. In the last hour, while I'd been at the seminar and then at the impromptu concert, about fifty ads had popped into my inbox.

Andrew scratched his head. "I don't know, Dr. Knowles, this looks tough."

My shoulders sagged. Until I caught the gleam in Andrew's eyes and knew he'd already aced the job in his mind.

Andrew grinned. "Kidding. It'll be done this afternoon, but"—he put his hand on his stomach—"do you mind if I run over to the Mortarboard first and grab a sandwich?"

I hadn't noticed the time. Growing boys and all. Plus hungry professors. "Great idea," I said. I dug in my purse and came up with money for a gourmet campus lunch for two. "Would you mind picking up a turkey and Swiss for me?"

"No problem."

Andrew had to be talked into taking the money, but I told him it was worth a lot more than lunch from the Mortarboard for me to be able to stay warm inside for another little while.

Andrew went off to take care of room service, and I decided to find more carillon music while he was gone. I clicked away on his laptop, going into his browser history.

Instead of clicking on the music files, I was drawn to a link to the installation of the world's largest bourdon, in the bell tower of the Riverside Church in New York City. I remembered seeing a photo of that particular bell in the Music Department hallway. This website showed the bell, weighing more than twenty tons, being hoisted onto a boat for its trip from a foundry in England in the early part of the twentieth century. With its more than ten-foot diameter, the bell towered, in a manner of speaking, over the men tugging on the ropes.

A clip of the foundry showed the steps involved in casting the bell. A frame appeared that showed the bell tipped on its side by a system of chains and pulleys, to give the foundry workers access to the inside surface. I remembered Pete Barker's attempt to sell me on a tour of our tower.

"You could hide a person in that big one," he'd said.

Or a load of money, I thought.

CHAPTER $\sqrt{22}$

It was a *duh* moment. I knew the police had searched places in the carillon tower where the robbers of twenty-five years ago might have hidden their spoils. Behind bricks, under floorboards, in the niches of dark stairways. But the real question was, where would a student, one who happened upon the money in the present day, hide it?

In a place that no construction worker would need to go, and no visitor would appear until the tower officially reopened—by which time, little by little, the money would have been "withdrawn," as from a bank, and spent, or otherwise appropriated.

Inside a bell.

I grabbed my phone, left my office, and walked to the southernmost end of the building where the windows faced the fountain and the back of Admin. On the way, I punched in Virgil's number on my smartphone.

No police cars on campus. No answer on Virgil's cell. I was left with no official outlet for my brilliant thought. Or, not so brilliant, given my track record in this case. Virgil had been a step or two ahead of me all along. I should have been pleased; wasn't that what my taxes were for? He was doing his job; I had my own. I had equations to solve. Puzzles to create.

Either the police had found the money or they'd given up and left campus. I called Virgil's number again. This wasn't exactly a nine-one-one emergency. I could simply leave him a message. Saying what? *I found the money.* Not really true. *Come back to the tower. I know where it is.* Risky. A waste of taxpayers' money, unless I could figure a way to use only my contribution to the city's coffers, especially if I turned out to be wrong.

I could always go up in the tower myself. Why not be sure before I caused a fuss?

My new plan, formulated as I walked back to my office, was to eat lunch, find money in tower, go to hospital to see Jenn, have dinner with Bruce. As I was cementing the plan in my head, item number one, lunch, had arrived.

Andrew agreed to a working lunch since we both had projects we were eager to get to. He held something that smelled spicy with one hand and pecked away on my laptop keyboard with the other. I bit into my turkey and Swiss between texts and phone calls, attempting to raise people who could help me out with access to the tower: Virgil, who should be on duty twenty-four-seven for me, if not for the entire city of Henley; Pete Barker, who'd given me his business card but clearly wasn't conscientious about answering his phone (though I realized he had a real, full-time job); and Randy Stephens, our music chair, who was probably the least culpable of all, with no reasonable way of knowing that I'd need him. Any one of them could help me gain access to the tower. It seemed they'd all decided to take a real lunch hour.

"What are the chances that the tower would be unlocked in the middle of the day?" I asked Andrew.

"Zero. Dr. Stephens runs a very tight ship. I can run over to his office and sign out a key card if you want."

I considered Andrew's request, which, it seemed to me, would loosen Randy Stephens's tight ship. "Thanks, but I think I'll head over to the hospital first and talk to Jenn. If no one gets back to me by the time I return, I'll ask you to let me in then."

My unspoken hope was that Jenn would tell me if my guess about the location of the robbery money was correct, or if not, where it was. She'd had a lot of time to reflect on what she'd done and should be ready to share. It was time for tough love. Too bad I wasn't medically or psychologically qualified to make that pronouncement.

"I wonder when they'll let us see her," Andrew said. His emphasis on *us*, that is, mere students, caused a twinge of guilt to attack me, but there was nothing I could do about the rules. Or the Marshalls. "You'd think they'd at least let her roommate see her, but not even Patty can get in," Andrew continued. "I understand, though. Will you tell her we're all still thinking of her and hope she comes back soon?"

"She'll be glad to hear it," I said, as I bundled up for the brief trip from Franklin Hall to my car. Another round of snow flurries was due today, though last night's deposit was mercifully short-lived and picayune.

I left the building feeling good. Andrew the Hacker, or Unhacker, was at work on my laptop, and I had a police-authorized mission to talk to Jenn. By later this afternoon, Andrew would have solved one thing that had been nagging at me. And though the small violation of my privacy was insignificant compared to the major crimes of the last few days, checking that one off would go a long way to bringing me a measure of satisfaction.

After a few minutes of bone-chilling, serious clearing of my windshield, I drove toward the campus exit. I slowed down as I passed the carillon tower, giving one last thought to attempting to enter now. Too low a probability of success, I decided, and off-the-charts cold out there. I pushed the temperature lever on my heater to Hi, waved to Morty, and drove onto Henley Boulevard toward the hospital.

With any luck, Virgil would have arranged for Mr. and Mrs. Marshall to be otherwise occupied while I had a serious conversation with their daughter. I sighed, realizing there was probably nothing he could do about Jenn's large, overprotective nurse.

I stopped to buy flowers at Henley General's gift shop then made my way along a too-familiar path to Jenn's room. I unwrapped my scarf and stuffed my gloves into my pockets as I walked, switching the pink and red bouquet from one hand to the other as I rearranged my clothing. I sniffed the air and wished I could plan my visits to avoid food carts, coming or going.

I arrived in time to see an orderly stripping Jenn's bed. The young man pulled a top sheet off the mattress and dumped it into a hamper on wheels. He bent over and loosened the bottom sheet and did the same, then reached for the pillow.

My heart raced. How could Jenn have gone from waking up and recovering, to . . . I couldn't say, or even think the first word that comes to mind at the sight of an empty hospital bed. Instead I switched to happy thoughts—Jenn was so much better, she'd been moved to the wing for nearly recovered patients.

"Excuse me," I said, squeaking out the words as if I had a bad winter cold. "I'm looking for Jenn Marshall?"

The orderly, a tall guy who could have passed for fifteen years old, shrugged his shoulders and pointed down the hall in the direction I'd come from. "You'll have to ask them."

I hurried back and addressed my question to the very busy crew behind the desk.

"She's been discharged," said a woman with a headset. Surely she was talking to the person on the phone and not to me.

"Jennifer Marshall," I repeated when I had her attention.

"She's been discharged," she said, more slowly, looking me straight in the eyes.

I was flustered to the point of asking a silly question. "Where did she go?"

Just in time, the large nurse I'd interacted with on my first visit to Jenn entered the workstation. "She's been discharged," I heard again.

"I just saw her last night. I didn't think she'd be ready to leave so soon." Not to mention that the police haven't gotten all they wanted from her.

"Her parents took her about an hour ago," a different nurse, nicer, told me.

"Do the police know she's gone?" I asked whoever was listening.

"Not our problem," one of them said.

Thanks, I knew that. Flowers in hand, I stood in front of the desk, a wall, really, with its busy worker bees behind it, and recognized that I'd get nothing more from the staff.

I laid the bouquet on the high counter. "Here," I said. "Please pass these on to a patient who might like them." I strode off before they could refuse me that small service.

I made my way to the hospital cafeteria, not for the quality of the coffee, but because the place was warm and I needed to make some phone calls.

A nasty image made its way into my head as I pictured Jenn making a stop at the bank on her way out of town.

It was a good thing I'd had lunch, since the offerings in the cafeteria were slim and unappetizing. I bought a mug of tea, which was harder to ruin, and carried it to a table in a corner. The cafeteria was so crowded that the cleanup people couldn't keep up, so I helped out by clearing my table of several large drink cups and a pile of napkins. I used a hand wipe to finish the job and took a seat, my back against the pale yellow wall.

Happy to have my phone back, and charged, I checked my messages and listened to a voice mail from Randy Stephens. He wasn't planning to go to campus today, he said. He'd taken a long weekend at the Cape. Lucky Randy. Even in winter, the Cape was a haven of both natural and shopkeeper-made beauty.

"I can come if it's urgent," he'd added.

Not exactly. I'd had second thoughts about asking Randy in the first place. Did I really want anyone other than the cops with me when I pulled the money out of the bell?

I had the same question about Pete Barker, who hadn't responded yet to my message. Rather than have him give me the tour he was so hot to give me, I'd prefer to wrangle a key from him and make the trip up to the belfry myself.

I supposed I could trust both of them to use discretion, but I had no idea how much either of them knew about the money or the past.

I sipped my tea, trying to let the bland aroma supersede that of the over-garlicky soups and pastas at tables all around me.

A call to Virgil worked this time.

"Did you know Jenn Marshall was released from the hospital?" I asked.

"I just found out. Did you get a chance to talk to her first?"

"I just missed her."

"Too bad. But we couldn't keep her. She claimed not to know her attacker and she didn't commit a crime. Her bank records are clean, by the way. The recent deposits are consistent with her pay from the college."

"She was so close to telling me more," I said, regretting that I'd lolled around listening to carillon music in the Ben

Franklin hallway and even had lunch in my office instead of heading straight for the hospital after my seminar. I consoled myself by noting how unlikely it was that I'd have been able to fend off Mr. and Mrs. Marshall if they were determined to take their daughter home to safety. I wondered if we would ever see Jenn again.

"Maybe yes, maybe no," Virgil said, referring, I realized, to my statement that Jenn had been on the verge of telling me more.

"What about her dorm room?" I asked, ruing the fact that Jenn was now on my list of suspicious characters whose life had to be dug into for evidence of a crime.

"Clean," Virgil said. "We got permission to look around from Patricia Reynolds, her roommate, who said Jenn never even went back to get her belongings. Her clothes and books are still there." I heard Virgil flipping through pages of a notebook. Or else I imagined it from seeing him do it too many times in person. "And speaking of striking out, the address that Warnocky—the one you call Einstein—gave to his boss is bogus. It's a vacant lot by the airfield."

"So there's no lead on Ponytail's killer?"

"Alleged killer. In any case, I doubt we'll ever see the guy again."

"Right."

A feeling of hopelessness took over my spirit and flooded my mind. Wendy Carlson was gone. Ponytail was dead. Jenn Marshall was gone. And now Mr. Einstein Warnocky had also eluded our grasp. I couldn't have felt worse if puzzle pieces kept falling into cracks in the floor, leaving gaping holes in the picture I was trying to put together.

Virgil echoed my thoughts. "We're hitting a wall. I'm not sure there's any hope now for finding the money either."

I perked up, remembering why I'd called Virgil in the first place. "I think I know where the money is," I said.

"Of course you do."

"Can you meet me at the tower later today?"

"I'm going into a meeting. I'll call when I get out."

"Bring your badge," I said. "Or whatever it takes to get a key card."

I almost ended with "How's Judy?" but thought better of it.

Instead, I called Bruce next and asked him if he knew anything about the now legendary date between his buddy and mine.

"I didn't think you liked gossip," he said.

"This isn't gossip."

Bruce laughed.

I waited while a sudden burst of loud laughter, appropriately timed, erupted from a table close to mine. It looked like an office party, with wrapped presents at one end of the table. A strange choice of venue, I thought, but who was I to talk?

"I'm simply interested in my friends' welfare," I told Bruce. "Both of them. So, have you heard anything from your buddy?"

"My friend's not talking," Bruce said.

"Mine either."

And we both laughed. The hospital cafeteria had become a happy place.

We moved on to dinner plans. I longed to do something normal and shop for food. A selection of cheeses, veggies, bread, and cookies sounded good. Nothing that involved a hospital, a police station, a barricaded hotel room, or an unfinished tower; no computer problems or home break-ins; no funny nicknames, injured students, or former students; no missing librarians.

"I was thinking pasta primavera," Bruce said. "Penne, broccoli, zucchini, carrots."

"Perfect," I said.

"Okra."

"Eeuw," I said and clicked off.

I took a last sip of tea from my mug and grabbed my jacket, ready to take off for campus.

I stopped when I heard "Hey, Dr. Knowles."

Andrew the Hacker rushed toward my table.

"I didn't expect you here," I said.

"Jenn's gone." Andrew looked crestfallen.

I nodded. "I was too late, too," I said. "But she's on her way home. That's the good news." In other words, we could be mourning her death.

"Yeah, I guess that's good. I texted Willa, Brent, and the others. They're all upset that she didn't even say good-bye."

"It might be a while before we figure out what's happened," I said, preparing myself for that truth at the same time. "Jenn probably needs some time. It's not just physical recovery that matters now."

Andrew heaved a heavy sigh. "Yeah, I guess you're right."

"How did you know I was in the cafeteria?"

"The nice ladies at the desk told me you were headed this way." It was good to know the ladies' type—cute young guys. "Anyway, I really came to tell you that I fixed it so you won't be getting that spam."

"That was fast," I said, unsure why Andrew had made the trip here to tell me in person.

"Stopping the spam was easy. I started to dig around and I found out who did it."

"Someone did it? I mean, of course, *someone* did it, but you mean you could tell exactly who?"

"Not always, but this guy wasn't that good."

"Okay. But you didn't have to come all this way to tell me."

"I couldn't tell you over the phone. The person is . . . You're not going to believe what I found."

"What is it?" I asked. I didn't need another blow to my psyche.

I'd expected Andrew to come up with a string of numbers as the source, or a code that he could use to filter out future spam. Not a person, not someone he knew, apparently. I took a deep breath. Was Einstein stalking my email? No, Andrew didn't know Einstein.

"I mean, seriously, Dr. Knowles. You're not going to believe me."

Dramatic Andrew. "Tell me."

"It's too . . . it's too . . . too crazy."

Andrew showed no signs of giving up his results.

"Tell me, Andrew," I said, more harshly than I meant to. He flinched. "Dr. Morrell did it."

My turn to flinch. Ted? What could Ted have to do with my email? "Are you joking, Andrew? Did Dr. Morrell take away some credit on your lab report again and you're getting even?"

He held up his hand, scout's honor style, his boyish features emphasizing the sincerity of his words. "Dr. Knowles, I'm not joking." He reached into his backpack and extracted several pages of printout.

I dropped my jacket on one chair and sat down on another. Andrew stayed standing. How could this be? Maybe Andrew himself hacked my email. He had all the skills not only to hack into my computer but also to pin it on someone else. Except why would he choose Ted as his victim? Why not another student, which I'd have been more likely to accept without question? He could even have blamed the meter maid who patrolled downtown Henley.

I was getting so far off-track that I was accusing anyone of anything willy-nilly—from thinking Pete Barker was part of the old gang to now thinking it was Andrew who'd set out to make my life miserable with spam. Who was next? Morty Dodd, our gatekeeper, as a bank robber? Woody, our trusty Franklin Hall janitor, mugging Jenn? Maybe Virgil and Judy weren't dating at all, but entering into a conspiracy to drive me crazy.

I'd lost control.

"I've been through this, like, eighteen different ways,"

Andrew said, smoothing out the printouts, his expression becoming more and more somber. "I can show you exactly how I traced it."

"Not now," I said.

"Maybe Dr. Morrell is playing a joke on you?"

I shook my head. "He doesn't joke like that." Riddles and brainteasers, yes, but pranks that caused real inconvenience? No. I thought a minute. "Andrew, could Dr. Morrell also have sent emails claiming to be someone else?" Someone like a copyeditor.

"Absolutely. You can use a Unix command and it's, like, no problem to impersonate someone else, so it looks like it came from anywhere you want."

"And using someone's credit card information."

"Do you ever shop online?"

Only about eight times a day. "Yes, I do."

Andrew shrugged his shoulders, as if to say, "There's your answer."

He pointed to the printouts again. "I can show you—"

"Andrew, I need a minute."

To his credit, Andrew caught on immediately. "Sure. I'm going to grab a coffee." He looked at my empty mug, a soggy, shriveled tea bag hanging from its rim. "I'll bring you another tea. And how about a cookie?"

"Thanks," I said.

I doubted that would do it, but it would be a start.

CHAPTER $\sqrt{23}$

I was grateful for Andrew's sensitivity in giving me time to digest the new information. Henley General's busy cafeteria wouldn't have been my first choice of meditation site, but I felt my legs wouldn't carry me out the door until I put things in some kind of order in my mind.

Ted Morrell, mild-mannered chair of the Physics Department and my colleague in Ben Franklin Hall for fifteen years, had hacked into my computer and sent me down three separate paths of annoyance and concern. That I knew of. What else had he inflicted on me that I was unaware of or blamed on others?

I put my elbows on the table, my head in my hands, and breathed deeply. A picture formed that began to make sense. Ted was certainly computer savvy enough to send me phony emails. In other words, he had the *means*, the first element in *means, motive, and opportunity*, the familiar summation of criteria for developing suspects in criminal cases. Ted also had *opportunity*, though I wasn't sure he'd even need physical access to accomplish the job; he'd asked to use my computer the day the group of students and faculty were at my home, the first day Jenn was in the hospital. He'd claimed that his laptop battery was dead and I'd nonchalantly sent him down to my home office, with instructions on the use of my equipment.

Motive was another story. Why would Ted annoy me with spam copyedits, fill my email inbox with junk, and steal my credit card ID? It was clear that whoever had hounded me hadn't meant to wipe me out; he'd wreaked just enough havoc to keep me busy and distracted. I thought back to my spam email and the ads I'd received. For eyeglass repair—check, Ted wore glasses. For golf clubs—check, Ted played golf. For chess software—check, and ditto. For pets—I wasn't sure about this one, but it didn't necessarily matter. He could have chosen a few ads at random.

I remembered something Ted had said in the lounge when I complained about my annoying copyeditor and the spam ads. He'd commented on how I might have to drop the investigation, meaning, at the time, my curiosity about Kirsten Packard's fall from the tower. Was that Ted's motive? To distract me? Was this just another aspect of the big cover-up of twenty-five years ago? Maybe that cover-up wasn't for the sake of Kirsten's father, the DA, after all, but for Ted himself, in the middle of a promising career. Ted would have been in his early forties, the right age to be seeking tenure at the college.

Great. Now I had Ted throwing Kirsten off the tower and asking Wendy to help him out by not telling the police anything that would instigate an investigation. I wished now that I'd confronted Ted earlier, asked him why he lied to me about knowing Kirsten Packard and her family. It was a long way from the "I might have met her once or twice" that he admitted, to "Her father was my roommate and best friend in college."

I was about to accuse Ted of the crime of B&E, breaking into my house, to add to my level of distress. But I couldn't imagine his doing that. That would connect him to the money in the tower, and, in turn, to the attack on Jenn.

I had to draw the line somewhere.

Just in time, I noticed Andrew hovering a few tables away, giving me space. I waved him over.

"Thanks," I said, meaning for the space and for the fresh mug of tea. I didn't think I could handle a hospital cookie, however. I put it in my purse and told him I'd enjoy it later. Not likely.

Andrew put his coffee on the table and took a seat. "I'm really sorry, Dr. Knowles. I'm still kind of, like, shocked. I can go over it again, or I can get my friend Doug back in Berkeley to look at it. I didn't want to get anyone else involved without asking you first."

Good choice. "It's okay, Andrew."

"Do you still need a tower key?"

"I'm all set. Detective Mitchell is going to meet me there."

"The cop Dr. Donohue is going out with?"

I laughed, enjoying the release it brought. Judy would be happy to be part of campus gossip so quickly, I thought. Virgil, not so much.

As for me, I was ready to take on a physicist.

Andrew and I headed to the parking lot together, then parted ways. I hinted that he should keep our little project confidential and told him I owed him one—at least one.

He zipped his lips, then unzipped them to say something about being glad to help.

I drove toward campus, having decided that it was better to approach Ted in person, with no warning like a phone call or a voice mail message. I did also consider getting

Andrew's help to spam him two hundredfold, but that would be mean, and not very useful in the long run.

I pulled into the entrance on Henley Boulevard and surveyed the parking lot. Ted's car was one of the few faculty vehicles still on campus. I remembered that he had an afternoon lab on Mondays from two to four; it should be breaking up any minute. I'd give him a little time to wrap up the session, then barge into his office.

In the meantime, as luck would have it, I saw another opportunity—Pete Barker talking to a couple of workers. Shouting at them, would be more accurate. Ted wasn't going anywhere. I could talk to him whenever. Now would be the time to get into the tower. I checked my smartphone one more time to see if Virgil had reported in after his meeting. Nothing yet.

I lowered my window and waved at Barker. He waved back and held up his hand to indicate that I should wait for him. No problem. I wedged my car into a small spot near the library, grabbed my purse, and walked toward the fountain. The sun was low in the sky, soon to disappear and leave us even colder.

Barker yelled a command or two and the men walked off toward the diminishing fleet of industrial vehicles by the east wing of Admin. Dismissed, I guessed, by Barker's orders. Barker was barking orders, I mused. Funny.

Then not so funny. I stopped in my tracks. My mind flew back to my visit with Wendy and her story about long-ago days with Kirsten and her pals in the diner. The nicknames of the men Kirsten pressed her into meeting came back to me. Ponytail, because he had one. Einstein, because he was smart. And a third guy who split from the group. I gulped. Big Dog. Not Smoky, a name I'd made up when I'd briefly considered that Barker, the smoker, might be involved. Not an imaginary Smoky, but Big Dog. Einstein's competition for the role of leader. Big Dog, because, as Wendy had said, he was always barking orders.

Coincidence? I thought not. Hard as it was to grasp, the three men in Kirsten's and Wendy's life had all been circling the money in the tower for twenty-five years. The Warnocky cousins roamed New England furthering their career in crime until the tower was reopened. Big Dog had obviously made a career change to construction, keeping clean, but staying close to ground zero.

But Barker had been in the best position to grab the money for many months. He must have charged up to the tower in the middle of the night every chance he got, as Bruce had suggested Einstein and Ponytail might do. Who knew how many times he'd searched, to no avail. Now that his job—and his possession of a key card—were coming to an end, he was desperate. And thanks to the urgent message I left on his phone, he figured out that I knew where it was.

Barker's interest in music and smooth talk wasn't his way of flirting at all; it was an interview, to see if I knew more than he did.

Was it Barker, not Einstein, who attacked Jenn for her key? Which one killed Ponytail? It was pretty clear that he'd sent the police on a wild-goose chase to a vacant lot they thought was Einstein's address.

Shivering, I woke up to the present and realized that Barker was closing the gap between us. My car was behind me. I turned to gauge the distance to my car, and Barker moved faster.

"Sophie," he said. "You've come to take me up on my offer of a tour of the tower." He pointed to the sky. "A perfect time of day to see the city lights."

Before I could react, he was upon me, taking my arm, steering me to the nasty entrance to the tower. "I got your message. Let's take a walk."

I felt a hard object poking my left side. I was sure it wasn't a carillon dowel. My purse hung from my right shoulder. I couldn't figure a way to reach my phone or anything else in the purse that I could use to defend myself. If I screamed or tried to break away and run, I'd be dead, but Barker would be caught. Would he take that chance? Would I?

The campus was nearly deserted. The only people in sight were Barker's own men, packing up at the far end of Admin. For all I knew they were in on it, waiting for their cut. The administrators in the offices far above me weren't likely to be looking out their windows. In fact, they'd be packing up to go home soon, too.

"This isn't a good time," I said. Playing it cool. Maybe it wasn't a gun prodding me along. Maybe Barker didn't know I had a good guess about the money. And maybe three hundred and thirteen wasn't a prime number.

Barker—Big Dog—squeezed my arm harder. "You're wrong," he said. "It's the perfect time. I've waited many years for this moment. And you're going to take me to what's mine."

"I'm not sure where it is," I said. No use pretending I didn't know what he was talking about.

"But you have a pretty good idea, I know, or you wouldn't all of a sudden want to go up to the tower. I watched those cops come down empty-handed. But you're a smart one. I don't know how, but you figured it out. And now we're going to get it."

He pulled me along, seeming to push the gun farther into my ribs with each step. "Move. I don't have time to waste."

Barker used his key card to enter and pushed me ahead of him into the cavernous tower entrance. We climbed the steps more slowly than Barker wanted, I knew. I pretended to be winded, clumsy, tired, anything to avoid ending up in the belfry. Ending up like Kirsten Packard.

"Did you kill Kirsten because she wouldn't tell you where she hid the money?" If nothing else, I'd die smart.

"I don't know who did that," he said. "I wouldn't have been so stupid. I'd have gotten the money first."

Like now. I felt a symphony of shivers, from my toes to my head.

"And Ponytail?" I asked, a touch of sadness in my voice, as if the smarmy-looking man had been a friend.

"He had to go. But I didn't do that either. Ponytail was a stupid, stupid man. He attacks the girl at lunchtime with guys all over the place. He told me he didn't think she'd put up a fight. He saw her come down from the tower and head for the bank, so he decided on the brilliant play of stealing her backpack in broad daylight." Barker paused, then shouted, his voice echoing down the dark, dank stairwell. "Which had all of two hundred dollars and change."

I wondered if I should feel bad that Jenn's backpack hadn't been full to the brim with hundreds like the one I'd found in the bushes. If it had been—in other words, if Jenn had been greedy—I wouldn't be on my last outing.

We'd reached the lobby floor and entered the museum area. After the near blackness and cold of the stairway, the brightness and warmth of the room was startling. I saw Barker's ruddy face clearly now, the determined look, every muscle set in place.

I saw the gun, too. But he'd denied killing either Kirsten or Ponytail. Did that mean he wouldn't kill me either? He had no reason to lie to me at this stage.

Barker caught me looking at his gun. "I know what you're thinking. Will I kill you after I get the money? Maybe throw you off the tower?" He laughed, enjoying his position of power. "We'll see how it goes."

"You mean if the money is where I think it is?"

"I like you, Sophie. We might have had a thing, you know, in another life." I tried not to show my disgust. "We'll talk after you show me the money."

Show me the money. From the movie *Jerry Maguire,* though I doubted Barker realized it. I thought of Bruce, who would have been able to quote the next line, whom I might never see again. I struggled to hold back tears. I thought of my friends and my students. Would they even know what had happened to me?

"So where do we go from here?" Barker asked.

I could tell him we'd passed the money on the way. Send us back down the stairs, point to a corner on a landing, and make a dash for the door. I could . . . No, I couldn't. Nothing like that would work.

"To the belfry," I squeaked out.

Barker motioned for me to climb the indoor spiral stairway.

"All of these attacks and killings, and you're innocent?" I asked, intent on filling my last minutes with information.

"I didn't say that. I racked up my share of felonies over the years. But it was Einstein who knocked off Ponytail. Not that I blamed him. Ponytail was impatient, bringing attention where it was not desirable, if you know what I mean. Einstein is like me. He takes his time, plants himself in the basement of that building to stake out the girl."

"And me."

"Yeah, you. You have kind of a reputation, you know."

I didn't want to hear that I was the subject of conversation among thieves and killers.

"Where's Einstein now?" I asked.

"They'll never find him. He knows how to disappear and show up again when and where he wants to. He took off after he broke into your house. Believe me, when he figures out I have the money, he'll find me."

"You're pals, huh?"

Barker's hoarse smoker's laugh came from behind me as we made our way up the stairway single file. If I had any confidence in my physical fitness, I would have back-kicked him, knocked him down the stairs, jumped over the railing—and all before he had the presence of mind to simply shoot me.

"Pals. You could say that. Me and Einstein make it work."

We climbed and climbed smooth stairs, interspersed

with landings that I assumed led to the music library, the practice rooms, and Randy Stephens's studio. I no longer had to pretend that I was winded and tired; the stressful climb took its toll on me. Barker showed no signs of wear, however, and uttered the occasional gruff, "Move."

When we arrived at the floor that housed the carillon, I felt it was almost worth the trip. The magnificent instrument was enclosed in a transparent shield, its batons highly polished, its system of wires and levers shining, even in the dim light coming down from the belfry. Maybe I'd already been shot and had arrived in heaven. In my mind I heard again the beautiful music from Andrew's laptop. My own private concert. I hated that I had to witness the majesty of the carillon tower under the threat of death.

In any case, the inspiring vision didn't last long.

"Move it," Barker said. "If you behave, you might live to hear the thing."

Right above us now was the belfry, with its fifty-three bells. And its bag of money. Or so I supposed. I hadn't given any thought to what would happen to me if I was wrong. I couldn't imagine Barker would simply take off and leave me with a great story to tell.

We stood looking up at the large metal framework that held the bells in place, some of them stationary, others able to swing. The network of wires, loops, and rods that connected the bells to the carillon keyboard looked like a giant three-dimensional puzzle, like the ones that spilled from my purse in the first moments of my meeting with Wendy Carlson.

We were at the point where the belfry windows began, where Kirsten Packard had fallen, or been pushed to her death. I looked across the multilevel roof of Admin, over to the Paul Revere dorm, and past the campus to nearby buildings. Lights twinkled, cars sped by, and, though I couldn't see them, people were living normal Monday evening lives.

Barker pushed me in front of him. He laughed. "Now I

get it," he said. "I can't believe I didn't think of that." I turned slightly as he hit the side of his head with his gun hand, as if to berate himself for being so dull. For a hopeful moment I thought he'd lost focus, but he recovered quickly. "The money's up there, inside a bell, or taped to the outside. Brilliant. I'll bet the kid moved it after she found it, so no one else would see it." He clucked and chuckled in a way that sounded like admiration of a young woman's cunning. "Then she could use the money, a little at a time, until they had the final inspection before they opened the tower."

Barker wasn't asking for my confirmation, so I didn't give it.

"I think I can take it from here," he continued, his smile broader than ever in the short time I'd known him.

He shoved me ahead of him and adjusted his arm accordingly, ready to fire. So much for his hints of leniency. I was now expendable.

I seemed physically unable to turn my body around completely and look down the barrel of the gun. Maybe he wouldn't shoot a lady in the back and I'd gain a few more minutes.

But I had to make a move. I had nothing to lose by trying.

In the dwindling light, I could just make out the bells' frame. The giant puzzle wasn't completed yet and I could see that I'd be able to reach into the clapper of the nearest one. *Here I go.* I dashed swiftly toward a bell, startling Barker. I grabbed the giant clapper, pulled on it with all my might, then let it go.

A peal rang out, stinging my ears. I pulled it again, and again, and then rushed to the back wall of the belfry. I'd at least made a call for help, sounded an alert. If nothing else, someone would investigate and Barker might be caught as he exited the tower.

Barker was on the move, readjusting his aim, while I dashed in and out among the pieces of the frame around the bells, my ears still ringing on their own.

"You can't get away," Barker said, stepping back to the top of stairs where we'd entered.

I knew he was right. All he had to do was wait. Around me were the open windows of the belfry, and it was a long way down. One hundred and seventy-six feet, give or take, according to the brochure.

"First Kirsten, now me," I said. "You can't get away with it again."

Surely someone had heard and was already on his way up. If I kept him talking another minute, help would be here.

"I told you, I don't know how Kirsten died," Barker yelled. "Maybe she jumped like they said. I didn't kill her."

"I did," said another voice.

What? I peered between the rods and levers and saw the source of the new voice.

Wendy Carlson, with a large wooden slat that she sent crashing down on Barker's head. He fell to the floor, his gun flying out of his hand. Wendy bent to pick it up and aimed it at him, though he showed no signs of moving.

Wendy Carlson, from out of nowhere, dressed all in black, had saved me. "I did," she'd said. Did what?

Then I saw it clearly: a young, straitlaced physics major, Wendy Carlson, sick and tired of Kirsten's offbeat, losing lifestyle, fed up with covering for her roommate, not wanting to be dragged into questionable, if not criminal, activities with Einstein, Ponytail, and Big Dog. I saw Wendy in the tower that morning, twenty-five years ago, arguing with Kirsten, trying to talk sense into her. Things get out of control and the next thing she knows Kirsten is on the ground below and she's frantic, hysterical. And calls her mentor, Ted Morrell.

Now Wendy was in the tower again. She was still holding Barker's gun by her side. I crawled partway out of the labyrinth of beams, not completely sure I was safe.

"You didn't mean it," I said, and I knew she got that I

was referring to her struggle with Kirsten Packard and not to her current defensive attack on Big Dog.

"No, I didn't mean it. I loved Kirsten."

"I know."

"I'm so sorry."

"I know that, too. And I'm so grateful that you're here now. But why did you come? I know it's not for the money."

She winced, as if the idea of touching money from the past was disgusting. "I hated that they were so hung up on money that wasn't theirs. Kirsten certainly didn't need it."

I looked at the fraught librarian, her hair a mess. Her eyes had wandered to the opening in the belfry. I realized I was safe from her hand, but she herself wasn't. I had to distract her.

"Why did you come up here, Wendy?" I asked again. "Did you know I was in danger?"

"I came up to use the practice room one last time. This was my happiest place. I could be myself with no one watching, no one trying to change me." She smiled, a strange, sweet sight over her deathly black turtleneck sweater. "One very hot day in August, during summer school after my junior year, I came up here and played 'Let It Snow.' I knew everyone below was laughing. I loved entertaining people without having to see them, you know?"

"I get it," I said.

"I was playing today, practice style. Pieces I wrote in music class a long time ago. Then I heard you and Big Dog and I hid, until I realized he was going to hurt you." She let out a long sigh. "And now I've done something good. I've saved you."

The look in Wendy's eyes was too serene, her posture as perfect as when we first met, her walk slow but determined. She took steps toward the tower opening.

"No!" I said, struggling to extricate myself the rest of the way out of the metal frame that secured the carillon bells. I cut my arm on a broken rod but went forward.

Wendy didn't stop her slow walk to the window in the belfry.

I made it out of the frame and threw myself at a woman larger than me and taller by a head. I landed on the back of her knees, bringing her down within inches of the tower opening.

"Police!" Cops announcing themselves as they ran up the stairs.

I stayed spread out on Wendy's back until one of the officers picked me off and another tended to Wendy.

A wave of dizziness came over me when I realized the blood on Wendy was mine. My arm was in worse shape than I thought. I collapsed onto a stretcher that had made its way up the stairs on the backs of EMTs.

I could have sworn I heard the bells ringing out a joyful tune.

CHAPTER $\sqrt{24}$

A messed-up arm from a gouge by a metal rod seemed a small price to pay for satisfaction on a large scale—having a quarter of a century's worth of puzzles solved. I was glad it was the HPD's job and not mine to take care of the disposition of all the parties. Who went with what crime and what punishment should be meted out would take a while to sort out.

We thought we had it straight, but the next morning Bruce and I reviewed the order of things one more time as we sat in my den with mugs of coffee (Bruce) and hot chocolate (me).

Bruce started.

"Wendy catches Kirsten hiding a large bag of money behind a loose stone near the top of the stairs to the belfry," he said, summarizing Virgil's report to us after interviewing Wendy.

"Wendy and Kirsten fight over the path Kirsten is traveling, and Wendy accidentally pushes her roommate to her death," I said. It hadn't been easy for me to adjust to this scenario after all the others I'd concocted to describe Kirsten's last moments.

"She calls her teacher and mentor, Ted, and together they decide it's better for everyone if they let the police think Kirsten jumped."

"I still can't get over that," I said.

"Because you're honest, because you're not running for office, because you have no image to protect, and, I guess, because you don't read those sections of the newspapers where you'd learn that this stuff happens a lot. You're too busy with more noble pursuits."

"Let's move on," I said.

"Okay, so then the tower is walled off," Bruce said. "Until a bunch of money nudges it open again."

"Enter Jenn Marshall, twenty-five years later. She finds the money during a practice session, and decides to hide it in a different place. She splits it up and tapes the packages to the outside of the larger bells."

"In other words, she knew what she was doing," Bruce said. "Taking precautions in case the owners came back for it."

"Pretty daring."

"And calculating."

"It looks that way, doesn't it?" I admitted.

"When the three Nicknames from the diner can't find the money, they patrol the tower, essentially, trying to figure out what might have happened to it."

"They probably make several unsuccessful searches of the obvious places," I said.

"Then Ponytail, the loose cannon in the group, sees Jenn and suspects something. Maybe she goes up empty-handed and comes down with a bundle? Something like that."

"And he attacks her, grabs her backpack."

"And bells go off," Bruce said, demanding a point for his punny humor.

"Einstein can't deal with Ponytail's erratic behavior, maybe for decades, and kills him."

"But he realizes Ponytail didn't even get any money out of the attack. The backpack is nearly free of cash. So Einstein breaks into your house. Thinking Jenn might have brought you in on her job? He couldn't have known how unlikely that was."

"Then I leave Big Dog a message, basically alerting him that I might know where the money's hidden." I shook my head in shame.

"You couldn't have known," Bruce said.

The review made me tired and I wrapped it up quickly. "Finally, Wendy, who's been hotel-hopping between Boston and Henley, comes back to atone for her sin and ends up saving me."

Bruce hugged me and I knew how glad he was of that.

Ted came to my home later in the morning. It was the first time I saw him since I learned that he'd been my cyberstalker all along.

I'd anticipated this moment and run through many possible responses. "How could you?" "I trusted you." "I'll never share a hot plate with you again."

But at the sight of him, more despondent than I'd imagined, on nearly bended knees, I buckled and accepted a first-time-ever embrace from the chairman of the Physics Department.

Bruce refilled my coffee mug, poured one for Ted, and disappeared.

"I tried my best to keep you distracted and busy without hurting you," Ted said. "I couldn't risk having you unearth the past." He threw up his hands. "What a terrible choice."

"Then or now?" I asked.

"Both." He shook his head. "We were all under so much pressure at the time. Kirsten's losing her way, her father's campaign, Wendy's vulnerability."

"It's going to take me a while," I said.

"I understand. Just don't cut me out of your life. That's all I ask."

As aggravated as I was with him, his desperateness twenty-five years ago and his genuine contrition now softened me. It was up to the HPD to make any further judgments.

I pointed to the clock on my kitchen wall. "It's almost time for the Franklin Hall party," I said.

"I think I'll sit this one out if you don't mind."

"Good choice," I said, giving him a conciliatory smile.

Tuesday was declared a day off from Intersession classes. The administration had covered itself by announcing that the impromptu holiday was in honor of Benjamin Franklin, whose birthday it was. Good planning on the part of all the criminals and sleuths involved? Or a lucky break for the Henley College PR office?

Day off or not, those who cared sat around the lounge of Ben Franklin Hall, the best place we knew to celebrate. Students, faculty, friends, and colleagues was all it took. Plus a cake in the shape of the carillon tower and carillon music pouring forth from Andrew's laptop.

Virgil graced us with his presence, and we were all sure that it had nothing to do with the fact that Judy Donohue "lived" here. They both wore significant grins today, but specifics had yet to be revealed.

Virgil satisfied our curiosity about the justice system by

letting us know that Pete "Big Dog" Barker, who'd lived through Wendy's two-by-four attack, had worked out a deal where he'd contact Einstein and draw him out using the money as bait.

"The money was from their biggest score," Virgil said. "No word on the exact amount yet."

"I practiced up there all the time. I can't believe I didn't know about the money," Andrew said. It was hard to tell whether he wished he'd taken a bite of it or not. "Where's all that money now, anyway?" he asked.

"Being added up," Virgil said. "Safe in police custody. Until all the banks across New England that were robbed in that era trip over themselves claiming it."

"Nice," said Willa in her uniquely sarcastic way.

We discreetly avoided talk of Jenn, who'd stolen only what she needed, in my decidedly nonlegal view. The day Ponytail attacked her as she crossed campus, her backpack contained only enough for a couple of textbooks for spring semester. I felt bad for Jenn, who wasn't out to get rich. But her willingness to do anything to survive had already cost her—and others—dearly.

Wendy was under close observation at a hospital in Boston, both by authorities who would decide her fate, and by doctors and counselors who would help her survive. I knew I owed her my life, and I hoped that would go part of the way to having her value her own life from here on. My first trip once I was off serious pain meds would be to visit her.

With everyone relaxed from the warm, comfortable environment, we enjoyed a few rounds of riddles, all of them old and corny.

Then Andrew had a better idea.

"Hey, we should come up with some cool nicknames," he said.

"Yeah," Brent said. "Too bad 'Big Dog' is taken."

"And Ponytail," Lauren said, tugging at her long locks.

"I'm going with 'Hack,'" Andrew said.

"Too obvious," Patty remarked.

We tossed around "Binary Dude" and "Prime Geek" (for Andrew), "Rich Cat" (for Willa), and "Biochick" for Judy. "Hypatia" came up for me, until I reminded everyone of her unhappy end.

In the end, none of the nicknames were as satisfying or as colorful as the three that recently made their appearance on our campus.

We turned again to riddles, this time with an offering from Bruce ("Sky Guy" had come and gone for him).

"I have a math riddle," Bruce said.

"*You* have a math riddle?" I asked.

"Uh-huh. From one of the MAstar nurses. Actually, from his six-year-old kid."

"Let's hear it."

"What's the difference between a new penny and an old quarter?" Bruce asked.

We all laughed and shouted a chorus of "Tell us."

Bruce faked a frown. "Nah, I can tell every one of you math and science geeks already knows the answer."

"Sorry," we said, in one form or another.

"That's okay. I should have known better. You guys have the world's best teachers."

The students who knew enough yelled, "Woot, woot," their voices soaring over the miniature carillon concert that filled the room, and delivered more cake to their teachers. Andrew made sure I got the largest piece.

On the way home, I leaned back against the passenger seat in Bruce's car. "I wish I'd been able to pick up the penne and veggies for dinner," I said.

He smiled. "I did it. And I'll cook, since your arm is out of commission."

I rubbed my arm, which was hardly sore at all, thanks to pharmaceuticals. "I don't know how long it will be before I can do any work," I whined.

"I'm taking the rest of the week off, so you can have three more days of pampering," Bruce said, in the nicest tone.

Music to my ears.

FUN (EXERCISES)

First, here's the answer to the math riddle in Chapter 24.

Bruce asks, "What's the difference between a new penny and an old quarter?"
A: Twenty-four cents!

Sophie Knowles doesn't expect that everyone will be able to unwind with arithmetic, but she feels that doing puzzles, brainteasers, and mental arithmetic keeps you sharp, and improves your memory and your powers of observation. Here are some samples of puzzles and games that exercise your wits.

Browse in your bookstore, library, and online for more brainteasers, and have some fun!

BRAINTEASER

Here's a combination of wordplay and number play. What do the items in the following list have in common?

Too bad I hid a boot.

2002

Was it a car or a cat I saw?

111,111,111 x 111,111,111

RIDDLES

1. Here's an ancient riddle, The Riddle of the Sphinx. (Be aware that metaphors are often used in riddles!) In Greek mythology, the Sphinx sat outside of Thebes and asked this riddle of all travelers who came by. If the traveler failed to solve the riddle, the Sphinx killed him. And if the traveler answered the riddle correctly, then the Sphinx would destroy herself. **What goes on four legs in the morning, on two legs at noon, and on three legs in the evening?**

2. Here's a cute riddle that physics professor Ted Morrell might introduce when he's in a good mood: **Where does bad lighting end up?**

   (Hint: It sounds like the place where Big Dog and Einstein are headed!)

MATH PUZZLES

1. Okay, Sophie admits this is not really a puzzle, but a simple algebra problem that might have been taken

from your middle-school textbook. But Sophie gets a great deal of pleasure when numbers work out right. She hopes you do, too. Try it!

A car travels at a speed of 64 mph and its fuel consumption is 28 mpg. It has an 11-gallon tank, which was full when it started but at that very moment began to leak fuel. After 112 miles the car stops with a completely empty tank. How many gallons per hour was it losing?

2. A short, easy math puzzle: Move only one digit in the following expression to make a correct equation.

   $62 - 63 = 1$

3. Have a little fun at a party with this calendar "trick."

   Ask a friend to choose four days that form a square in any month on a calendar. Then, ask the friend to tell you only the sum of the four days. Using basic algebra, you'll be able to tell her which four days she picked.

ANSWERS

ANSWER TO BRAINTEASER

All the items in the list are palindromes—a word, phrase, verse, or sentence, that reads the same backward or forward. Note that $111,111,111 \times 111,111,111 = 12,345,678,987,654,321$. (The answer is a palindrome, though the equation taken as a whole is not.)

ANSWER TO RIDDLE #1

A man, who crawls on all fours as a baby, walks on two legs as an adult, and walks with a cane in old age.

ANSWER TO RIDDLE #2

The riddle that Ted might use when he's in a good mood.
    Where does bad lighting end up?
    In a prism!

ANSWER TO MATH PUZZLE #1

The Speeding Car

ANSWER: 4 gallons per hour.

SOLUTION:
Distance ÷ Speed = Time for the trip.
    The car took 112 miles ÷ 64 mph = 1.75 hours to travel
the 112 miles
    In that time, the car used 112 miles ÷ 28 miles per gal-
lon = 4 gallons of fuel.
    The car started with 11 gallons of fuel; thus, 7 gallons
of fuel were lost (leaked) in 1.75 hours.
    Therefore, the car was losing fuel at a rate of 7 gallons ÷
1.75 hours = 4 gallons per hour.

ANSWER TO MATH PUZZLE #2:

The tricky equation

$2^6 - 63 = 1$

ANSWER TO MATH PUZZLE #3:

Fun with Calendars

Let x be the first date your friend chose. (Sophie says not to groan; it's easy and fun!) The next day will be x + 1, of course. That's the top row of the square. The first number in the bottom row of the square will be x + 7 (the first date, plus 7 days); the second number in the bottom row of the square will be x + 8.

Forming the equation, we have:

x + x + 1 + x + 7 + x + 8 = T (total given to you by your friend).

Simplifying:

4 x + 16 = T

This is as far as we need to go!

You can see that no matter what x (the first date) is, to figure out what it is, simply subtract 16 from the Total, and then divide by 4.

For a method that's easier to remember, simplify the last equation further, by dividing by 4:

x + 4 = T/4

You can find x, then, by dividing the total by 4, then subtracting 4.

Try it and let Sophie know how it goes!

WELL-CRAFTED MYSTERIES FROM BERKLEY PRIME CRIME

- **Earlene Fowler** Don't miss these Agatha Award–winning quilting mysteries featuring Benni Harper.

- **Monica Ferris** These *USA Today* bestselling Needlecraft Mysteries include free knitting patterns.

- **Laura Childs** Her Scrapbooking Mysteries offer tips to satisfy the most die-hard crafters.

- **Maggie Sefton** These popular Knitting Mysteries come with knitting patterns and recipes.

- **Lucy Lawrence** These brilliant Decoupage Mysteries involve cutouts, glue, and varnish.

- **Elizabeth Lynn Casey** The Southern Sewing Circle Mysteries are filled with friends, southern charm—and murder.